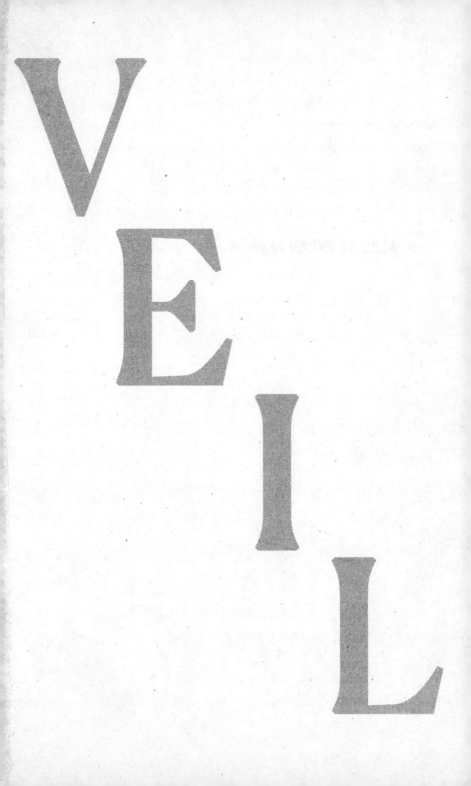

VEIL

ALSO BY DYLAN FARROW

Hush

DYLAN FARROW

VEIL

A HUSH NOVEL

WEDNESDAY BOOKS
NEW YORK

First published in the United States by Wednesday Books, an imprint of St. Martin's Publishing Group

www.wednesdaybooks.com

Map, endpapers, and interior illustrations by Rhys Davies

Library of Congress Cataloging-in-Publication Data

Names: Farrow, Dylan, 1985– author.
Title: Veil : a Hush novel / Dylan Farrow.
Description: First edition. | New York : Wednesday Books,
    2022. | Sequel to: Hush. | Audience: Ages 14–18.
Identifiers: LCCN 2021052237 | ISBN 9781250235930
    (hardcover) | ISBN 9781250235947 (ebook)
Subjects: CYAC: Fantasy. | LCGFT: Fantasy fiction.
Classification: LCC PZ7.1.F3697 Ve 2022 | DDC [Fic]—dc23
LC record available at https://lccn.loc.gov/2021052237

Our books may be purchased in bulk for promotional, educational, or business use. Please contact your local bookseller or the Macmillan Corporate and Premium Sales Department at 1-800-221-7945, extension 5442, or by email at MacmillanSpecialMarkets@macmillan.com.

First Edition: 2022

10 9 8 7 6 5 4 3 2 1

For Mom & Sue

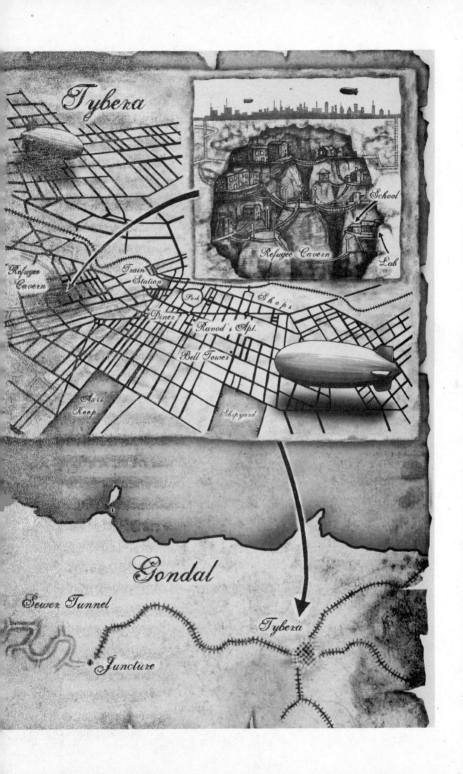

VEIL

EXCERPTS FROM THE DIARY OF A ROGUE BARD

14th Sun / 9th Moon

Martin is dead. I heard through the caravan yesterday: he was discovered in the woods outside the village of Valmorn with a distinctive golden dagger in his chest. Last we spoke, I told him he was paranoid. I mocked him for always looking over his shoulder. Now I think I may have been the crazy one, for believing we could strike against High House and simply disappear into the populace to lead regular lives. I was so confident.

The traitor, that dirty rat killed him. I know it.

The merchants will no longer assist us. I can't say I blame them. It's too dangerous. Martin's coin was the only thing persuading them to aid our efforts in the first place. And just like that, the system of safe houses we carefully set up is now defunct.

Tonight, I remember our merry little band of rebels. So very pleased with ourselves, our dreams and plans and conspiracies. The world feels lonelier without them. There are only two of us left.

I hope Victor is okay. Perhaps I should . . . No. If there's even a minuscule chance that they know my whereabouts and not his, sending a message might lead the Bards, or worse, the plague, straight to his doorstep.

Maybe Martin had the right of it after all. I must remain vigilant. Paranoid, even. I swore an oath to my friends who are now gone. I will not die until I've ensured the complete and utter destruction of High House.

I should leave Aster. I no longer have a safe house to oversee. Even if I did, there is no one left to make use of it. High House's deceit has taken root too firmly amongst the people. No one wishes to flee to a place they don't believe exists.

I struggle to accept this. Does it mean that we lost? That everything we fought for, all the sacrifices we made, were for nothing?

I've now spent two hours staring at my own words and the letters are starting to swim in the candlelight. I could have used that time to pack my things and disappear into the night.

This is silly. I know why I'm still here. There is no sense denying it any longer. I'm waiting for a certain young carpenter to knock at my door and convince me to stay.

What a fool I am.

21st Sun / 9th Moon

For better or worse, I have decided to stay.

Is it the best decision? Probably not. But for the first time in years, I've remembered what it is to live instead of merely survive. I've found something here beyond anything I discovered in my time at High House—beyond even the camaraderie of my friends and fighting for a worthy cause.

It's a decision that has shown me who I am. Perhaps, more accurately, it's shown me who I truly want to be.

I hid my tracks well. I spent years doing so. Cathal—or the traitor, Niall—can try to find me here. He can send his Bards and his manufactured plague. I'll do whatever I must to remain prepared and protect this new life I'm forging for myself—free of High House, and the Telling, and the conspiracies. Free of keeping watch over an empty safe house.

The more I think about it . . . the more I like the idea. Freedom was what it was always about, wasn't it?

And with that, I bring this record to a close. I'll need to conceal it someplace safe. Someday someone may want to know the truth, but for now I have other priorities to attend to.

I'm getting married!

8th Sun / 11th Moon

I don't know why I dug up this musty old journal after so long. Or why it feels so comforting to read these words, see my own handwriting, or to set pen to paper once more. Perhaps I needed a connection to something in this madness. Even if I know intellectually that doing so, especially now, is incredibly dangerous.

A great depth of emotion exists in the decade between this entry and the last. Serenity, bliss, joy, pride . . . as well as pain, sorrow, and grief beyond anything I'm qualified to put to words.

My husband is dead. My son is gone.

The home I built is in ashes. It took all my strength to remain composed when I saw the Bards approaching. One of the locals must have tipped them off. But I did not recognize their faces—nor they mine. I thought for sure that . . .

There's no reason to speculate. Cathal finally sent the Blot. He must have hoped to flush me out of hiding. He's afraid of . . . something. Or perhaps planning . . . something. It was never easy to know with that man, even when I trusted him.

My best analysis of the situation: He knows I yet live, but not where. His final threats haunt me. He'll never stop searching. And now I don't just fear for myself what he may find if he succeeds.

I'm watching my daughter sleep on a cot near our campfire. My earnest, stubborn, curious, sweet child. She has no home. The fearful villagers won't let us near the town in case we "infect" them.

Every second, I'm a hair's breadth from screaming at them all: They have no idea how any of this works. They cling to their superstitions, but I learned through years of bloodshed and treachery that those laws they hold so dear are nothing but the fabrications of a madman.

Then I remind myself that even if I shared the whole sordid truth, no one would believe it. They'd cast me and my daughter farther out. Or remove my tongue, as they are so fond of doing to those who don't toe the line. Fools, all.

None of that matters now. My only concern is my little girl. I swore once that I would not die until I'd as-

sured High House's destruction. Tonight I'm amending that oath. I will keep her safe. Perhaps one day she will be ready to hear the truth and choose to continue what my comrades and I started so long ago.

I know what I must do.

At the farthest southeastern corner of Montane lies a small village called Valmorn. It comprises two roads that intersect in the middle, lined with homes and businesses, encircled on the outskirts by struggling farms. At the center of the crossroads is a large textile factory, where the majority of the townsfolk work feverishly to produce their next tithe to High House in the hopes that some of their suffering will be alleviated in return. It is entirely unremarkable in many of the same ways as the village I came from, and all too familiar.

Only the most daring of travelers will ever see this place, which is cut off by the dreaded expanse of wasteland that encompasses most of the country.

At least, I try to think of myself as a daring traveler. It's a bit more glamorous than "terrified fugitive" or "vile seditionist." I am those things, too.

A cold, damp wind blows from the east, past the hilltop overlooking the town. It crawls down the collar of my shirt and along my spine to where I sit on a patch of dead grass. I shiver it away, pulling my black cloak a little closer around my shoulders. It's only wind, but it feels like a quiet warning.

I keep my gaze on the town and not my traveling

companion, who paces in small circles to my left. Without even looking in her direction, I can practically see her rolling her spectral amber eyes at me, bright yellow glints in the light, as though my reaction to the cold has betrayed some deep inner weakness.

I try to imagine this view as it could be, free of the trappings of death, fear, and sickness that were implanted long before my time. Streets bustling with people working for the betterment of their home instead of existing to appease a distant power that cared nothing for them. The buildings painted with vibrant colors, window boxes housing herbs and flowers, instead of hung with dead vines and walls caked with the grayish brown dust of the wasteland.

A faint whistle by my side nearly causes me to jump out of my skin. I screech in alarm, rolling out of the way. Turning around, I see a small throwing knife embedded in the dirt inches from where I was sitting.

I look toward my companion, concerned we might be in trouble, only to hear her bark a laugh at me.

"If you keep spacing out, you're not going to be alive much longer," she says. Her bright eyes and white teeth stand out in stark contrast to her dark skin as a long grin spreads across her face.

Of course this was her doing. She's delighted in vexing, threatening, and insulting me since the moment we first met. I take a deep breath, trying to purge myself of my desire to scream in frustration as I get to my feet.

"I'm not *supposed* to fear for my life from someone I'm traveling with." The words grate out through my teeth.

"Naivete like that will also shorten your life substantially."

"I'm not your student anymore, Kennan." My temper rises at her dismissive tone. "And even if I was, I don't exist purely for you to derive whatever sick enjoyment you get out of torturing me!"

Kennan lifts an infuriatingly calm eyebrow. "Touchy, are we?"

"I swear—"

"Calm down, both of you." A welcome, amiable voice carries over the hilltop as two familiar figures, laden with equally welcome supplies, make their way toward us. "Can't we leave you alone for ten minutes without returning to you at each other's throats?"

"Sorry, Fiona." I feel like I'm apologizing more to a displeased parent than a concerned best friend.

"I'm not apologizing," Kennan states to no one's surprise.

"Look, let's not lay blame." Mads pulls his rucksack over a broad shoulder and sets it heavily on the ground. "We need to get some food in us, and we need a plan. That's more important right now."

"Yes, I agree." I nod, relieved to set aside my argument with Kennan. "Did you learn anything in town?"

"Not much more than we learned in the last few towns we've passed." A grimace passes over Fiona's seraphic face. "They did say there was a weird old hermit who used to live on the outskirts of town, but he died ages ago."

"From the Blot?" I ask. I can't help nervously running my fingers over my wrists.

Fiona and Mads shake their heads in unison, sharing an apprehensive glance. I'm about to ask again when Mads speaks up.

"He was murdered. Stabbed through the heart with a golden dagger."

My blood freezes in my veins. The wind picks up again, somehow colder than before.

For a split second, the scene flashes through my mind, only it's not some old hermit's house—it's mine. And the body is my mother's.

The floor is covered in blood. The smell is overpowering. The silence is deafening.

My legs are shaking.

"Shae." A gentle hand on my shoulder brings me back to the hilltop outside Valmorn. Fiona's gentle green eyes are locked on mine. "It's okay, you're safe."

I grip Fiona's hand over my shoulder and squeeze it, letting her warmth seep into me. I focus on the familiarity of her face—high cheekbones, pale blond eyebrows, small, upturned nose, and reassuring smile—letting her ground me in reality. Gradually, I feel myself return. I remember how to breathe.

"That's it?" Kennan drums her fingers irritably on her crossed arm. "I could have turned up twice that information in half the time."

"So you keep insisting," Mads says as he crouches to unpack his rucksack. "But that doesn't change the fact that you're a Bard, and thus instantly memorable, and asking about stuff that people will remember when High House inevitably comes through here looking for us."

She knows he's right, but Kennan just sniffs and looks in the other direction.

I approach Mads alongside Fiona. The supplies they managed to get are meager, but I know it took all their skills, and possibly the remainder of their coin, to even get that much.

I'm not sure what to say as I sit back down on the cracked earth, watching as Mads and Fiona take inventory of our supplies. Gratitude mixes uncomfortably with guilt. They are here because they care and want to help me. But that meant leaving everything they knew and loved behind.

Unlike me, they have families back in Aster. Fiona's father and brothers are probably worried sick and Mads's parents must miss him terribly. I can't even bear to ask if their loved ones know they left because of me—the town's favorite pariah.

"We have about three days' worth of food—if we're careful," Mads states. In front of him is our water supply in tin canteens, an unimpressive tower of canned beans, and a few strips of jerky.

"We still don't know how much longer this journey will take," Fiona says, her pale brows creasing with worry as she turns to me.

I understand her fear. My hand tentatively reaches toward my pocket where our only guide, a scrap from the *Book of Days,* rests.

When we escaped High House, the page seemed animated, as if alive. Words and images wove themselves on the surface, showing us our path. It led us past two safe houses in a little under a week. As the days passed and our journey progressed, however, the movement of those images became sluggish and the words faded. The safe house we just came from, we found by dumb luck.

The prospect of uniting the page with the rest of the book grows more unlikely the farther we travel. The thief could be anywhere by now. With no clue as to his motivations, I can only blindly continue along the path before me.

What are you up to, Ravod? I wonder. He is irritatingly never far from my thoughts. I know he's out there, somewhere, with the *Book of Days.* If his plan was to use it to rewrite reality, I assume he would have done so by now. It seems odd to put such an idea past him. But then, I never thought he'd steal the book, either. When we meet again, I plan to give him a very stern talking-to. Hopefully that's all I need to do.

I pull the page out and examine it, hoping my worry isn't too obvious. There's a dark smudge in one corner—my blood—that I can never look at for too long. Otherwise, it is an ordinary piece of torn paper, with a faded glyph of a house surrounded by trees and a single word: *East.*

"We've got to keep heading east." I try to muster as much confidence as possible when I add, "If we look for trees, the next safe house should be there somewhere."

I don't have to look up to know that Kennan is rolling her eyes as she approaches.

"You sound about as reliable as a cheap fortune-teller at a bazaar."

I blink at her, unsure whether to feel enraged or surprised that she's already picking another fight.

"Kennan, that's not helpful," Fiona says. "We're all tense. We need to work together."

Kennan fixes Fiona with a stare I remember all too well from the days she trained me at High House. I find myself rising to my feet, prepared to defend my friend if even one golden strand of hair on her head is threatened.

"What's not helpful is traveling in a group this size with no way to ensure our survival," Kennan hisses. She's launched into this diatribe before, about how one skilled individual could ensure success better than three bumbling kids. "We're not making good time on reaching Gondal—*if* it even exists—and three days of provisions for four people would last two weeks for one."

I know she's not wrong, but I still stare at her in disbelief. She really would leave us, just like that.

"Look," I begin, forcing myself to sound calm. I can't believe I'm playing peacekeeper, but if even Fiona's powers of diplomacy are ineffective against Kennan, the least I can do is try to keep our ragtag group unified. "You're the most skilled among us, Kennan, there's no question. But we all have a stake in this journey, and we deserve to see it through. So instead of arguing this again, let's eat and get back on the road before we lose daylight."

Kennan shifts her gaze between me and Fiona before mercifully turning away.

"She really knows exactly how intimidating she is; I'll give her that," Fiona whispers to me.

I nod. "So do I, believe me."

When all this is over, I'll be very happy never to eat cold canned beans ever again. A few hours' walk east and I still can't get the taste out of my mouth. Even if we were willing to start a fire to cook them, they probably wouldn't have tasted much better, and Mads made the excellent point that a campfire would make us easier to track.

That we've seen neither hide nor hair of High House is starting to get worrying. The longer we travel without being ambushed, the more imminent an attack feels. From a glance at my companions, I know I'm not the only one who thinks so.

As the sun begins to wane overhead, the flat, dusty ground gives way to dead shrubbery and strange, twisted overgrowth. By my side, I hear Fiona's quiet growls of annoyance whenever her skirt catches on the thorns. By the time we reach a ragged line of trees, the pesky article is knotted well above her knees and her long, pale legs are covered in scratches.

In all my life, I've never heard Fiona complain and, apparently, she's not about to start now. She waves off my concerned look with a gentle laugh.

"I guess the first casualty of this adventure is my skirt!" Her tone is light, but her lips twist as she passes me.

I know better than to insist upon anything with her when she's set her mind to something. Instead, I fall in step alongside Mads as he scans the area.

"Never seen terrain like this, even up in the wooded areas of the mountains back home," he says thoughtfully. "We're at a number of disadvantages here."

"We'll just have to tackle them as they arise," I reply. I can't help agreeing with his assessment, though. The dead trees and underbrush are growing denser the farther we walk, and the sky is rapidly darkening. All I can make out of Mads is the silhouette of his tall, muscular frame beside me, his blue eyes lost to the gloom.

He's handsome, in a rugged way that he takes confident ownership of. His attractiveness was never much of a barrier in our ill-fated courtship. By the time I refused his proposal of marriage, however, I had come to realize that a deeper problem stood between us—we were simply too different, in temperament and expectations.

Now that our trajectory is once more aligned, I still find it difficult to rekindle the spark we once shared. Come to think of it, I struggled to ignite it the first time. And I don't see any reason to try—I'm perfectly comfortable with the way things are.

Mads shifts his gaze from the trees to me with a slight frown, interrupting my thoughts. "The sooner we find this safe house, the better."

A low howl sounds from somewhere deeper in the dead forest, sending a shiver down my spine. Whatever predators live here will find four lost travelers quite appealing.

"What was that?" Fiona whips around to face us.

"Wolves," Mads states. "We don't have long before they start spreading out to surround us."

Kennan prepares the knife she threw at me earlier between her fingers. In a low voice she says, "Let's get a move on then, shall we?"

In one of our rare instances of agreement, we forge deeper into the forest. My heart thuds loudly against the wall of my chest as twilight casts the trees in a pale glow that makes them look like blanched bones rising from the earth.

I pull the torn page from my pocket and squint at it desperately in the dying light. The ink on the page warps into a dull, incoherent, and utterly unhelpful splotch.

"What does that mean?" Fiona appears over my shoulder, pointing at the paper.

I sigh and shake my head. "It doesn't mean anything."

"No, no, it looks like a hand!" Fiona peers closer. "And it's pointing!"

I squint, gasping when I realize she's right. The ink splotch has loosely taken on the appearance of a closed fist with one finger pointing to the right, but there's nothing on the paper to indicate what it's pointed *at*.

"Useless scrap of junk!" I hiss at the page and shove it back in my pocket before angrily raising my right arm to point. "How's a finger pointing supposed to . . ."

I let out a sharp breath. If you follow the path of my finger through the gathering darkness, there is a large shadowy shape set against the trees.

Another howl issues from the bushes, closer than before, followed by two more.

"Over here!" I call to the others, gesturing to the right of the path we've been tracing. Mads and Fiona follow without question. Kennan squints at the trees I'm heading toward, but a rustle in the underbrush nearby prompts her closer to the rest of us. Against a pack of wolves, even Kennan agrees there's safety in numbers.

The wolves are closing in. I hear them in the brush while I hurry as fast as I can though the brambles that claw at my legs. The form of a small thatched hut takes shape ahead. The safe house.

Wolves start to appear, thin and ravenous, in the bushes around us, growling menacingly. Mads reaches the door first and shoves it open, shouting for us to hurry. I grab Fiona's hand as a wolf snaps at her, pulling her through the thorns, gritting my teeth as they tear at my clothes and slice into my skin.

The nearest wolf prepares to pounce as we reach the doorway. One by one, we throw ourselves into the blackness inside the safe house, and Mads slams the door shut just in time behind us. The howls of the wolves are drowned out in the darkness beyond.

It quickly becomes clear that the safe house is long abandoned and probably haunted. I can barely see a thing in the dark. Our feet send shivers through the floorboards. Outside I can still hear prowling wolves. The pervasive smell of mold burns the back of my throat as I feel my way around. The first thing my hand contacts is Fiona's arm, and she screams.

"Ghost!"

At least I'm not alone in thinking this place is inhabited by some manner of restless spirit.

"Calm down, it's me," I assure her. Fiona grabs my hand, checking to make sure I'm corporeal, and issues a weak laugh.

"I guess it's slightly better in here than being eaten by wolves," Fiona says. Her tone is light, but her hand is still rigidly grasping mine.

"Enough levity." Kennan's voice issues from somewhere in the dark. "Find a place to rest and be ready to leave at first light. If I must sleep in this hovel, it will be undisturbed by your incessant banter."

Her words are punctuated by Mads tripping over something none of us can see. He curses more violently than I ever thought him capable of before I hear him get back up.

"Are you okay over there?" I venture into the darkness, pulling Fiona along with me.

"I think I found a lantern," he says.

I hear Mads rummage in his bag, then the sound of a fire striker. Moments later, sparks catch the wick of an old lantern. Fiona squeals with glee, clapping her hands together. The light even extends to the corner of the room where Kennan rolls her eyes at the display. Mads either doesn't see or ignores her, hanging the lantern from a hook on the wall. "We won't get much warmth from this, and there are only a few hours of oil left in here, but it's better than nothing."

"I'll take first watch," I say. "I want to look around. You all get some sleep."

I hear no complaints from the others as they find spots for themselves and settle in.

I fight back my exhaustion. I don't want to admit to my companions that I'm afraid to fall asleep. There's no need to worry them over a few bad dreams. Vivid, intense dreams that pull my strongest emotions from all corners of my psyche. Sometimes I remember them, sometimes I only remember the terror they leave me with. I've awakened gasping for air more times than I can count on this journey.

Fiona has mentioned my troubled sleep more than once, but I dismissed her worry convincingly enough that she stopped after a while. Even if I told her, the nightmares wouldn't vanish. Knowing

Fiona, the inability to solve the problem would only vex her. I'm not sure if Mads or Kennan have even noticed, which is a relief. I would have far more trouble talking about it to them. Mads was never a very emotional guy. And Kennan is Kennan.

Truth be told, sleep is less troubling to me than the sickness lurking beneath my skin. Cathal's parting gift: the Blot.

Thinking about Cathal still stings. It's another thing I'm not sure how long I'll be able to avoid. Sooner or later, the pain of his betrayal will eat me alive, if the plague doesn't get me first. Continual Tellings have been keeping it under control; my veins only look slightly darker than normal.

For now.

I stretch my arms over my head, yawning. I need to focus on something else. Mads said there's only a few hours of oil in the lantern, so I decide to search the house while I can. I stand on my tiptoes and unhook the lantern from the wall.

I'm not sure what I'm looking for, but secrets tend to lurk in unlikely places.

I quickly take stock of my immediate surroundings. The house isn't much bigger than the one I grew up in and is not dissimilar from the other safe houses we've come across. To the naked eye it would seem like an ordinary cabin in the forest.

There's a deeper story here, though. I feel it in my bones. After everything that's transpired, I like to think I've gotten pretty good at sensing these things. At trusting some greater instinct instead of how things appear.

Drawing on the information I have so far, I recite what I know of the story to myself as I walk through the house. The person who lived here was part of a network that assisted people fleeing from High House to Gondal. My mother was part of the same network.

She did not speak for most of my life. After my brother, Kieran, died from the Blot, she refused to say a word. Knowing what I do now, it makes sense. I always thought she was afraid, and maybe she was, but it was a lot more complex than that.

I wonder if they knew each other, or who my mother might have been to the resident of this house. Maybe he was a rogue Bard like she was. Maybe she even visited here at some point. My eyes strain into the dim light as though hoping to catch sight of their phantoms, as if my desperation alone can— somehow—will them into revealing what they know.

All I see is the dilapidated interior of an incredibly old, musty house, no matter how hard I look. What's left of the furniture is collapsed and covered in dust. Lichen has started to grow on the wood in some areas. The house was built for sturdiness, but it clearly won't be around much longer.

I narrow my eyes. A tall shelf in the farthest corner seems suspiciously untouched by the ravages of time. I tread carefully, trying to keep the creaking to a minimum so as to not disturb anyone, lifting the lantern higher to get a better look.

Whatever used to be on the shelves is gone. Given its proximity to the rusted stove in the corner, I would guess this was where the rebel Bard kept his food. A few cooking implements are scattered on the floor nearby, confirming it. Apparently, Mads tripped over a tin pitcher earlier.

I return to the shelf. There's an odd metal fixture at eye level in the back, like the handle of a mug. It would have been easy to conceal if the shelves were full.

I hook one finger of my free hand around the cold, rusty metal. It jiggles a bit. There's a small give, suggesting it's not completely fused to the wood. Pulling it would probably send the shelf toppling over onto me.

Instead, I try lifting it. Nothing. Pushing yields the same result. I try rotating it like a doorknob.

Click.

A soft noise issues in the wall, muffled by the wood, and the shelf gently sways toward me. A trick door.

Except there's no room behind it, just a recessed wall of plaster with peculiar painted-on markings. Strange, but oddly familiar. The light is so dim, and the colors so faded, I practically have to press my nose to the fresco to decipher it.

It's a map. The same as the one I've been following on the page from the *Book of Days*. And like the

Book, there is a path marked by the symbol of the crescent moon—the safe house network—charting a path south and east. My mother's house was the northernmost point on the path, and this house is the second to last safe house before the end.

It's mysteriously beautiful in a way I've never quite seen before. The colors and patterns flow together in striking uniformity. The person who lived here obviously spent many hours toiling at it. Each icon is painted lovingly on the plaster. It's not just a representation of geographical locations—it's a work of art.

I trace the road with my finger, following the path, memorizing it. We have to continue southeast through the forest to the very edge of Montane. Beyond that final safe house denoted by the crescent moon, the map is marked with a brilliant golden sun.

That must be Gondal.

"Good find."

Kennan's voice behind me nearly sends me bolting straight out of my skin. When I return to my senses, I am doubly surprised by how she was, apparently, giving me praise.

"One of these days, you're going to scare me to death," I grumble, turning from the map to face her. Kennan's amber eyes practically glow in the soft light.

"Probably." She nods, curtly. "You are astonishingly weak of heart, after all."

"And *you're* full of—" I cut myself off as I hear

Fiona mumble and shift in her sleep. As always, it's a struggle to keep Kennan from goading me. I take a deep breath and lower my voice, hoping to redirect the conversation somewhere useful. "Take a look at this map. If we chart a course to the southeast, we'll hit the edge of the forest and be halfway to the final safe house."

Kennan steps closer to the map, reading it quickly. "See these markings? They're different than the ones indicating the wasteland. The terrain is going to change." She points to the area beyond the forest, where sure enough the icon of a flat line used for the wasteland has altered to a wavy one, with a few vertical strokes protruding from odd intervals.

I've seen a fair bit of Montane. So far, it's been almost entirely mountains, wasteland, or dead forest. I'm not sure what else there could be.

"Good to know," I say. "We need any information we can get."

"And any advantage," Kennan adds, casting me a meaningful look over her shoulder. "Now we can erase this map."

Her words twist something inside me. "What? Why?"

Kennan regards me with a cocked head, clearly trying to put words to her opinion of my stupidity. It takes effort to stand firm beneath her stare.

"It's a *map*." She says it as though speaking to a small child. "It shows people where to go. Us, yes, but also *them*."

The Bards. If they tracked us this far and read the map, they would know exactly where we're headed. It's a good point, but I can't shake the feeling of unease that destroying this map gives me.

"Then we hide it again," I counter. "It was an accident that I found it in the first place."

"That's a chance you're willing to take?" Kennan crosses her arms over her chest. "What if they follow us? Ambush us at the next safe house? Kill us? Or worse?"

"And if we destroy it, how are we any better than High House? We'd be wiping this information from existence, just like they do." My fists shake at my sides. "This feels *wrong*."

Kennan pauses, and for a moment, I wonder if I've swayed her. Then she shakes her head.

"You don't get to decide whether I become a martyr," she says.

"Kennan, wait." I choke on my own words. "Maybe there's another way."

"Funny that you should feel the need to deliberate this, after what you did to Niall."

My mouth locks shut. Cold chills penetrate my core as I recall that, not too long ago, I erased a person from existence. I could justify it however I pleased, but in the end, that was a choice I made.

"How . . ." My voice comes out as a frail whisper. I clear my throat, try to start again and fail.

"How do I know?" Kennan finishes for me. "You've

been apologizing for it in your sleep every night. I'm surprised most of Montane doesn't know, the way you carry on."

No wonder Fiona's worried.

For her part, Kennan ignores me and approaches the map, running her fingers over the surface. A barely audible Telling issues from her lips. The surface of the fresco begins to chip, peel, and crack. Mold crawls along it, distorting the image until it's completely indecipherable.

She pauses afterward, frowning at the wall, her fingers flexing at her side and then running over her hair in frustration. The motion frees a single coil of black curl from the otherwise perfectly tidy bun atop her head. Something like worry clouds her face before it passes.

She's clever. From a Bard's standpoint, it's a masterful Telling. Her words alone would not destroy the fresco, not permanently. Instead, she sped up years of decay by Telling the mold that was already there to destroy it for her.

Even so, the erasure of the map leaves a bitter taste in my mouth. It was the only remaining fragment in this world of the person who created it. Now it's gone, like him. Like he never mattered.

I'm not sure why I feel such a connection to some person I've never met. Perhaps it's because we were trying to achieve the same thing. The only difference, so far, is that he failed.

I'm terrified that his fate is what awaits me.

Kennan's words stay with me through the night, haunting my already troubled dreams. Inky blue veins coil inside me, then burst from my skin and branch out into the darkness, trapping me like a fly in a spider's web. The mention of Niall conjures him from my subconscious, faded and distorted but no less terrifying. It doesn't surprise me that I can't see him clearly—he no longer exists. Because of me.

I scream myself to exhaustion at the ghostly figure in my mind. He was a murderer. A monster. He didn't deserve to live. I did the right thing.

Didn't I?

The only answer I receive is Niall's specter brandishing a golden dagger at me, then driving it into my chest.

I wake in a cold sweat, my heart pounding. I battle my body's desire to return to sleep until sunrise. When Kennan rouses the others to leave, I'm equal parts relieved and exhausted.

I mumble a Telling to banish the plague, like I've done every day since we set out, and haul myself to my feet. It takes a bit more effort than usual, but I dismiss the thought and blame my fatigue.

The wolves have given up on us as gray daylight starts to seep through the trees. The forest is eerily quiet, save for the cawing of crows in the gnarled treetops and the crunch of our footsteps through the underbrush.

This early in the morning, none of us have the

energy to speak. I'm surprised when Mads draws level with me and clears his throat, catching my attention.

"Hey, Freckles." Hearing that familiar nickname somehow puts me more at ease.

"Hey," I respond in kind.

"Mind if I ask you something?"

The simple act of turning my head makes me yawn. Luckily, Mads and I have been friends long enough that I know he won't take it personally.

"Sure."

"I . . ." His voice suddenly falters and gets quiet. "I overheard you talking to Kennan last night."

I take a deep breath of cold, damp morning air. I was not looking forward to this.

Mads was there. He saw what happened to Niall. At the time, we'd been too busy fleeing for our lives to talk about it. A part of me hoped we never would.

A lot of things have turned out differently than I hoped. I've learned to adapt.

"You want to know what happened to that Bard, back at High House." I voice his question for him.

Mads frowns. "That's the thing," he says, "I remember we were fighting our way out of High House. I mean, it wasn't that long ago, it's still pretty fresh. I remember there was someone there. And then there wasn't. But it's weird. Clouded. Like I fell asleep and dreamed the end of the fight."

I suppose that makes sense. I wrote Niall out of existence, out of the *Book of Days,* no less. All traces of him must be gradually fading from reality. Including Mads's memory. If Kennan still remembers him, Bards must be somehow immune to forgetting people erased by Telling.

"I'll do my best to explain." I take a deep breath. I try to keep the tale brief, since we're still tired and trudging through the woods, with no clue who might overhear. Nonetheless, I share with him about Niall—that he was a Bard, that he murdered my mother and tried to pin it on Kennan, that he tried to kill us when we escaped High House. Before I can let myself get choked up, the momentum of my story carries me into describing how, during the fight, I used my blood on the page from the *Book of Days* as a Telling to wipe him from existence.

Mads is quiet, absorbing the information as we walk. His brow is knit in a thoughtful frown as his eyes inspect something past the ground. I've known Mads my whole life, and this level of consideration is typical of him.

It's one of many traits I thought made him an appealing marriage prospect. That time feels so long ago now. Given the ease of our friendship, it almost feels strange to have ever considered him anything else.

"Do you think I'm a terrible person?" I ask, barely above a whisper. My voice wavers. I'm not sure I want to know the answer.

Mads fixes me with a look I know well. He's trying to say something delicately. He made the same face the first time he tried my cooking.

"I'm not a Bard or anything, but if you used the page from the *Book of Days* to erase this guy couldn't you do the same thing to bring him back if you wanted?"

"I . . . Maybe?" I falter. "I don't know. But—"

"My point is . . ." Mads cuts me off, recognizing the uncertainty in my voice. He stops me with a large, gentle hand on my shoulder. "You made your decision. And it was a tough call you had to make under a lot of pressure. That you struggle with it says a lot about who you are." He leans down slightly, eyebrows raised, making sure I'm looking him in the eyes. "Between us, as your friend, I agree this guy sounds like a piece of garbage and deserves what he got."

I manage a tiny smile. "Thanks, Mads."

"Anytime."

A sudden noise of complete disgust interrupts us. Up ahead Fiona cries out, "What *is* this?"

Mads and I share an identical look as we pick up the pace to catch up. Kennan and Fiona have both stopped at the edge of the forest, looking out over a wide expanse bathed in midmorning light.

Kennan was right—the terrain *has* changed.

The smell hits first, like rotten waste, even worse than the mold in the abandoned safe house. Dark, fetid water, punctuated by swampy earth and decaying vegetation, stretches before us as far as the eye can see.

"Disgusting." Kennan grimaces.

"Whatever's beyond Montane was supposed to be *better*, not . . . this." Fiona covers her nose with her sleeve.

"We have no choice," I say, trying to conceal my queasiness. "We have to cross to get to the next safe house."

Something whizzes past my ear. Then another near Kennan's arm. She darts out of the way, eyes wide as they meet mine, both of us realizing what this means.

Bolts.

We've been ambushed.

3

Tremors of fear radiate through me as I catch sight of Bards closing in on us. Both sides are shouting, but sound distant. I'm trapped in my shuddering body, unable to move.

Mads pulls me and Fiona behind a fallen log before another volley of bolts reaches us. The log jolts as projectiles hit from the other side. The sudden force pushes out the breath I was holding, and I feel my senses return.

"Stay down!" Kennan orders as she vaults over the log to join us. "Wait for them to reload, then make a run for it!"

"What about you?" I ask, flinching as the log shakes again.

"The Telling is weakened here, for some reason," Kennan says. "But we don't have any other choice. I'll cover your escape."

"No." I shake my head. "I'm with you."

Kennan levels a look at me that I can't quite read. Finally, she nods once.

"Follow my lead and don't get in my way."

I nod back.

Beside me, Fiona looks even more terrified than

I am. She's never been in a life-or-death confrontation. I've never seen her eyes so wide or full of fear. She reaches for me, gripping my sleeve with all her strength.

"Please be careful, Shae," she whispers.

Another bolt hits the log and a brief silence stretches over the bog. In the distance I hear the Bards order their crossbowmen to reload.

"Go," I say to Mads and Fiona. I see them start to scramble out of the way before I turn back to Kennan.

She rises to her feet, stepping atop the log with her usual air of deadly power. The bright morning light enfolds her, making her look as though she's glowing. From where I cower in the mud, she almost looks like one of the heroic statues of Bards I saw at High House.

"Ready?" Kennan's glare is fixed on the enemy, but her question is directed at me. I take a deep breath.

When I join her atop the log, it's to a view of a half-dozen Bards closing in and eight more behind, readying their weapons against us. I'm not thrilled with the odds, but Kennan seems unnaturally calm.

The enemy continues their advance. As they draw closer, I see many of their lips moving, performing Tellings to aid their movement through the muck that swirls around their calves. They are still struggling against the bog, however.

It must be as Kennan said. The Telling is weaker

here. It would explain why the Blot in my veins has lessened, and why it's been harder to use my gift to keep it at bay.

At my side, Kennan has begun to whisper a Telling of her own. The sound resonates deep in her throat, casting a low hum into the ether.

I recall her directions to follow her lead. If we're both weaker here, we stand little chance individually against a squad of fully trained Bards, even if they are, too. Our only chance lies in doing together what we can't do alone.

I take another deep breath, calling upon my training and issuing a Telling of my own—not against the enemy, but to strengthen Kennan's.

The waters begin to ripple in front of us. The Bards stumble, losing their concentration as the combined might of Kennan's Telling and mine starts to shift the fabric of reality. A moment later, one slips beneath the surface, followed by another. Then a third. They thrash in the bog before disappearing into the water. A few bubbles rise, but nothing else.

The Bards are thrown into disarray. Those closest to us try to double back and regroup but one of the three falls victim to our combined Telling and sinks into the bog.

The crossbowmen scatter, and I feel myself tense. I turn to Kennan.

"Don't move," she says. "They want to separate us."

They still have the advantage with their ranged weaponry, however. In very little time, they manage to surround us. Still outnumbered, I'm not convinced even a combined Telling is strong enough to repel their bolts. The only reason they haven't yet fired is because they are still gauging what we're capable of.

I try unsuccessfully to swallow the lump in my throat. An eerie stillness settles over the bog. It seems like the only sound for miles is my ragged breath as I look from Kennan to the Bards and back.

A high-pitched whistle suddenly sounds through the air. My gaze darts in every direction, trying to find the source. I'm surprised to see the Bards doing the same.

Before I can question the sound, it's followed by an even louder shriek.

Almost too fast to see, a falcon dives from the sky to assault one of the Bards. The cries of bird and man tangle as the Bard tries vainly to battle the talons in his face. Nearby, one of his companions readies his crossbow and fires a shot at the creature.

Its work done, the bird flies off as the Bard slumps into the mud, a bolt protruding from his bloodied face.

I turn to Kennan again. For the first time, she appears utterly confused, but she's looking in the opposite direction.

A large figure in a rough, black coat, his face hidden by a dark hood, has taken advantage of the confusion to sweep up behind another Bard. My eyes can barely follow the figure's movements, save for a flash of steel. A moment later, the Bard falls into marshy water.

Kennan leaps into the fray. The pandemonium has turned the fight in our favor.

It feels like mere seconds later we're alone again. Except this time, we're covered in foul-smelling bog water, caked with mud, and breathless.

I haven't moved from the log. I feel like if I do my legs might forget how to hold me upright. Out the corner of my eye, I spot Fiona approaching Mads and Kennan. Everyone is alive and uninjured.

The cold bite of a blade against the skin on my neck diverts my attention, followed by a firm, gloved hand tangled in the back collar of my shirt.

"Your name," a deep, rasping voice issues from behind me.

In the jumble of thoughts that follow, I immediately feel foolish for assuming the cloaked man was a friend simply because he fought our enemies.

Fiona notices and gasps sharply, looking to Mads and Kennan, who remain where they stand. Mads is obviously more frustrated than Kennan, who holds her arm out, signaling them to remain still.

It's probably for the best. One wrong move and this stranger is ready to press his knife into my throat.

"I'll ask once more before I lose my patience, kid," the voice says, enunciating each word slowly and deliberately. "Who are you?"

"My name is Shae," I say on the off chance that knowing my name will humanize me enough to give the stranger pause. He seems to have no qualms killing nameless Bards.

"Shae," he repeats, slowly and quietly. The dagger at my throat retreats.

The cloaked man steps back and I turn to face him. I still can't see his face through the dark shadow of his hood, but I can feel his eyes locked on me. He stands completely still.

Then he starts to laugh.

My companions and I watch the cloaked man convulse with laughter, confused expressions on our faces. The sound of the man's guffawing echoes uncomfortably through the otherwise silent bog.

"You can stop now, her name's not *that* stupid," Kennan mutters, just loud enough to hear.

Kennan's words seem to jolt the stranger out of his hysterics. As his laughter dies, he glances at her as though he just remembered she was there.

"Shae . . ." A final chuckle escapes the dark hood as the man sheathes his knife in his boot. Righting himself, he lifts his arm and his falcon perches atop it. "Small world, isn't it?" he asks the bird, who merely trills happily in reply.

"Are you okay?" I can't help asking, but common sense assures me that I probably already know the answer.

"Of all the crazy things I didn't think would happen when I woke up this morning," the stranger says as he shakes his head, still in conversation with his avian companion, "here she is, little Shae, all grown up."

"Do you know him?" Fiona mouths at me. I shrug helplessly.

"Follow me." The stranger turns suddenly and begins trudging south through the bog.

I hesitate, conferring silently with the others. Fiona and Mads mirror my trepidation in the grimaces on their faces. Kennan, however, seems curious and starts after him.

"Really? We're following the suspicious bog man?" Mads asks, giving voice to my concerns.

"Am I the only one who pays attention around here? *Look* at him," Kennan says, sighing as she turns around from a few paces ahead. She points at the stranger, still walking ahead and chatting with his falcon.

I squint at the figure, noticing for the first time the distinctive boots and ceremonial golden dagger protruding from one. When he turns to beckon us onward, I realize that he, too, wears the uniform of a Bard, dirty, patched, worn and mended time and again, but unmistakable.

"He's a Bard." The words slip out on a breath.

"What's more"—Kennan spares a meaningful look at each of us—"I'd wager we just found the overseer of the safe house we're looking for."

Without another word I set off following the

stranger, trusting my companions to keep up. Suddenly I can't catch up to him fast enough.

He *recognized* me. That can only mean one thing.

I stumble in my haste to reach him, as though being closer to the lone, faceless figure trudging through the muck ahead of me will bring me closer to my lost mother. It's a desperate, gnawing feeling deep in my chest where the oldest of my hurts still linger.

He doesn't wait but spares me another glance from under his hood when I finally manage to catch up.

"Figured it out, did you?" he asks. I'm nearly breathless from fighting my way through the bog to reach him and can only manage a short nod. When he replies, his voice is quiet and distant, more as though he's talking to himself than anyone else, even his falcon. "But how much, I wonder?"

"Did you know my ma?" I ask.

The stranger tilts his head, but all I can see is a broad chin covered in dark stubble.

"Yeah." He seems to realize I'm about to bombard him with questions and he raises his free arm. "Listen, kid, I'm old and tired. Cranky. It can wait until I'm back in my chair."

I clench my jaw, sealing my questions in my mouth for the time being.

The stranger leads us through the bog for what seems like hours. I curse the muddy water only to feel a stab of residual guilt. Back home in Aster, water was the most precious resource we had. I can still remember how it felt to live in fearful limbo, uncertain of the next day. Droughts were common, a way of life for us. It wasn't so long ago that I celebrated a small rainfall like it was the greatest blessing ever bestowed on our little town. Part of me wishes there was some kind of Telling to transport all this nasty bog water up north and dump it on Aster.

Clouds the same color as the gaunt, withered trees sticking up from the bog eventually overtake the sky, making it difficult to gauge the time of day. Somehow it makes our surroundings even murkier. The only sounds are our boots in the fetid water, so cold I stopped feeling my feet after a while. Even the stench has stopped bothering me, or maybe I've completely lost my sense of smell, too.

Every time I chance breaking the silence and questioning the strange man at my side, his falcon glares daggers and screeches at me. In the heavy quiet, I can hear my friends whispering.

"You don't think anything lives in this bog, right?" Fiona asks Mads a short distance behind us. "And it definitely wouldn't try and attack us?"

"I don't think anything could survive out here, no," Mads replies. Glancing over my shoulder, I see him nod toward the cloaked man. "Except maybe that guy."

"Ever heard of leeches?" Kennan asks with mock innocence.

"No." Fiona's voice shakes.

"I read about them in a book back in the scriptorium at High House. Little predatory worms that live in swamps like these and latch onto your skin to suck your blood." Underlying Kennan's grim words is a hint of enjoyment. She laughs when Fiona squeaks in alarm. "I'm sure none of them live here, though. They definitely won't wiggle into your boots . . ."

"Cut it out, Kennan," I call.

Kennan smiles in self-satisfaction, her work done. Fiona has already started to beg Mads to carry her. Mads, in turn, tries vainly to convince Fiona there's no such thing as leeches.

Daylight wanes as a small hill rises into view over the dank water that now reaches our knees. Atop the summit is a small, rickety hut. After slogging through the bog for the better part of the day, I have a similar feeling upon seeing it as I did when I first saw the magnificent castle that is High House.

"Here we are," our guide says, punctuating his words with a sharp whistle. His falcon launches off his arm toward the hut. "I suppose the least I can do for an old friend's kid is let you and your companions rest the night here."

"Thank you," I reply, gratefully stepping out of the bog water and onto the stone pathway ascending the hill. My boots make an audible, incredibly disgusting squishing noise as they contact dry land.

We can't get inside fast enough, each of us eagerly anticipating the prospect of warmth and dryness. Kennan shoulders past me as I wait for Mads to set Fiona down—he wound up carrying her a fair distance—and the two of them hurry into the hut.

This safe house is much cozier than the last one, due to it being half the size and well cared for. The walls are hung with dried plants and furs, and insulated with moss. The falcon sits on a perch built

into the wall near a small, circular window, keeping
so still it almost passes for a hunting trophy. We'll
have just enough room if we sit shoulder to shoulder
around the small woodstove in the center. An old
carved rocking chair stands in front of it, the only
item in the hut that doesn't seem strictly utilitarian.

Our host lights the fire in the woodstove, and the
space is instantly cast in a warm, welcome glow.
Kennan, Mads, and Fiona crowd around it like moths.

I take the opportunity to step around them, over
the pelt on the floor that serves as a carpet, to the
other side of the stove. The cloaked man has kicked
his boots off, stretching his long legs toward the fire
as he sinks into his chair. His hood still covers his
face, but he's likely trying to keep the light out of his
eyes so he can sleep.

I clear my throat.

"You're in your chair," I remind him, "care to
answer some questions now?"

"If I must," he half sighs, half groans, but doesn't
move.

A small burst of excitement rushes through me.
I'm not even sure where to start. I take a deep breath,
trying to order my thoughts.

"Let's start with your name." I take a seat on
the floor slightly in front of the rocking chair, an-
gling myself so I can see him without sacrificing the
warmth of the stove.

"Victor."

"Victor," I repeat, finally deciding where to start

my line of questioning. "Has anyone else used this safe house recently?"

"Sounds like you're asking about someone specific."

Great. I'm pretty sure he's toying with me, and already knows exactly who I'm asking about. "Actually, yes." I decide on directness, hoping against hope that it will prompt him to be direct in return. "Has a fellow about my age—tall, with black hair and a serious disposition—passed through?"

"Ah, you're looking for Ravod." Victor hums with amusement. My breath catches at the name.

His face briefly flickers in my memory, pale and handsome, with piercing dark eyes and silken black hair. His voice carried with it a strange, otherworldly reverberation in its controlled depth, like he was always holding back a powerful Telling. Even the memory feels like an earthquake in my chest. Perhaps it wasn't so surprising that I found myself so attracted to him. He was kind, smart, intriguing, and unreasonably gorgeous.

Ravod was the first Bard I ever met. It took some time, but I came to learn that beneath his stern exterior lay a sensitive, vulnerable young man.

It stings that I still feel so strongly about him after everything that's happened. Ravod rebuffed my affections, albeit in the most gentlemanly way possible. And right when I thought we might be becoming allies—*friends*, even—he stole the *Book of Days* and vanished.

I still have his note in my pocket alongside the page he left for me to find. I couldn't bear to throw it away. Somehow it would be more painful to give up on him than to contemplate his baffling disappearance.

"You've seen Ravod?" I try not to let my voice crack and fail miserably. Victor's mouth quirks up at the sound.

"He came through here not too far ahead of you. He said he'd likely be followed," Victor says. "Didn't say by whom."

"Did he have anything with him?" I ask. Knowing whether Ravod still has the *Book of Days* would be useful information, but I'm still not sure if sharing that with Victor would be the best idea.

"He did seem pretty protective of his bag, but it's not my business what's in there so I didn't ask."

"Fair enough." I bite my lip, ready to dive into the question that's been burning in my chest since meeting this man. "And my mother? How did you know each other?"

Victor sniffs irritably, shifting his seat. For a second, I'm not sure he's going to answer.

"We met at High House," he says finally. "Trained and served as Bards together."

"I figured that much out, but . . ." I trail off, unsure whether I'm asking the wrong questions or if Victor is just a frustrating conversationalist in general.

"Back then, there were only four women in the ranks." Victor maintains his posture in his rocking chair. Perhaps I imagine it, but I think I hear a shift in the tone of his gravelly voice. "She was the fifth. And she was special. One day she's a trembling little girl in rags getting hazed by Bards three times her age, next thing you know, she's practically Cathal's right hand. No one had ever seen a Bard like her. Fearless. Gifted. Devoted. Everything a good Bard ought to be. That was Iris."

It's strange hearing her name spoken. It's been so long since I've heard it. But also, the woman being described sounds so fundamentally different from my mother. When I think of Ma, I see her tending sheep and spinning wool. I remember her gently smiling, brushing her fingertips over the freckles on my face and braiding my hair.

I can still remember, with a foul taste in my mouth, the cruelty I faced at the hands of the Bards when I started training at High House. One of those Bards is sitting five feet away. And I can't picture my mother in that scenario, no matter how hard I try.

Maybe she was Iris, a fierce Bard, once. To me she was only Ma. I guess she did that on purpose.

If I'm being completely honest, it stings that she never shared this secret history of hers with me. Instead, I must hear it from a stranger, long after her death, and feel like we're remembering two different people who happened to share a name.

"What happened?" My question feels heavy in my throat.

Victor sighs, crossing his arms over his chest.

"There were two people in this world who Iris adored more than anyone. The first was Cathal, and I'm guessing since you're here you're probably familiar with why *that* could have been. The second was her mentor, another woman. Long story very, very short: Iris's mentor pulled back the curtain on Cathal's chicanery. Such a thing was previously unheard of. Iris was tasked with bringing her own teacher to justice and putting down the resulting insurgency." He pauses, before adding, "She did her duty, but something changed in her after that. She was never quite the same."

"So, the Bards were already rebelling?" I ask.

"Not for long," Victor replies. "Cathal purged our ranks. Anyone he decided was a traitor was executed by their fellow Bards. No one's hands were clean. Eventually, enough was enough. Myself, Iris, and a handful of others began quietly discussing what was going on."

I nod. "You rebelled."

"Got it in one," he says. "We even managed to steal the *Book of Days* from Cathal and seal it somewhere he couldn't touch. It was the best we could do. At the time, it felt like we'd dealt him a major blow. Word was starting to spread about us. Our cause was gaining momentum. People were fleeing to Gondal, and for the first time, Cathal didn't have his precious *Book of Days* to learn our secrets or manufacture a plague for the dissidents on a massive scale. He didn't even know which of his Bards had turned against him. It was the springboard that launched our rebellion in earnest. We started trying to completely dismantle Cathal's power base from the inside, in the shadows."

"But you didn't succeed."

Victor is quiet. "We were betrayed," he says eventually, and the pain in his voice is audible. "One of our own tipped off Cathal that our operation had started sending refugees to Gondal to seek aid in overthrowing High House's regime. We were intercepted and defeated. In the end, there were only six of us and we were forced to flee."

"But you couldn't resist keeping up the fight, and set up your safe houses," Kennan says, listening intently. The light dances in her eyes, making them look like they are made of flames.

"Want to guess whose bright idea that was?" Victor asks.

After hearing the story, warmth fills me at what I know to be the answer. His words linger in the quiet hut. For a few minutes, only the crackle of flames, the quiet rustling of Victor's falcon, and sounds of the night beyond the walls can be heard.

I twist my hands in my lap, lost in thought. There's so much I want to know, but the strange, writhing tightness in my ribs makes me wonder if I should ask.

When I look up, Victor is sitting perfectly upright, and I see his face for the first time. His skin is tanned and wind-scarred, but his eyes are large and brown and surprisingly gentle. His dark hair is long, thick, and mostly matted.

I swear I see a flash of the person he was when he knew my mother, a scrappy young Bard. Someone who fought for something he believed in alongside people he cared about.

"You really look just like her," he says quietly. "Except for the freckles."

Stupid freckles. Even so, his words cause me to smile.

"You really cared about each other, didn't you?" It's less a question and more a realization. He's looking at me with such fondness, I have to believe that it was how he looked at Ma.

The question seems to take him aback. He cocks his head and quirks an eyebrow as he struggles to form his next sentence.

"I don't think you want to hear about *that* part," he says finally, with a slight grimace.

Shock and curiosity battle within me, causing my jaw to slacken. "Wait, were you two—"

"It's in the past, kid," Victor groans, interrupting me. "Let's just say I'm glad she found happiness and leave it at that."

"So you *were*—"

"Go to sleep. I'm kicking you out tomorrow."

Despite him cutting me off a second time, the silence that settles around us seems to allow the story to fall into place as well.

"Thanks, Victor," I reply. "I'm really glad I wound up finding you."

Victor chuckles ruefully, leaning back in his rocking chair but keeping his dark eyes fixed on me.

"Don't thank me yet," he says. "You still haven't made it through the tunnel."

Morning comes abruptly, as does the toe of Kennan's boot against my arm. Her nudging isn't painful, but certainly unwelcome. I groan, sitting up where I curled on the floor last night. Automatically, I check my wrists for plague veins, preparing my Telling to ward off the sickness another day.

The indigo discoloring my veins is even less noticeable than it was yesterday. I barely feel any pain at all. It reinforces my suspicion that the closer we get to Gondal, the less effective the Telling becomes. I worry about why this is, and what that might mean going forward.

Victor is nowhere to be seen, but a delightful smell beckons me to the small table beneath the far window. My companions are already crowded around it, Fiona and Mads vigorously tucking into a meal that's been prepared.

At the center of the table is a scratchy note that reads simply: *Gone Hunting. Made food. Eat. Back soon. V.*

Breakfast is vegetables and small game roasted lightly in oil—very similar to the fare back home in Aster. It's not the titanic portions one would find at High House, but there's plenty for the four of us. I glance out the window, realizing that Victor must have cleaned out his stores to prepare this. No wonder he needed to hunt. His gruff kindness is strangely touching.

I squeeze in beside Fiona, who smiles at me.

"Been a while since we've had a proper breakfast together," she says.

She's not wrong. I remember after Ma died and Fiona's family took me in, we ate breakfast together every morning. There is something pleasant about the thought that we're doing so again, now. Perhaps it is even more comfortable without the rest of her family shooting me dark looks across the table. Instead, it's only Kennan.

This time, her frown isn't leveled against me, it's directed at Fiona. I brace myself for the accompanying complaint, but as she opens her mouth Mads clears his throat loudly and deliberately.

"So, does anyone have any idea what we can actually expect in . . ." His voice falters. He's not used to even saying the word "Gondal." It doesn't come as much surprise; we've been raised to believe that the name alone would cause some kind of catastrophe.

I shake my head. "All I know are the stories. Knowing what I do now, I guess it's not really surprising that my ma told me about it when I was younger. I just always thought it was made up."

"I was too afraid to ask." Fiona's voice is small, betraying her lingering fear.

"I definitely believe *that*," Kennan interjects, leaning back in her chair.

"Well, what about you, then?" I cross my arms over my chest, leveling a pointed glare across the table. "Does the mighty Kennan have anything useful to contribute to this discussion?"

"Do you recall how I collected a number of Gondalese relics within a tower at High House?" Kennan returns, arching one dark eyebrow at me.

I nod. I also vividly remember that Kennan tried to kill me in that tower.

"Your mother handed me that little stone ox idol you like so much, just before she died," Kennan states. "She told me it was from Gondal. That it was a real place. She was struck down before she could say more."

I glance quickly at my backpack, lying on the floor at the other side of the hut. The idol she mentioned is tucked safely inside. Before I lost Ma, it was my only remnant of Kieran. I feel a familiar stab in my heart when I try, and fail, to recall my little brother's face. He's little more than a blur in my mind. Soon I'll only be able to recall Ma's face the same way.

Kennan's words feel like a finger poking at a fresh bruise. It's the same hurt I felt when I listened to Victor's story last night. My mother trusted everyone but me. "She gave you—"

"Don't interrupt me." Kennan cuts me off. "When I was discharged from the sanitarium, I began to search the castle for more evidence. I concealed what I found in that tower with a Telling. I performed exhaustive tests on the relics, hoping for some clue. Obviously, my research was hindered by Cathal razing the tower that was my first hiding spot, and then *you* bumbling into my second and messing around. What I did manage to discover was rather interesting." She pauses with a meaningful look. "Gondal is *nothing* like Montane. If I had to hazard a guess, I would say that they wield a power that dwarfs even that of Telling."

"You have no idea."

Victor's silent entrance and unexpected voice causes us all to jump visibly. The former Bard stands nonchalantly in the doorway, wrapped in his thick cloak, falcon on his shoulder. He carries a stained burlap game bag in his hand, which he sets down before closing the door. "I almost wish I could see the looks on your faces when you see what Gondal *really* is."

"The entrance into the tunnel that leads to the legendary land of Gondal . . . is under your outhouse?"

Fiona's question is innocent enough, but the slight edge of disbelief in her voice mirrors the rest of our thoughts. Following breakfast, Victor announced it was time for us "damn kids to leave me in peace" and led us around the back of his hut toward a nondescript outhouse.

Dense mist had settled over the bog, obstructing our view beyond Victor's small, elevated plot of land. A drizzle of cold rain began as we stopped in front of the ramshackle structure.

"Clever, right?" A smile plays at the side of Victor's mouth. "Not a lot of people would think to look for it here. Besides, it's more appropriate than you think. The tunnel will deposit you in the sewers beneath the Juncture. You'll be well over the border by then, so it won't take long for the Protesters to find you."

"Juncture? Protesters?" I've never heard these terms. My brow knits as I repeat them.

"The Juncture's where the tunnels will spit you out. The Protesters is the fancy, if not terribly imaginative, name our allies in Gondal adopted," Victor explains. "It's been a while since I've been in contact with them, but last I heard they were trustworthy."

"Last you heard?" Mads winces.

"Like I said, it's been a while." Victor shrugs. "You probably noticed people aren't exactly tripping over themselves to make use of this safe house."

"Your confidence is certainly overwhelming," Kennan murmurs under her breath.

"I'm sure it will be fine," Fiona replies, but she doesn't seem all that confident.

Victor either ignores them or did not hear. He grips the handle to the door of the outhouse. Like he did with the mechanism from the safe house before this one, he rotates the handle instead of pulling. A hollow clicking sound followed by a sharp hiss issues from somewhere deep beneath our feet. The outhouse itself starts to lengthen, pushed into the air by a hollow compartment built into the hill. Inside is a simple wooden ladder.

"Anything else we should know?" I ask, turning back to Victor.

Victor starts to reply but is interrupted by a shriek as his falcon reels overhead, cutting through the mist.

"The Bards!" Victor hisses through his teeth, motioning us rapidly toward the tunnel entrance. "They either missed their friends from yesterday or they really want to find you. You need to get out of here, *now.*"

He doesn't have to tell us twice. I force myself to breathe to keep my pounding heart from overcoming me. Kennan shoves her way past Mads to the ladder and promptly descends into the darkness, followed by Fiona.

The falcon emits another warning screech, circling above. Before I can object, Victor starts leading me to the ladder with a firm hand on my elbow.

"Victor? Are you going to be okay?" I ask.

"Aren't you sweet, worrying about an old man you just met in a bog," Victor says. He rolls his eyes at me, but his deflection does little to set my mind at ease.

Their cover blown, the Bards forgo stealth. I can hear them, at least as many as yesterday, if not more, issuing commands and initiating Tellings as they close in on us through the mist.

"Victor, wait," I cry, turning back to him as we reach the opening. "Let me help . . ."

"You can help by going to Gondal and finishing what you started." Victor's voice is firm but surprisingly gentle as he presses something small and cold into my palm before gripping my upper arms. "I'll buy you as much time as I can and permanently seal this passage so no one will follow."

"No." I shake my head. "No, you can come with us . . ."

A shout pierces the fog. The falcon screeches again. They're almost here.

"When you get to Gondal, find Stot. Tell him you spoke with me," Victor says, squeezing my arms as though to emphasize the importance of his cryptic statement.

"Victor . . ." My jaw quivers as his name passes my lips. Whatever I'm about to say is interrupted by the sound of the Bards' rapid approach, and yet another call from the falcon.

"All you need to know going forward . . ." Victor pauses and looks steadily into my eyes. There's a small, peaceful smile on his face. "Is that your mother would be incredibly proud of you, Shae."

He says nothing more, just pushes me into the darkness. The last thing I see overhead as I fall is Victor turn and vanish from view. A second later, the gray sky disappears as the entrance closes in behind us.

I brace myself for impact, expecting something hard and probably painful. My eyes squeeze shut, my fists clench, and I grit my teeth to keep my heart from escaping out my mouth. Distantly, I hear my name.

I yelp as something breaks my fall, and it yelps in turn as we crash to the floor.

"Mads!" I roll off my friend, both of us groaning. "I'm so sorry! Are you okay?"

Mads grunts. "I'm fine," he says. "Maybe warn me next time?"

My laugh comes out in a weak burst that's half sob. Mads picks up on it immediately, placing a large, steadying hand on my shoulder.

"I'm not hurt." I shake my head, answering his silent question. "I just . . ." I trail off into silence.

Mads squeezes my shoulder gently. "I'm sure Victor will be fine," he says. "You'll see him again when this is all over."

I try my best to believe him. To have faith that my only connection to my mother will be okay. Eventually, I manage to lift my head and look Mads in the eyes. There's a dim, distant light from farther away. It makes his features difficult to see, but his steady gaze grounds me.

I'm so glad I'm not alone anymore.

"Let's get a move on." Kennan's command echoes in the air from a short distance away. "The old man bought us time. We'd do well not to waste it."

I nod and let Mads help me to my feet. By the time I'm standing, my eyes have adjusted to the dimness around us.

We are standing inside a large metal tube, rusted in some spots and adorned with smaller tubes and pipes in others. Behind us is a dead end where the ladder deposited us, leaving us no choice but to follow the pipeline. A small current of water flows along the curved ground in the center, as though guiding us along. Lights flicker behind portholes welded in the wall, casting eerie shadows. Aside from our movement, the only thing I can hear is a steady drip of water and a faint buzzing noise. The tube is big enough to walk through, but not *quite* tall enough for Mads, who is forced to bend forward slightly.

Kennan takes the lead as we file through the tunnel. There's a small spring in her step, I notice, not sparked by joy, but curiosity, if I had to guess. A minuscule smile plays at the corners of her mouth as she runs her fingers over the curve in the metal.

"Does she not remember Victor saying this tunnel was part of a sewer?" Fiona whispers to me.

I wrap my arms around myself protectively. I hope Mads is right and Victor's okay. Even if I've only known him for a total of one day, he's given me the gift of kindness and a connection to my mother; one thing I was mostly unaccustomed to, and the other something I did not even know I'd been missing.

I realize my hand is still balled in a fist around whatever he gave me. Drawing level with the nearest light in the wall, I release the tension in my fingers.

An oval-shaped brass locket glints up at me with a faint inscription of a crescent moon, the same symbol that I had come to associate with my mother's group of rebel Bards. It's been worn down, as though it were thumbed at for number of years.

"Did Victor give that to you?" Fiona asks from behind me, resting a hand on one of my shoulders and her chin on the other. I nod, leaning my temple against hers, hoping to convey silently how grateful I am for her presence. "It's beautiful."

"It is," I agree, carefully flicking it open with the edge of my nail. Like most lockets, there's a tiny black-and-white portrait of a woman inside, although it looks unlike any I've ever seen. The detail is vividly lifelike. I squint a bit to see it properly in the dim, flickering light.

A young woman, no more than a few years my senior, grins back at me. Her hair is tied away from her face except for a few wispy tendrils framing her cheeks. Her eyes sparkle with mirth. The creases in her skin from her broad smile are instantly familiar. It's a face I have both never seen before and never thought I'd see again.

Fiona gasps. "Is that . . ."

"Ma." My voice escapes in a whisper.

We fall silent, unable to tear our gazes from the tiny picture in my palm.

Somehow, seeing my mother as she was long ago finally drives home the fact that her secret past was a real part of who she was. Even if I was never made aware, she was Iris the Bard even when she was Iris, my mother.

I gently close the locket and slip the chain over my head. Fiona smiles gently as we link arms and hurry farther through the tunnel to catch up with the others.

The tunnel is endless. Hours, maybe even days, are lost in the dank monotony as we forge onward. The path never splits or changes, but after rounding turn after turn with no end in sight, we have mostly given up on ever seeing the end. Even Kennan's original curiosity has dimmed after passing hundreds of the same circular light affixed to the same metal wall. Mads has complained several times that he thinks his neck is permanently bent from having to angle his head downward. The endless dripping sound is fraying our last collective nerve.

The longer we travel, the tighter the knot in my gut squeezes. Every step recalls memories from High House that I'd rather forget. With them come the flood of questions left unanswered and the terrifying possibility that, no matter how hard I try, I'll never succeed in ending Montane's suffering.

Before, that failure only meant my own suffering. It would have been undesirable, but a part of me had always accepted that. Now it means the suffering of those closest and dearest to me, and the weight of that possibility is unbearable. And when I think back on my mother's journey—how she and her friends set out to achieve the same thing, long ago—their failure only compounds the heaviness in my heart. What awaits my group could possibly be even worse if we can't pull this off.

"First that bog and now this," Mads mutters. "Wish one of you'd told me in advance how soggy this little adventure was going to be."

The current at the center of the tunnel is getting deeper, rising to ankle depth. It's just enough to make trudging through that much more uncomfortable. I shiver against the damp cold running up my legs as we round what feels like the hundredth corner.

Each of us issues a unique, audible sound of relief when we see the tunnel widen out, with small platforms creating a channel on either side of the stream. It might as well be every single luxury contained within High House. We waste no time stepping onto the dry surface.

"Maybe we should take a break?" Fiona's question echoes through the tunnel, interrupting the rhythm of the dripping and buzzing we'd become used to drowning out our thoughts.

"That would be inadvisable," Kennan replies. "Any delays could be costly, especially if we're being followed."

We fall silent, but there are no other sounds in the tunnel. It's only us here. Kennan sighs irritably.

My feet are accustomed to this kind of mistreatment, but still throb angrily as I finally offer a reprieve. I angle myself sideways on the narrow platform, hastily removing my boots and wringing my socks out.

I dry my hands on my pants and gingerly reach into my pocket and remove the page from the *Book of Days*. As I suspected, the paper is completely inert. I fold it back up, frowning at my bag for a moment. I pull it toward me, opening a side pocket, and pull out the stone ox that once belonged to my brother.

The stone used to be the color of gold, with small, shimmering veins along the surface. Now it's a dull gray, like it was carved from any old rock.

Something about Gondal really does diminish the powers that work in Montane. I wonder how such a thing is even possible as I squeeze the little ox once and return it to the safety of my knapsack.

Fatigue strikes not long after. I lean back on the cold metal, propping my head on my bag like it's a pillow. The others have assumed similar positions. Even Kennan leans back against the tunnel wall, stretching her long legs over the water current to rest her ankles on the opposite platform.

My eyelids are so heavy they drift closed on their own to the sound of the rushing water. Before I know it, I've drifted into a dreamless sleep.

"I have a question for you."

Kennan's voice pulls me unhappily into wakeful-ness. I fell asleep with the crook of my elbow over my eyes, which I open only slightly. That's when I realize she's not talking to me, she's addressing Fiona, who is also awake. My friend sits near my feet, mending a tear in her skirt.

Fiona raises her pale eyebrows as she lifts her gaze from her needle to Kennan. "Yes?"

"What are you doing here?"

Keeping my arm over my face, I flick my eyes over to Kennan, who is watching Fiona with the same naked contempt in her eyes that I remember from my first days of Bard training.

I can't hate Kennan, not after learning what she'd been through. Cathal tried to use her, like he did with me, to find the *Book of Days*. Niall manipulated her into believing she was guilty of his crimes. I'm pretty sure the combined weight of that mental abuse landed her in High House's sanitarium. No one should be treated like that. It's no wonder she doesn't trust me, us. However, despite what we've been through together, Kennan is still frustratingly determined to maintain her distance from everyone as a result.

"I'm not sure what you mean." Fiona ties off her thread and cuts it with her teeth. To her credit, she's handling Kennan's intensity far better than I ever did.

Kennan's nose twitches as though she smells something vile, but does not take her eyes off Fiona. Neither of them notices my jaw clenching as I ready myself to step in on Fiona's behalf if needed.

The energy between them is charged. It almost seems like, if the pause lingers any longer, sparks will start shooting across the space where their eyes lock.

"Well, for starters, you're utterly useless. Even more so than those two over there, and that's saying something." She nods in Mads's and my direction. "When I was instructed to fetch you from your dismal little village, I assumed you had some practical skills that just weren't apparent. But you surprised me. You managed to be even *more* worthless."

"Is that so?"

"Your flippancy doesn't change the fact that you contribute nothing to this endeavor."

"According to you, perhaps." Fiona does not flinch. "So, I suppose it's a good thing I'm not here for you. I'm here for Shae."

"Adorable." Kennan rolls her eyes. "The power of your friendship will save Montane. Who knew? All we needed the whole time was to enlist a vain fool in a skirt to prop up Shae's ego in order to succeed."

I'm about to sit up and intervene. Instead, I'm surprised when Fiona's response is to laugh. The sound echoes lightly through the cramped tunnel.

"Are you quite finished?" Fiona asks. "I don't think you realize how many times I've had some version of this conversation. Or did you really think you're the first girl to take out her petty insecurities on me?"

The tunnel goes very quiet. Kennan abruptly gets to her feet, glaring over her shoulder at Fiona.

"Enough lounging around. Let's move," she states, loud enough to jolt Mads out of his slumber. He grumbles under his breath, rubbing his eyes as he gets to his feet.

I sit up and manage to catch Fiona's eye in the dim light. A tiny smile flickers at one corner of her mouth.

"How did you *do* that?" I whisper to her as Kennan strides ahead of the group and Mads lags somewhat blearily behind.

The smile on Fiona's face softens as her eyes find Kennan. "Under all that bluster, she's just a person."

"A terrifying person," I correct her.

Fiona shrugs. "I'm not so sure."

As we continue walking, I glance back at Fiona, feeling like I'm seeing her for the first time. She was always kinder than me. Seeing something in others, in me, that I could not. That's why everyone in Aster loved her so much. It was why, even though she was taller, prettier, and more outgoing than me, I was never able to properly resent her the way some girls in town did.

I'm beginning to wonder if she felt like more of an outcast there than she let on.

The thought stills when I see that Kennan has stopped walking and is holding her hand out behind her, instructing us to do the same. We come to a halt as she turns around, her brow knit tightly with concern.

"Do you hear that?" she asks.

I hold my breath, trying to listen as my pulse quickens. Fiona and Mads glance warily around, trying to locate any sign of disturbance.

Then I hear it. Distant voices. Footsteps. They're headed this way.

Except they're coming from up ahead.

I recall what Victor told us. *The Juncture's where the tunnels will spit you out. The Protesters is the fancy, if not terribly imaginative, name our allies in Gondal adopted.*

Have we reached Gondal at last?

The sounds of footsteps and voices grow louder, followed by lantern light casting chaotic shadows around the nearest bend in the tunnel. Moments later, I count six figures blocking the path ahead. An unexpected blaze of light shines in our faces, and I raise my arm to shield my eyes. After trudging through the dim tunnel for so long, the harsh brightness summons tears to my eyes.

As my vision readjusts, I notice that the group before us is fixated on me and Kennan. The looks on their faces are something between fear and disgust.

"Bards!" a man at the front hisses. Their weapons are pointing at us.

At least, I assume they are weapons. They look like crossbows with none of the components, just a single long hollow metal tube attached to a trigger.

I keep my arms raised, hoping to convey that I present no threat, and Mads and Fiona follow my lead. Kennan opens her hands, holding them out to her sides, which is probably the furthest she'll go toward capitulation.

"We mean no harm," I say, shifting myself in front of Kennan, Mads, and Fiona. There must be some way I can salvage this situation peacefully. "We're unarmed. We are just trying to reach Gondal."

The man doesn't answer, signaling to his comrades with a tilt of his head. They step forward, closing the distance between our groups. Before I can continue, a man grips my wrist and twists it behind my back.

"Don't touch her!" I hear Mads shout, and a moment later his muscular frame hurtles between me and the one holding my arm back. My assailant is no match for Mads's size and raw strength and is quickly subdued in a choke hold.

The strange weapons click menacingly as they are suddenly trained on Mads and his hostage.

"Release him, or we will not hesitate to use lethal force against your companions," the leader instructs. He has an unusual, musical accent, which clashes with the coldness of his tone. I feel as though I've heard it somewhere before.

"Don't hurt them," Mads says, "and we'll come quietly."

The charged stalemate lingers heavily in the air before the leader of the group nods once. Mads releases his hold on his captive and pushes him roughly away.

"They have the upper hand here; we should play along for now," Mads whispers to me. I nod, grudgingly, as we're separated by one of our captors.

"Hey!" Fiona's objection is silenced as she's pushed ahead of me through the tunnel.

"Fiona!" I try to grab for her, but I'm stopped when one of the Gondalese weapons is held against my temple. Up close I see the darkness inside the narrow metal tube. It's too small for an arrow or bolt. I wonder how such an armament is meant to work, but I definitely don't want to find out like this.

"Don't take any chances," the leader says. "Remember, the last one didn't seem suspicious at first, either."

I start to ask what he means, but I'm prodded into step ahead of our captors. I have a pretty good idea of who "the last one" might have been, anyway.

Ravod, what in the world have you been up to?

I lock eyes with Kennan, who to my surprise is cooperating quietly. She flashes me a meaningful look I'm not entirely able to interpret before fixing her gaze ahead of us.

Two more armed figures are silhouetted by a shaft of cold white light. Behind them is a metal ladder built into the wall. I shiver as a feeling of unease settles over me.

The end of the tunnel.

The men up ahead ascend the ladder. Once they disappear up and out of sight, the rest of the group silently spurs us forward one by one. Fiona climbs up first, followed by Kennan and Mads. A lump of apprehension forms in my throat as I'm pushed forward.

I place one hand on the ladder, then the other. My breath echoes heavily in my ears as I climb up toward the light above.

I clamber out of the tunnel onto a cold stone platform. The light, I realize, is not daylight at all but a long, slender metal streetlamp that curves over me as though weeping. Behind it is a starry sky.

When I turn around, I see my companions staring off into the distance with some version of the same awestruck expression on their faces.

Out in the night are the distant lights of a sprawling town. My breath hitches at the sight.

It was one thing to learn it, but quite another to see with my own eyes. Gondal is *real*.

My reverie is abruptly halted by the loudest noise I've ever heard. It sounds half like a whistle and half like a scream. Fiona and I instinctively grab each other by the arm, shrieking in alarm. Even Mads, who almost never gets rattled, jumps a bit. Kennan clutches her ears, searching her surroundings for the source of the noise, ready to assess a threat.

Next, I hear raucous laughter. Our captors are nearly doubled over, their amusement surrounding us in addition to their bodies.

My first reaction is anger. My memories of the hazing rituals enacted by the Bards at High House are still fresh. For a split second I feel as though I'm back there, suffering their jeers.

"That never gets old," one of the men says as the merriment tapers off.

"Right? Nothing like seeing a Montanian's first reaction to the Juncture," another replies.

"You think this is funny?" The question bursts out as I round on the laughing men. "Do you have any idea what we've gone through to get here? This is *not* a joke!"

The men regard me as one might a small, yapping puppy. In the stark light, I finally get a better look at their outlandish clothes. I've never seen so much leather, or so many buttons and buckles before. The stitching is perfect in a way I've only seen at High House, never adorning common folk.

They don't answer me, and the deafening sound issues again, somehow even louder than before. It's accompanied this time by steady chugging machinery and a light even brighter than the one overhead. The rest is simply a black mass in the darkness, growing larger with impossible speed.

What kind of Telling is this? I can barely register my rapidly slackening jaw as several enormous metal carriages, linked together, come into view with one more burst of noise. As I take in the sight, I realize it runs along a pair of parallel metal beams on the ground. It emits a hissing sound as it grinds to a halt in front of the stone platform where we stand, steam billowing from a large cylinder at the front.

Doors open onto the platform and people step out, some carrying luggage, others more interested in staring at their small, leather bracelets. Their clothes are even more strange and exotic than our captors'. None of them cast much more than a cursory glance at the four astonished foreigners gaping at their surroundings.

The leader of the Gondal group whispers to his comrades, and half of them slip back into the tunnel, leaving us with the four most intimidating men. I have to assume Mads's display earlier, coupled with whatever stunt Ravod pulled, has made them extra jittery.

When the doors are clear, our captors motion us to board. When we hesitate, they rest their hands on their weapons. The brief, silent conversation conveys their intent to use force to maintain our compliance.

Kennan, Mads, Fiona, and I all share a look before stepping up to the doors and passing through.

The area inside is larger than it looked from the platform, lined with seats facing one another in smaller sections, and large windows. Like the tunnel and platform, the space is lit warmly with glass orbs over each section of seats. Outside is pitch-dark, so the polished glass reflects our images back at us—dirty, harried travelers from another world. My reflection is completely at odds with the stately, ordered rows of brown leather seats that almost look more like armchairs.

"Sit," the leader of the group behind us instructs.

He doesn't have to tell me twice; my backside sinks into the cushioned seat as though it was made for me. I haven't felt this comfortable since I discovered the mattress I slept on in the dormitory at High House.

It seems like an eternity ago, in another life, full of different people. My thoughts swim in circles as I try to reconcile how all this exists in the same world.

"Welcome to Juncture Twelve," a slightly garbled, disembodied voice issues from somewhere I can't see. *"Next stop, Consonance Station."*

The group that brought us here takes the seats across from us, clearly comfortable with their surroundings aboard this moving metal fortress. One is whistling while another checks his hair in the reflective glass. The leader pulls an engraved metal circle, much like an oversized locket on a gold chain, from his coat pocket, flicks it open, glances absently at it, then returns it to his pocket.

"Where are you taking us?" I ask, breaking the silence between our groups.

The leader points up with one finger, as though that's supposed to mean something. "Consonance Station," he says, mimicking the disembodied voice from before. I ball my hands into fists on my lap to keep from shaking with fear at the overwhelmingness of it all.

"And after that?" I persist.

"We'll see what the others make of you." He shrugs, earning a chuckle from his companions.

"I want to know—"

I'm interrupted as a tall man in a dark blue uniform steps into view. I recoil from the color instinctively, along with Mads and Fiona. Even Kennan's eyes widen at the sight. Dark blue was strictly forbidden in Montane after the plague ravaged us. Even knowing the truth, old habits die hard.

The uniformed man seems too tired to either know or care. He sighs through his nose into his handlebar mustache. He turns to Kennan, who is sitting closest.

"Tickets," he says simply, extending a white-gloved hand. Kennan merely holds his gaze, her widened amber eyes, the color slightly darker, perhaps from fatigue, only betraying the barest hint of confusion.

"They're with us," the leader says, drawing the uniformed man's attention and producing several small pieces of paper between his fingers. He hands them over with little ceremony. I see a flicker of recognition pass between them, as though this is a regular occurrence.

"Should have known." The uniformed man shakes his head, pulling an odd contraption from his belt. He feeds the tickets in and it clicks a few times. "Have a pleasant evening, Mr. Emery. Regards to your father." Then he continues down the aisle.

"Friend of yours?" I ask, determined to be a nuisance if I'm going to be forced to endure being a prisoner.

"Not really." The leader, who the uniformed man called "Emery," makes a face and shrugs. "I see him and the other conductors from time to time, I suppose, during tunnel operations when I come down here. Helps that my father owns this railway." I understood most of that, I think. But before I can respond, Emery leans forward on his knees, leveling a dark, serious look at me. "So, I suggest you don't get any funny ideas about trying anything, got it, *Bard*?"

"I suggest you adjust your tone." To my surprise, it is Kennan who speaks up. Her voice is just icy enough to draw Emery's attention.

"Or what?" the man to Emery's left pipes up. "His father owns the railway, he's one of the most important businessmen in the city."

"And that means less than nothing to me. If you threaten us, we *will* fight back," Kennan states.

"I'd be careful if I were you," Emery cuts in. "You're not in Montane anymore."

I notice, however, that his hands are trembling very faintly. Kennan holds his gaze unblinkingly as the conversation dies.

That does not leave us in silence, however. Whatever Telling works the massive machinery roars to life. The shrill piercing sound from before is muffled in the strange metal compartment, which lurches suddenly into motion. There is a low rumble that courses through the cabin, picking up speed. Within a few short seconds, although we cannot see outside, it feels as though we are moving at an impossible velocity.

I grip the edge of the leather-padded seat with white knuckles. Beside me, Fiona seems even paler than usual. Mads looks slightly ill.

Kennan keeps her gaze locked on Emery from beneath her knitted eyebrows—a look I know all too well. She *loathes* him. I only hope that however that manifests will not get us into even deeper trouble.

I'm not sure how long we spend traveling, or how far we've gone. Despite the tension, the rhythmic movements and deceptively comfortable cushions of the machine lull Mads and Fiona to sleep. It's not long before I have a blond head resting on each of my shoulders. Kennan maintains her fearsome glare at Emery, who is either remarkably unperturbed or simply very good at ignoring such looks. A couple of his men have drifted off in their seats opposite us.

No one says a word until we start to decelerate and finally hiss to a stop. Even then, it is only the crackling, invisible speaker from earlier.

"Welcome to Consonance Station. This is our final stop. As you disembark, please ensure you have collected all luggage and personal items. Have a pleasant evening."

The sound rouses Mads and Fiona, who look around anxiously.

"We're here," I whisper to them. "Wherever 'here' is."

Emery and his men get to their feet and motion us to follow with a not-so-friendly reminder that they are armed and potentially dangerous.

We step off the machine into a large, tiled chamber. A sign hangs from an ornate metal frame attached to the ceiling. It reads MAIN CONCOURSE AND TICKETS in fancy black letters, with a large arrow pointing down the corridor ahead. Beneath my feet is stark, gray cement. The tiles along the wall of the corridor repeat the number 15 in a mosaic at regular intervals. Words and letters are commonplace here, not like home where they are feared and reviled.

The area is well lit, the same as the platform we

departed from, with bright glass orbs of light shining behind elegant wrought-metal sconces. For the first time, I can properly see the massive vehicle that transported us. The metal hull looks like plate armor and steam swirls around the giant, cog-like wheels like mist. It emits a loud sighing sound, as if catching its breath. I find it almost impossible to believe that only a few short moments ago such a huge machine was moving as fast as it did.

The people stepping out of it create a river of bodies that we join, moving quickly to keep up with the current. I've never seen so many people, outside of High House. The entire population of Aster could fit in this room and have a great deal of space.

These people are not at all like the townspeople I grew up with, and not just because of their outlandish clothes. It is difficult to discern any social status from the clothes alone—everyone looks equally outrageous, from the frilly, layered skirts of the women to the rigid suits of the men. The single commonality seems to be their equal fondness for elegant hats and gloves.

This is normal to them. I try to wrap my head around the thought. No one seems remotely as impressed by their surroundings as they should be. The Gondalese walk in the same direction but keep to themselves and do not acknowledge or even so much as look at one another. There is no familiarity between them at all. Many seem tired or distracted. They don't even notice that I'm staring.

A tight grip on my upper arm steers me back as I start to drift away from the others. I turn to see one of Emery's buddies glowering at me. He must have thought I was trying to escape, or something. I can't imagine where he thinks I would go in this completely foreign place. I'm more worried I'll drown in this sea of people and never surface.

I shrug away his grip on my arm as we pass through a tall archway into a space that's easily twice the size of High House's entrance hall and a thousand times more crowded. A vaulted ceiling rises above the crowd, held aloft by symmetrical metal columns, which I soon realize are heavily stylized statues.

Above it all, another invisible voice hovers, magnified to drift over the crowd. It could almost be a Telling, but there is no trace of power behind it. Instead, it sounds more like instructions.

"The nine thirty express train with nonstop service to Juncture Five is now boarding from platform twelve. Have a pleasant evening."

How do they keep all these numbers straight? My awed gazing is cut short when I am once again shepherded through the crowd by a strong, stiff hand. Glancing to my friends, I see that we're being navigated toward a large door, which I assume is the exit.

"Where, *exactly*, are you taking us?" I hear Kennan ask Emery through gritted teeth.

"You're going to meet the rest of our happy little group so we can decide what to do with you lot," Emery replies in kind.

"And you decide that for all my countrymen who come here?" Kennan's question is laced with venom. At her sides, her hands are balled tightly into fists. A few steps behind, I see Fiona cast a worried look from Kennan to Emery and back. She's worried that the Bard's questions might get her into trouble. I'm worried about the same thing.

"Don't be so melodramatic. Your countrymen are helpless refugees. We assist them. But you?" He finally turns a suspicious glare at Kennan. "You're not so helpless, now, are you?"

He's right about that, at least. Kennan is the least helpless person I have ever met. I maneuver my way closer to her, catching her gaze and dropping my voice so only she can hear me through the din of the crowd.

"Let's not do anything foolish," I say. "We should wait to meet the group and try and convince them we're not the threat they think we are. Maybe we can work together."

Kennan holds my gaze for a long moment as we walk, and, to my surprise, nods slowly.

"For once, we agree on something."

We are led outside the enormous building we arrived at only to halt on a bit of crowded pavement not far away. One of Emery's goons pries open a metal grate near the edge of the structure, revealing a ladder leading somewhere dark.

"Joy of joys. Here I was worried I'd never see another tunnel again," Mads grumbles, leaning closer to me so I can hear his complaint but not Emery or his friends. I grimace, mostly to myself. Mads tends to get sarcastic when he's cranky.

I can't say I blame him. For all the legends and mystery, so far Gondal is a lot less hospitable than I imagined.

I think back to the illegal tales Ma used to recite to me and Kieran. In retrospect, she always knew exactly what she was describing. As a child, I was fixated only on certain details, the gardens full of flowers the size of men, insects that would speak to travelers, nobles in splendid raiment, and magic that defied all imagination. At the very least, I don't recall so many tunnels in those stories. It never occurred to me that I might one day set foot in the very place my mother described in her bedtime stories.

I clutch the locket around my neck through my shirt. I haven't seen much of Gondal yet, since night has fallen and we are being held captive, but I'm beginning to wonder if anything she told me matches what Gondal actually is.

At the bottom of the ladder is another tunnel, much like the one that led us here, but bigger and lit more brightly by large buzzing glass orbs suspended from the ceiling. There's a platform built into the side, where the words MAINTENANCE TUNNEL 014C are stenciled in chunky black letters on the rusty metal. The Gondalese sure do love designating things numerically.

The platform leads over a river of rancid sewage. The smell doesn't seem to bother Emery or his lackeys; they're probably used to it. Fiona covers her face with her sleeve, while Mads and Kennan scrunch their faces uncomfortably. I grip my locket tighter, my free hand diving into my pocket and clutching the scrap from the *Book of Days* just as tightly. No one speaks.

When the platform ends, the tunnel plunges downward, creating a thunderous waterfall of waste. And beyond the scope of the light, I finally see a hole, blasted through the side of the tunnel and leading away from the sewer.

Emery's group leads us through silently, and we know better than to venture questions.

The path through the rock is surprisingly short, emptying onto another platform. Unlike most of the structures I've seen in my brief time in Gondal, this one is made of rickety wood. The slats creak under my boots as I step onto it alongside everyone else.

"What is this place?" Fiona's whisper fades into silence as she looks over the side of the platform.

The space beyond is massive, cut from the rock into a rough oval. Countless metal pipes cross the space between the walls, which are lined with platforms, catwalks, and little wooden shanties. Lanterns of every shape and size light the windows and walkways, looking almost like a hive of fireflies.

There are people—hundreds of them. When I strain my eyes toward the other side of the cavern,

I can just make out a small, bustling marketplace. Children scramble deftly, yet terrifyingly, over the web of pipes, their laughter echoing through the air. Others mill about on the various catwalks and platforms, going about their lives as a small underground civilization.

"Are all these people from Montane?" I ask Emery, who is already hurrying us over to the nearest wooden bridge.

"Or their descendants," Emery says. It is difficult not to notice the indifference in his voice.

"Why don't they live aboveground, like everyone else?" I persist.

"They aren't citizens, that's why," Emery replies. He pauses before elaborating. "The government doesn't want to handle an influx of refugees, so they fell through the cracks. This is where they landed. The Protesters do what we can for them, both aboveground and below."

I close my mouth, considering his words. As impressive as this setup is, it doesn't seem fair that after everything they've been through, these people are forced underground by an apathetic government.

"Pathetic. This is the best you can do?" Kennan's words are quiet and cold. Her nose is wrinkled in disgust. "What a load of manure."

Emery stops walking, halting the entire group so he can round on Kennan with a snarl on his face.

"What did you just say to me, Bard?"

Kennan is a few inches shorter than him but

maintains her piercing glare as though she were several feet taller.

"I said," she hisses back, "your best is garbage. You expect us to believe there is nothing more you can do when half an hour ago you were bragging about how your father owns an entire . . . What was it called again? *Railway?*"

There is a long but somehow very satisfying silence as Kennan's question lingers in the crackling air between their locked eyes. It only stretches a little further before Emery turns away with a huff.

To no one's surprise, conversation halts abruptly after that. We travel the rickety, winding paths that connect each block of shanties built into the cavern wall. The whole time, I have the strangest feeling that we are being watched.

Up close, Kennan's harsh appraisal becomes a lot fairer. The structures themselves don't seem all that stable. In four separate instances I overhear people we pass complain amongst themselves of being mugged or pickpocketed. Far more worry about where their next meal will come from. Most of these refugees seem to be growing angry simply from idleness.

"They escaped Montane only to find themselves in a different mess," I murmur, not even realizing I've spoken aloud until Kennan responds with a snort.

"If you stand around pitying them, nothing will change."

"I was just acknowledging what they're going through," I hiss back at her.

"Then you're no better than these imbeciles." Kennan jerks her head toward Emery, who doesn't appear to have heard our exchange—or is deliberately ignoring it.

I fall silent, unsure how to respond. Part of me is indignant, while the other part is forced to grudgingly admit that Kennan has a point. Pity never solved any of my problems—it won't solve any of theirs, either.

We pass over a rope bridge suspended by two large pipes. Lighting the path overhead is a long string of red paper lanterns, casting the path in an eerie glow. I hear deep rumbling beneath the metal as I try not to take a wrong step and topple into the darkness below.

My heart is in my throat until I see that we have all been deposited on the relative safety of the opposite side. Turning forward, I'm met with the sight of Emery opening a door into one of the larger shanty houses built into the wall.

The space inside could almost be described as a one-room home, very similar to the one I used to live in with Ma. Except for the pipes that run through the space, it almost feels familiar. A small kitchen is off to one side with a few bunk beds opposite, and worn furniture is scattered in between. The decorations are eclectic, some more native to Montane than others. I have to wonder if these belongings are things the people here managed to carry on their journey.

Spread around the room I count eight people, dressed similarly to Emery's group. Most are gathered around the large wooden table in the center of the room, but a couple linger in the kitchen. They look up as we enter, their eyes growing wide when they notice my Bard trainee uniform. Those same eyes are about ready to pop out of their sockets when they notice Kennan, dressed in the uniform of a fully trained Bard.

The flat of Emery's palm shoves me roughly into the center of the room alongside Kennan. Mads and Fiona stumble behind us.

"Found this group in the tunnels under the Border Juncture," Emery states. "Looks like Gondal's becoming a popular destination again."

The room is silent, everyone giving looks to one another before coming back to us.

"Are they in league with the other?" one young woman finally asks, frowning.

She must mean Ravod. Worry seizes in my chest at the prospect of him not being okay. It takes some effort to push those thoughts away.

"I thought it might be prudent not to interrogate them in public," Emery says. "They're not armed and have been cooperative. Mostly." He shoots Kennan a pointed glare alongside the last word.

I say nothing, but my gaze flicks to Kennan's boot where she keeps her throwing knives concealed. At least when she isn't testing them on me. She catches my gaze as I look up, holding it, before discreetly shaking her head. I feel my jaw tighten, understanding despite my frustration. It would do us, or the other Montanians here, no good to start a fight. We don't know enough about what is going on yet.

"Look," I say, holding up my hands and taking a small step forward. "We're not here to cause trouble for you. Truly. If anything, we want the same thing."

"We have no reason to trust you," a Gondalese man standing near the table says. He's barely finished his sentence before the next person starts talking.

"The last Bard who came through here attacked us for no reason!"

"For all we know, you were sent from High House!"

A girl standing next to the last speaker slaps him upside the head. "You idiot, don't you think they would have bothered to disguise themselves?"

"Perhaps we should put it to a vote?" another chimes in.

Soon, the whole room is talking over one another, with the exception of myself, Kennan, Fiona, and Mads. A chaotic argument starts building, but I am unable tell who is saying what as the din escalates.

"Enough!" Kennan is not using a Telling—she can't here in this strange land—but her commanding voice silences the room just the same. "Is this why your pitiful little group can't accomplish anything? You're so disorganized that I'd be astounded if you could agree on whether water is wet!"

The room is quiet, those gathered shifting their weight like unruly children being scolded by their mother.

"This isn't difficult," Kennan continues. "These

idiots brought us here and you don't trust us, correct? Take us into custody, treat us fairly, question us, and examine the evidence impartially to arrive at a verdict." She steps forward, holding her wrists out. "There's no reason we can't be civilized, no?"

"What are you *doing*?" Mads whispers. "You're *letting* them keep you a prisoner?"

"Not just me," Kennan says, furrowing her brow to cast a meaningful look at us.

"Are you nuts?" Mads seems ready to continue, but he's interrupted as Fiona steps forward to stand beside Kennan, holding her wrists out. She and Kennan share a lingering look that I can't fully interpret.

Mads turns to me. "Freckles, you're not seriously considering this, are you?"

I look from Mads to Fiona and Kennan. On the surface, what they are trying to do does seem crazy. Part of me worries if I let myself be taken prisoner that I will never get free.

I asked my friends to trust me when we left Montane. Now it's my turn to trust them. The thought slows the coiling fear in my chest.

I join Kennan and Fiona.

"I guess we're doing this." Mads heaves an exasperated sigh, throwing his hands up before following suit. I shoot him a small smile and he rolls his eyes at me.

"Yes, yes, we're adorable," Kennan groans, her gaze fixed on the people in front of her. "Are you going to take us prisoner? Or do you need me to repeat myself?"

The group hesitates. Finally, Emery speaks up.

"Well, what are you waiting for? Stot. Bind them."

Quiet descends, and a boy emerges from the back of the group. He's tall, but his features are youthful, making it difficult to gauge whether he's barely more than a child or older than I am.

Stot. The name rings a bell. It takes a second for the memory of Victor's voice to surface in my mind.

When you get to Gondal, find Stot. Tell him you spoke with me.

I watch as Stot collects a few lengths of rope from a chest before approaching us. He starts binding Kennan's wrists and methodically works his way down the line of us. When he finally reaches me, he keeps his pale eyes locked rigidly on his task, refusing to meet my gaze from behind the messy brown bangs that fall over his face like a wall between us. Once his task is complete, he steps back.

"Let's lock them down below while we deliberate," a young woman says.

"I'll take them." Stot speaks up, his voice quiet and a little hoarse. The main group collectively nods in assent, the first agreement I have seen since stepping into the room. Stot gestures for us to follow with a tip of his head, although he carefully avoids meeting anyone's eye.

We fall into step behind him as he leads us to a door at the side of the large room. It creaks open, revealing nothing but darkness. Stot casually flicks a small switch on the wall beside him and light blinks on. The golden glow of the small glass orb above the doorway reveals a short wooden staircase built atop another large metal pipe that descends through a hall cut into the dark rock.

Stot leads us down, pulling a ring of brass keys from his belt and unlocking the door at the bottom. It creaks on its hinges as it sways into a sparse storage room. We shuffle in, one by one, while Stot stands in the doorway, watching us through his unkempt hair.

"I'm sorry about this," he murmurs as I pass him. I pause, turning to face him. His eyes snap away from mine the moment they make contact.

"It's not your fault," I say.

"The Protesters, they aren't bad people," he replies, frowning at the floor as he fiddles with the key ring in his hands with long fingers, stiff with tension. "They're doing their best."

"You're not part of the group?" I inquire, hoping the boy might offer further information on the situation in which we have found ourselves, maybe a way to appeal to the Protesters and enable us to work together.

Stot shakes his head. "I'm from Montane, like you. The Protesters took me in after . . ." His voice cracks on the last syllable, betraying his age. He clears his throat quickly. "They saved my life."

"Did Victor help you get here, too?" I ask. The young man's eyes widen at Victor's name. Worried I startled him, I take a small step back. "When we came through the tunnel, he told me to find you."

Stot doesn't move, like a forest creature confronted by a hunter. When he speaks, his voice is almost too quiet to hear.

"I wouldn't be here without Victor."

"It's the same for us," I say. "I know that if he trusts you, I can as well."

Stot is silent at that, his gaze dropping to the floor as he considers my words. Eventually, he looks up at me through a small gap in his hair.

"What are you doing here?"

"We came here to try and help fix things back home," I answer. "Is there any way you can relay this to your friends? That we only want to help?"

Stot is silent again. Finally, he nods.

"I'll try."

I reach toward him and place a hand on his thin shoulder. He flinches at the contact, his frame tense, but he doesn't pull away.

"Thank you, Stot."

I drop my hand, and the young man seems grateful to leave the room. Once the door closes behind him, I hear the soft click of a key turning before his muffled footsteps disappear.

As far as being imprisoned goes, we could have done far worse. At first glance, the space looks like a simple basement, but it is closer to a bunker. The windowless walls are lined top to bottom with shelves of provisions and locked crates labeled EMERGENCY

SUPPLIES. A distinctly uncomfortable-looking cot sits to one side. A wooden partition serves to create a bathroom, complete with a small sink that provides hot and cold water.

It doesn't take long for us to inspect the space before finally settling in different parts of the small compartment. At least we were allowed to keep our belongings, even if we are unable to reach them with our wrists bound.

It's hard to tell whether hours pass or only minutes. The silence stretches as Fiona and Mads finally curl up on the wooden floor and drift off to sleep.

I envy them. My body aches and my eyes sting with exhaustion, but my mind can't seem to slow down. Everything that has happened creates a whirlpool of thoughts and memories that rapidly circle one another without end.

I wander over to slump beside Kennan on the cot. She spares me her usual sharp glance, instead sighing softly and turning her attention somewhere past the opposite wall.

"I wasn't sure you'd go along with my plan," she says. "Perhaps you're growing more sensible after all."

My eyebrow rises at that. "Did you just say something nice?"

"Why do you constantly need everyone to tell you how great you are?" she asks, turning toward me with a look of genuine puzzlement.

I fall silent beneath the heavy blanket of her question. I've spent enough time around Kennan to realize when she's issuing an insult meant to end a conversation, and that's not what she's doing here. Her eyes are narrowed at me more in inspection than condemnation. The difference is remarkably subtle, but noticeable.

She's never asked me about myself. Part of me wants to shut down and close her out. I've tried so many times to open up to her, and she rebuked my overtures of friendship every time. My cheek briefly stings, remembering how she struck me with the pair of embroidered gloves I tried to give her as a peace offering.

If I had known then what I know now, I wouldn't have bothered. Not because Kennan is unworthy of such gestures, but because that's just not who she is. She's stoic, but not completely. I've seen things that moved her. She respects intelligence, power, and confidence. I am still at a loss when it comes to figuring out the rest of the puzzle, however.

I take a breath, ready to try to open up to her yet again but steeling myself for the inevitable censure.

"Back home, everyone hated me. They believed I was cursed by the Blot. With the exception of my ma, Fiona and Mads were the only people who were willing to come near me or spare a kind word. I suppose it's made me somewhat insecure." I chuckle a bit when she arches her eyebrow at my statement. "It's made me *very* insecure," I amend. The eyebrow lowers. "So now I treat people the way I want to be treated in the hopes they'll believe I'm kind, and therefore be kind in return."

"Do you not believe yourself to be kind?" Kennan asks.

"I try to be." I shrug. "But sometimes I wonder if it's worth it."

Kennan is quiet before saying, "I may not be the right person to answer that."

"What about you?"

"What about me?"

I am surprised she allowed the question at all, and I shift in my seat, unsure how to encourage her to keep speaking. I cling to the vague hope that she'll let me attempt to understand her, that we can finally be—if not friends—then proper partners in all this.

"How did you become the way you are?" I ask, finally.

"Say what you mean." The hardness in Kennan's voice is returning.

"Fine. You're pessimistic, rude, and generally insufferable," I reply. "And also, terrifying. Please stop glaring at me."

"No."

"Then will you answer my question?"

True to her word, Kennan keeps her signature glare affixed to me, but she leans back onto the cot very slightly, as though reassessing me. The golden lamplight shines on her dark cheeks, casting her in a warm glow that seems at odds with her hostile disposition.

It takes all my willpower to hold her gaze. Perhaps I am imagining it, but her eyes seem darker than before. *Could their color be a Telling that has faded now that we're in Gondal?* I push the thought away, unwilling to allow it to distract me.

"I'm pessimistic, rude, insufferable, and terrifying because I must be," Kennan states. "It was the only way to survive growing up at High House."

"You grew up at High House? How did that happen?" I keep my voice gentle, hoping it will prompt her to elaborate. When the silence lingers, I continue, "It's okay if you don't want to talk about it. But I'm willing to listen if and when you do."

Kennan scoffs and rolls her eyes, turning away from me. But now I'm not sure if it's because she's closing off or because she isn't.

"It's not your problem," she says.

"Well, no," I admit. "But the offer stands all the same. I want to believe we can still see our way to being friends someday."

"We're not friends," Kennan mutters.

"Well, why not?" I ask, lowering my voice when Fiona stirs where she's curled up on the floor. "Not everyone is trying to use you like Cathal or hurt you like Niall."

"You think I told you about that because I *trust* you?" A familiar sneer is beginning to turn Kennan's lip.

"Then why *did* you?" I barely manage to keep my voice to a whisper. My sympathy is quickly replaced by flickers of anger that bite at my heart. Trying to get through to her is like talking to a very insulting, mistrustful brick wall. I can't help feeling stupid for thinking her brief moment of openness was a step forward for us.

Kennan opens her mouth to retort when a resounding, unexpected crash breaks through the stillness. The sound is promptly followed by yelling, banging, and loud thuds, as if bodies are falling to the floor.

Mads springs to his feet, and Fiona looks around anxiously, both roused from their sleep. They turn from the door to me and Kennan, as though expecting us to be able to explain the sudden commotion.

"Sounds like a fight." Mads grimaces.

"But who is fighting whom?" Kennan's quiet question is nearly drowned out by the din.

I hiss in pain as an unexpected searing flash runs across my thigh. I shove my hand into the pocket where the sensation originated.

The page from the *Book of Days* comes free in my fingers. I grit my teeth against the burn of the paper, which looks otherwise normal, and gingerly unfold it. Though previously inert, symbols and text now flash across the page. Whatever message it is sending is completely indecipherable.

"What in the world is going on?" I whisper, half to myself and half to the page.

I barely notice when Kennan steps closer to peer over my shoulder, her brow furrowed tightly as she inspects the page in my hands. Then her gaze snaps to the door, planting a new seed of fear in my already chaotic chain of thoughts. The paper trembles in my hands as my eyes follow Kennan's toward the door—and the violent sounds outside.

"It's reacting to whatever is out there . . ."

I push the page back into my pocket. The ebb and flow of the sounds of an altercation consumes our small prison. It presses against the silence in the storage room, heavy with our worry and fear.

Then, just as suddenly as it began, it stops.

The Bards. They've found us. My mind races and I find myself frozen where I sit, my eyes riveted on the door—our only escape. Any previous thoughts are replaced by the icy, slithering fear in my gut that the Bards are here.

The rhythmic sound of feet slowly descending the staircase beyond the door meets my ears, and I can only imagine it is Cathal, come to finish us off.

My jaw clenches at the memory of those cold, cruel eyes. My teeth grind together uncomfortably at the thought of seeing them. Somehow, the painful recollection of Cathal's true colors is heightened by the simultaneous memory of his gentle, paternal kindness toward me—kindness that had been nothing but a lie.

The sound of footsteps stops, replaced by the frantic beating of my heart. I remain paralyzed, not sure if I'm about to faint or throw up.

The door handle rattles. Once. Twice. Then there is nothing but suffocating silence.

The door explodes. Shards of wood fly into the room and the metal handle spins impotently across the floor, coming to a stop in front of a frightened Fiona, whose eyes are widened beyond what should be physically possible.

The figure of a man stands in the doorway, and my heart stops beating altogether as he steps into the room.

Unbidden words leave my mouth on a whispered breath.

"It's you . . ."

Ravod takes a single step into the room. The uniform he wears is almost black, but in the light it shows hints of a dark olive green beneath worn brown leather armoring, gold buttons, and buckles. The clothes are completely foreign—the fashion here in Gondal—but the man wearing them is unmistakable.

It occurs to me that I have been trying, unsuccessfully, to forget how handsome he is. His face is a perfect marriage of soft and angular features; high cheekbones and a square jaw set against a subtly curved nose and delicate mouth. The fight we heard messed his hair up slightly. A few curved ebony locks graze his pale forehead near distinctively arching black eyebrows, which knit together in a stern expression that I have come to associate closely with him. His dark eyes flash over the room methodically.

There is a flicker of familiarity when his stiff gaze lands on Kennan. Then his eyes meet mine and his features soften somewhat. I awkwardly shuffle my weight from one foot to the other. For a breath, my heart is indecisive on whether to leap into my throat or burst out of my chest.

Then I remember he stole the *Book of Days* and disappeared without warning, and my excitement at seeing him dims somewhat. The memory makes my heart sting with each new beat.

"You followed the trail. Good," he says with a nod of his head, his melodic voice finally breaking the stillness that permeates the small storage room.

"Ravod." His name cracks in my throat as I stand up, drawn to him. I barely make it more than a step when a stiff arm shoots out before me, blocking my way forward.

Kennan rises to her feet, suspicion narrowing her eyes as she watches Ravod.

"How are we supposed to trust you after what you did?" she demands, her voice low and icy.

"I'm the reason you're here, aren't I?" Ravod doesn't miss a beat. "Look, I promise I'll answer all your questions, but right now we need to leave."

As though to punctuate his words, the sounds of a mob approaching begin to stir in the distance.

Ravod turns his attention to Mads and Fiona, as if suddenly realizing they are there, and frowns at them.

"You, too, I suppose," he says. He turns on his heel, heading for the door.

I start to follow but pause when I notice Kennan is not doing the same. I throw her a questioning look.

"I'm staying," she says, as though it is the most obvious thing in the world.

"What?" I exclaim. "Why?"

"I believe I can get through to these people. Maybe help them." Kennan's gaze is steady as she speaks to me. "I'm asking you to trust me one more time."

I swallow a sudden lump in my throat. *Kennan is not my favorite person, but . . .* My thought trails off. There's no "but." We've been through a lot together, and I'm worried what might happen to her if I abandon her in captivity, even if it is at her behest.

"If I don't hear from you by tomorrow, I'm coming back," I say. "And I will burn this whole place down if it turns out you're not okay."

Kennan cocks her head, confusion flickering over her dark features before—to my complete surprise—a slow smile spreads over her face, as though the idea of my threatened rampage amuses her.

She nods once. "Go."

"Tomorrow," I remind her as I step back, keeping my gaze on Kennan's for a moment longer, to which she rolls her eyes.

"Yes, yes, you're terribly heroic. I feel giddy. I may even swoon. *Go!*"

I turn to Mads and Fiona, who are waiting by the door, their faces creased with worry. Fiona grabs my hand as I approach.

"Let's get out of here," I say, and we rush up the stairs after Ravod.

My jaw practically falls off its hinges at the sight that greets us. The space we had walked through not so long before has been completely trashed. The large table is split down the middle and two incapacitated bodies lie sprawled in its wreckage. Others are scattered amid the mess of overturned furniture and broken paraphernalia.

Ravod does not break his stride, walking through the fight's aftermath as though it's not even there. Mads, Fiona, and I share a look before picking our way carefully after him.

"They aren't . . ." Fiona grimaces as she gives an overturned bookshelf a wide berth. "They're not dead, are they?"

"They're alive," Ravod states over his shoulder, but I notice the very slight hint of defensiveness in his voice that could be easily missed by anyone unfamiliar with his past. Ravod is especially careful to prevent inflicting lasting harm on others.

Mads steps closer to me and whispers, "Who *is* this guy?" with equal parts suspicion, disbelief, and awe.

"He's a friend," I say. "At least, I'm pretty sure."

Mads frowns. "You might want to be *completely* sure before we follow him much further."

I nod and pick up my pace, moving ahead of Mads and Fiona to draw level with Ravod. It's a little harder than expected, with the combined mess on the floor and the Bard's long-legged gait. He pauses at the other door to the shanty, opposite from the one we entered through.

Outside, the underground dwellers mostly carry on as they did before, but there are a couple of small groups in Gondalese clothes rushing along the catwalks toward us. They are still far enough away to not pose too much of a threat, and they don't see us yet.

We can make it out as long as we can formulate a plan, but that hinges heavily on my faith in a certain Bard, which has been heavily damaged.

"I really want to trust you, Ravod," I say, drawing his gaze. It flickers over me briefly before he turns back to his assessment of the situation beyond the door. "I need to know you're not planning on harming my friends."

"Says the one who not so long ago was begging for *my* trust." A small, ironic smile tilts the corner of his mouth.

"That was before you took off," I reply. "You have no idea what I've been through to get here. Because of what *you* did."

Those dark eyes of his lock onto me suddenly, with an intensity he does not allow himself to show often but sometimes slips through the tiny cracks in his carefully constructed defenses. There is something more, though, in the way they glimmer faintly in the lantern light. Something I've seen once before from him. Regret.

"Follow me, or don't. It's your choice," he says finally. "But you told me once that you wanted answers. That is what I'm offering you, nothing more, nothing less."

He does not elaborate, instead darting into the shadows hugging the rock face and nearly disappearing altogether.

I cast a look toward Mads and Fiona over my shoulder as worry creeps through my chest. If I were on my own, I might have followed Ravod without a second thought, but things are different now. The full weight of my responsibility to them nearly makes me sway on my feet. They are here because of me— because they trust and believe in *me*. I can't let them down. I *won't*.

"I think we can trust Ravod, for now." I speak from the heart. "But it's not only my decision. Are you both okay with following him?"

"You take us on the strangest adventures, Shae." Fiona sighs in amusement before squaring her slim shoulders. "All right. Why not? He's cute."

"Just because someone's 'cute' doesn't mean . . ." The start of Mads' exasperated lecture tapers off as his focus drifts over my shoulder. "You know what? We don't have time for this. Let's accept the jailbreak and sort the rest when we're safe."

Glancing over my shoulder, I see the Protesters have started converging on the catwalks, heading toward us with raised voices and those bizarre weapons of theirs. I nod to Mads and Fiona, and the three of us slip out of the shanty and into the dark after Ravod.

Luckily, he's not too far ahead, as though he knew we would follow him. Ravod ushers us onto one of the upper catwalks ahead of him. Hurrying past silently, save for the creak of the wood and ropes, I quickly catch Ravod's eye. The regret in his gaze is gone, replaced with his usual stern focus. I wonder if I might have imagined it in my desperation to trust him.

A shout to my left makes me chance a look across the chasm to the other catwalks, where the Protesters are splitting up. Their familiarity with the bridges allows them to move faster than us, and by taking two directions they stand a very real chance of pinning us from both sides.

"We need to hurry," I say, urging Fiona and Mads ahead of me. They do their best to pick up the pace. We are all too painfully aware that one false step could send us plummeting into the dark.

I dare to look behind me at Ravod. Despite the businesslike frown, he, on the other hand, does not seem terribly worried.

What is he planning? I cannot help wondering. *What does he know?*

"Focus, Shae," he says in the same gentle tone he

used to instruct me with. I take a deep breath and turn forward, but I swear I see a small smile touch the corner of his lips as I do.

We reach the other side, my legs shaking even after stepping onto the relative security of the opposite platform. Our pursuers have reached the bridge we just crossed, and the second group is closing in on our path up ahead.

Ravod turns to the wooden post that secures the bridge, producing a hunting knife from his belt and shredding the rope that holds the bridge together.

"He's destabilizing the bridge! Turn back or it'll collapse!" I hear someone shout. They start to panic, rushing over one another in their haste to double back.

"That takes care of one." Mads nods approvingly. "We still have to get past the pack up ahead."

"I have a few ideas about that." Ravod sheathes his knife and takes the lead again.

Luckily, we seem to be done with rope bridges for a time. We dash up a flight of stairs leading to the next level of catwalks. They creak noisily, but at least they don't wobble underfoot. Unfortunately, it is the only way forward, and at the rate we're being closed in on, we won't be able to go much farther without a confrontation.

We converge on the platform at the top of the stairs, which empties into a small marketplace cluttered with colorful makeshift stalls. The shopkeepers and handful of patrons quickly and quietly shuffle out of the way of the confrontation as though this were something normal.

I wonder if things are as peaceful down here as they seem. The thought is rapidly swept away by the standoff beginning between us and the group more than twice our number.

"Let us pass," Ravod commands, stepping forward with his hand placed unmistakably over his weapon.

"The government abandoned these people. We don't recognize the authority of the military here," a young woman replies in a clearly rehearsed tone.

Looking over the crowd blocking our path, I notice they are not much older than us. Much like Emery, they are dressed and armed well. There is something strangely recognizable about the light in their eyes when they speak of their cause. It reminds me of home.

Maybe Gondal is not so different after all.

I look to Ravod, who seems neither surprised nor intimidated. He draws a deep breath, as though preparing to sigh. But he doesn't.

"*Rift.*"

My jaw slackens as his voice sends a tremor through the fabric of reality. The floor of the platform cracks with a sound like a clap of thunder. The wood bursts apart into splinters and collapses into a sizable gap between us and the Protesters.

A Telling. It should not be possible.

Mads and Fiona gasp in unison, but they are still less surprised than the Gondalese, some of whom scream in outright terror, pointing fingers in Ravod's direction. Others flee.

Taking advantage of the sudden pandemonium, Ravod ushers us off to the side, where a rope ladder hangs near the rock face, leading up to the next tier of platforms.

"These folks really don't like Bards, do they?" Mads frowns, looking over his broad shoulder before stepping onto the ladder.

"Not Bards," Ravod corrects him. "There are no Bards here. They fear the Telling."

Fiona eagerly steps onto the ladder, flashing a charming smile as Ravod holds the rope steady for her. He maintains his grip as I step forward to follow.

I try to channel everything I've seen Kennan do to level what I hope is my fiercest glare at him. I can't imagine it's very intimidating, since I'm a great deal shorter than he is, and far more unkempt from my days of traveling. At best, I probably look cranky and in need of a nap, but it will have to do.

"You have a *lot* of explaining to do." I jab the air in front of him with my index finger.

"I know." Ravod nods sideways to the ladder. "And the sooner we leave, the sooner I will do so."

My mouth twists to the side, but I obey while maintaining my glare as long as possible.

When I've gained some height and momentum on the ladder, I feel a short tug, signaling that Ravod is following. I try to shake away my lingering worry and old hurt, fearful that he is preparing to betray me the way Cathal did.

At the top of the ladder, I grab onto Mads's outstretched hand and let him haul me up to the platform. Regaining my bearings, I realize this is not the entrance we previously used to enter the cavern, but that there is another tunnel leading out nearby.

Once Ravod steps onto the platform behind us, we file into the darkness and out of the cavern.

At the end of another long walk through another long tunnel I am convinced that the nation of Gondal is composed entirely of infuriating tunnels. Ravod eventually halts below a ladder of metal rungs bolted into the rock. Looking up, I see a small grate overhead where faint rays of early morning sunlight peek through.

Ravod ascends wordlessly and detaches the grate. Tossing it to the side, he beckons the rest of us to follow.

I go first this time. As I reach the top, Ravod offers me a hand. I hold on tightly as he pulls me effortlessly out of the hole and onto my feet. The light stings my eyes as I get my bearings and his face comes into focus. Sunlight casts a faint halo around the paleness of his features, making him almost seem like he's glowing. His dark eyes and hair, on the other hand, seem to repel the light, standing out even more starkly against his other features. He watches me with a patient, but slightly amused, smirk. My breath hitches as I realize I haven't let go of his hand yet, and I bite back an apology as his fingers slide free of mine.

"Look around you," he says quietly.

I blink, turning away from Ravod to my surroundings, and try not to fall over as they come into focus.

Directly in front of me is a collection of rectangular towers rising into the early morning sky. The height of each varies, some only several stories tall while others disappear into the clouds. Some are made of brick, others of stone, and a few even look to be glass. Above the tops of these behemoth structures, I see enormous balloon-like airships of various types floating in the sky. Smaller aircraft zip by in the gaps between the rooftops and the larger crafts.

At ground level is a grid of paved streets, where loud carriages zip by with no horses or oxen to pull them. Despite the early hour, the area is abuzz with activity. Stores are open, lights flash in every direction without flame or fuel. Well-dressed pedestrians keep to their paths at the sides of the street and, just like the crowd at Consonance Station, completely ignore my prolonged stare.

I tear my gaze away, as though that could prevent my eyes from popping out of my head. Mads's and Fiona's stunned faces mirror my own. Only Ravod looks completely nonchalant.

"Welcome to Gondal," he says.

"This . . . This is . . ." I try to form a sentence and fail spectacularly. When I attempt again, I'm met with the same result. There simply are no words for this place.

"This is Seventy Fourth Street." Ravod appears to be enjoying himself as he tilts his chin up at a nearby sign that reads 74TH STREET in gold letters.

"There are *seventy-three* other streets like this?" Fiona splutters, finally finding her voice.

"Two hundred and fifty, actually," Ravod replies. "On this side of the river, at least."

"I thought High House was big," Mads mutters, his eyes roaming over the towers that surround us. "You could probably fit it three times over into that one building over there."

I shake my head clear of the clouds of disbelief that threaten to overwhelm me. Even having expected Gondal to be nothing like home, this is a lot to take in.

"We're not being followed," I say after the bustle slips into the stillness of realizing I'm not running for my life.

"The Protesters don't show their faces above-ground unless they're holding one of their rallies," Ravod explains. "If they were seen chasing us through the city, they would be apprehended by the *actual* authorities."

I take a deep breath, and it calms me until the city air burns in my windpipe. I cough it out.

"Perhaps we should discuss this somewhere other than the middle of a busy street?" I suggest.

Ravod nods, and a genuine smile flickers over his face for an instant before it is replaced by his usual stoic countenance.

"I know just the place." He gestures to us to follow him down the street, heading east. "It's not far."

We make it a few steps before a new question twists in my gut. I hurry to catch up with Ravod, frowning at him as I struggle to match his quick pace.

"How?" I ask.

Ravod spares me a glance. "Excuse me?"

"*How* do you know just the place?"

He swerves, rounding the street corner without breaking his stride. It takes some effort not to barrel into him or the ladies walking in the opposite direction. They sniff at me irritably from beneath their broad-rimmed feathered hats before eyeing my clothes with distaste and carrying on with their day.

I check over my shoulder to make sure Mads and Fiona are behind me. Their progress is a little slower, as they instinctually eye each lettered sign with suspicion. A few men leer at Fiona as they pass but lose interest when she steps deliberately closer to Mads.

This enormous urban plexus is nothing like the bedtime stories Ma used to recite. I sidestep an oncoming group of chatty friends, finding some difficulty in reconciling my thoughts and paying attention to the flow of the busy sidewalk. I draw a deep breath, closing my fingers around Victor's locket before forging onward.

Ravod is nearly at the end of the block, but he stops just short of the next corner, facing a large storefront built into the base of the tower that dominates this street. He looks at the sign above the large window, which reads DINER in curving letters made of steel.

I'm a little surprised there's no string of seemingly random numbers, given what I've seen so far of Gondal.

Perhaps more surprising is the look that lingers on Ravod's face as his gaze roams the storefront. At first glance it looks like contentment, but as I draw closer it's clear it is something deeper. He is smiling almost wistfully at the sign, like it's an old friend with whom he shares a secret. I did not think Ravod capable of such sentimentality, but there is so much of him that remains a mystery, even now.

"You must be hungry," he says. "In here."

Mads and Fiona waste no time following Ravod inside, but I linger as a tumultuous wave of uncertainty leaves me rooted in place.

"Come on, Shae!" Fiona reappears at the door and beckons me. "We're starving!"

I take a deep breath, which releases me from where I stand on the pavement, and follow her inside.

Ravod describes this place as a "kind of restaurant," but I have no idea what that is. Neither do Mads or Fiona. The three of us stare helplessly at Ravod, waiting for him to clarify.

"It's like a tavern, but for breakfast," he says finally, with a bit of a shrug.

That, at least, makes a little sense. But I've never seen a tavern like this before.

It smells like tea and fresh baked bread in here. The floor is tiled in black and white, and there are small, dark wooden booths of worn leather along the whitewashed walls and bright windows. Near the back is a bar, but it doesn't seem to be used for ordering drinks. Instead, some patrons sit on tall, comfy-looking padded stools eating breakfast. A few customers have large, loosely collected papers with small black print on them. The nearest one says THE GONDAL GAZETTE in big letters across the top.

A young serving girl in a bright yellow uniform with a white apron approaches us. She's chewing on something that she deliberately does not swallow.

"Four of you?" she asks with little enthusiasm.

Ravod, the only one of us not distracted by our

surroundings, nods. We are led to one of the nearby booths that aligns with the big window up front. Sunlight spills over the table where a stack of thin pamphlets labeled MENU sit.

Ravod slides easily into the nearest seat while Mads and Fiona take the spot across the table. I'm the last to sit, eyeing Ravod with a frown as we both shift to sit beside each other.

"Drinks?" the serving girl asks bluntly.

Ravod turns toward the girl with an uncharacteristically amiable smile. "Coffee, please."

"Coffee! I know what that is!" I blurt, unable to contain my relief at hearing something familiar. I turn eagerly to Mads and Fiona. "They served it for breakfast at—Ow!" I break off my overexcited explanation when Ravod kicks my foot under the table. I bite my lip, realizing that advertising our origins might not be the best idea. "I'll have a coffee as well, please."

The serving girl seems mercifully disinterested and turns to Fiona and Mads. "Two coffees and . . ." She trails off, waiting for them to finish her sentence.

"Water?" Mads looks like he half expects such a simple substance to not exist here. He sags in relief when the serving girl's attention drifts to Fiona, who bites her lip anxiously.

"May I please have what that young lady is having?" She discreetly points out a small child with her mother at the bar, who is being served an enormous pink beverage.

With that ordeal over, the serving girl drifts away. I wait until she is safely out of earshot to round on Ravod.

"You mind explaining all of this?"

Ravod draws a deep breath before resting his wrists on the edge of the table and tenting his long, gloved fingers.

"You recall I once told you about my mother? She was a physician?"

I nod, not really seeing where he's going with this. During one of the few instances Ravod opened up to me at High House, he had said his mother practiced medicine, which was one of the reasons he carried bandages and disinfectant on his person at all times.

Ravod tilts his head toward the window. "You see the drugstore across the street? That was her clinic."

I fall silent as my eyes widen. The signage was clearly slapped over an older façade reading FREE CLINIC, noticeable only if you look for it. I tear my gaze away to stare at Ravod. Across the table, Mads and Fiona do the same, only slightly more confused.

Ravod keeps his gaze calmly trained on me, watching as the pieces of the puzzle fall into their places.

"You're . . ." The word comes out as a ragged whisper. I find myself unable to complete the sentence.

Ravod has no such trouble.

"This is my home," he says. "I'm originally from Gondal."

A long, tense moment passes as Ravod waits for the revelation to sink in for everyone. Across the table, Mads looks between me and Ravod thoughtfully. Fiona rapidly opens and closes her mouth, like she always does when she is trying to figure something out.

"But . . ." Fiona says, her pale brows knotted together as she drops her voice to a whisper. "But you're a Bard . . ."

"It's extremely uncommon. Practically impossible, even," Ravod replies. "But yes, I possess the gift, and am able to use it here."

"But Kennan and I can't," I say with a frown.

"That is the norm," Ravod says. "It's even theorized that there may be other Gondalese who possess the gift but simply cannot use it here. Those like myself who can are sent to High House per a long-standing treaty with Cathal. So it has happened at least enough to warrant that level of official action. After that, Gondal washes its hands of us. We're effectively banished to Montane, and our options are to be either conscripted or imprisoned by High House."

There is a heaviness to his words that causes my frown to deepen.

"Is that what happened to you?" I finally ask.

"Yes. When my . . ." He trails off before collecting himself with another deep breath. This is difficult for him. A dull pang of sorrow lurches through me before he picks his sentence back up. "When my gift manifested, I was turned over to the military, who in turn brought me to High House. I thought I was being saved. Given a second chance."

"You were *six*," I recall, the words falling tactlessly from my mouth before I can reconsider them.

"I was old enough to know there are consequences for my actions," Ravod replies. "And because I felt indebted to Cathal, I turned a blind eye to his corruption. I can't change that. I probably can't be forgiven for it. I can't even forgive myself. But hopefully I can atone by trying to set things right."

I lean back in my seat. Suddenly, I feel like I am seeing Ravod for the first time. The specifics of his past—how his Telling banished his parents from existence, how he unquestioningly served High House, and probably the big question of why he took the *Book of Days*—make so much more sense. Every action he has taken, every word he has spoken, was produced from his profound, deep-seated guilt.

Biting my lip, I wonder if there's something I can say or do to help. My gaze drifts to Ravod's forearm, resting on the table. My fingers twist nervously in my lap as I simultaneously resist and question the thought of placing a reassuring hand on his. Or maybe his shoulder, so I don't seem too familiar? Or is that too familiar in and of itself? For as long as I've known him, Ravod has been reserved and proper. I can't help thinking that he'd find such a gesture inappropriate. He'd think I'm strange and desperate . . . wouldn't he?

My thoughts are brutally interrupted as Fiona reaches across the table and takes Ravod's hand, giving it a gentle squeeze. She has done this countless times for me, I know that. Yet the reasonable side of me completely falls apart.

When I told Ravod I had feelings for him, he couldn't *wait* to get rid of me. The memory of his rejection surfaces all too easily as I watch my best friend's fingers fold around his. Fiona's words reverberate in my head.

He's cute.

My fists ball in my lap, already complicated feelings bursting into chaos that almost makes me want to slap her hand away as rudely as possible.

"None of this is your fault," Fiona says in her usual warm, gentle voice that right now sounds like the screeching of the train we arrived on.

The moment proceeds without regard for my building rage. Ravod smiles gratefully at Fiona and she gives his fingers one last squeeze before releasing him.

The conversation subsides as the serving girl from before passes out our requested beverages. I barely notice when a mug of steaming coffee is set in front of me.

Fiona's drink looks better than mine, and I can't help scowling at it.

Afternoon sun warms the street as we depart the diner, some of us more satisfied than others. I hang back as Ravod leads us toward the outskirts of a lush, wooded area that looks supremely out of place amongst the buildings. The hustle and bustle of the city is a little muted here. People walk slower. There are more families with children. It's a small oasis of peace enclosed on all sides by buildings, industry, and vehicles of all shapes and sizes.

Ravod calls it a "park."

"The city itself is called Tybera. It's the capital of Gondal, the seat of its government," Ravod explains while we walk along a shaded street toward the park's entrance. "The rest of the country comprises fifteen smaller territories called the Junctures, which are connected by railways."

"Sounds a lot less isolated," Mads remarks. "Back home, we only got news of other villages from the Bards."

"And even that news wasn't entirely accurate," I add, recalling how Aster had been continually told it was the only village suffering when, in reality, it was the entire country.

"The government has a lot less control over the

day-to-day lives of its citizens here," Ravod replies. "Gondal is much larger. There are more people. Going from place to place is much faster and easier. Modern medicine ensures people live longer."

"Sounds like a much better system," Fiona says, pale brows shooting up.

Ravod grimaces a little. "On the surface, perhaps. Gondal is not without its issues."

"What are those?" Mads asks, incredulous. "Tybera looks like a paradise compared to Aster."

"The biggest issue here in the city is crime," Ravod says, not missing a beat. "And it possesses its fair share of corruption amongst the elite. Not to mention . . ." he trails off. Clearing his throat, he glances back at us. "Further discussion should probably wait until we've reached our destination."

"And where is that?" I ask, staring pointedly at him.

"Not far." Ravod seems perfectly aware that he's answering the wrong question as a small smile tugs at his mouth. He starts walking through the park again, carried swiftly on his long legs. He is joined by Fiona, with whom he chats quite happily.

"If looks could kill . . ." I turn to the side, noticing Mads smirking at me.

"I don't know what you're talking about," I snap. I regret it, but not enough to apologize.

Mads laughs, much to my surprise. Shaking his head, he directs his attention forward to Fiona and Ravod. "Sure."

I fall silently and comfortably into step beside Mads. Walking with him is a lot easier than back in Aster. When there were expectations, feelings . . . or perhaps it was the expectation of feelings that always drove a wedge between us.

If things had turned out differently, we might be married. It's a strange realization.

"You know, Freckles." Mads breaks through my thoughts. "I've seen you make that face about a thousand times. It's your 'I'm jealous of Fiona' face."

I roll my eyes. "Very funny."

"It's true," Mads replies. "You've always gotten yourself twisted into knots when you think she has something you want."

I sigh, and my gaze drifts over to Ravod. His head is turned to the side as he listens to some anecdote or other of Fiona's. A wayward strand of black hair has fallen out of place and sways gently over his forehead as he walks.

"But *that* face," Mads continues, drawing a circle in the air around my face with one finger. "That face I've never seen before."

I pull my gaze back to him and immediately feel my cheeks burning. Unable to prevent it, I stop walking altogether. Mads's smile is fixed firmly in place as he halts alongside me.

"This is awkward," I say to him. But like my comment from before, I'm not sure if that's really what I mean. "Is this awkward?" I amend, my head cocking as though the new angle will provide some answer I had not considered. It doesn't.

"You mean because I proposed to you and you rejected me, broke my heart, and ran off to High House?"

The words should sound accusing, but the way he says them sounds more like he's teasing me.

"Yes?" I venture. "And with all the goings-on, we never talked about it?"

Mads is quiet as we just . . . stare at each other.

He still looks mostly the same as he did before my world fell to pieces. He's tall, and his broad features complement his wide, muscular build. His short, messy hair shines golden in the sun, bleached even fairer by long hours working his father's mill.

He's far away from that mill, though, and the life he led there. It shows. He's more relaxed, more like the Mads I remember from my childhood who used to play with me and Kieran.

In much the same way, he assesses me. His blue eyes crinkle at the edges as he smiles down at me, and I wonder if he's thinking something similar about me. A breeze issues from the nearby trees of the park, momentarily chasing away the strange stench of the city and tousling his pale hair.

"Perhaps this *is* a little awkward." He chuckles softly as he rubs the back of his neck. "But maybe it's overdue?"

I nod in agreement. "Maybe it is."

"I guess I just don't want you to think I lied to

you about anything. About how I felt," Mads admits, and the rest starts rushing out like a broken dam. "I did love you. I do . . . love . . . it's . . . Well, it's complicated, I guess. I care about you, and want you to be happy, and back then I thought the best way to do that was to make sure I could always be there for you."

"And now?"

"Now . . ." He pauses, letting out a deep breath, like he's purging the toxicity of everything that came before. "Nothing's changed. Not really. I still want to be there for you, but I guess I understand that loving you and wanting you to be happy . . . aren't the same thing. You can take care of yourself, and you're good at it. Really good at it, actually."

I finally manage a smile. "Thanks, Mads."

"In Aster, things were different," Mads says. "I got caught up thinking there was only one way to do things, because that's how Aster's always been. My parents were childhood friends who got married even though they didn't really get along. They just made it work because that's what everyone told them was supposed to happen. I figured there was nothing else I could do but chart the same course. I told myself it was the right thing to do so many times that I believed it. You showed me I was wrong."

"I never wanted to hurt you," I say, hoping he'll understand how much I mean it.

"No, I needed to go through it." He shakes his head, the smile on his face dimming momentarily. "I know we care about each other enough that we would have been okay, but deep down we would have always wondered if we were only together because it was expected of us."

"True," I admit. "And that's our answer. We were just good friends trying too hard to be more than we should have been."

"Yeah, that about sums it up."

My chest hurts, but it's the kind of pain that comes when a badly treated broken bone has been reset and can now heal properly. Our conversation falls into comfortable quiet that's even more easy than before. Mads's smile broadens to a grin as I step forward and wrap my arms around him. He curls one arm around my shoulder while his other hand smooths over my hair.

Time stops and flows in reverse for a few peaceful moments. Instead of the events of Ma's murder and the subsequent trials and tribulations of High House, my problems are only Kieran calling me a name and saying I can't play with his toys. And Mads is here with a big hug to get me through it.

It suddenly occurs to me how long it's been. Last time I embraced Mads we were still roughly the same height. Now my ear is pressed against his sternum and I can hear the steady beat of his heart. I stopped getting hugs like this when our courtship began. I've missed them. The village elders deemed such displays improper.

The sharp sound of someone clearing their throat causes me to finally pull back. Ravod stands nearby, glancing between us with a furrowed brow.

"Pardon the interruption," he says almost awkwardly. "Our destination is somewhat farther past the park. In the interest of making good time, I think it advisable we get a move on."

Ravod's gaze lingers on Mads's hand resting on my shoulder. Both gaze and hand are snapped away at the same time, although Mads does so with a sheepish smile and Ravod looks mildly horrified.

"There is more I have yet to explain." Ravod's voice drops in volume and the clipped tone from before smooths out, his guilt edging in. He gestures for us to continue walking.

Fiona stands near the entrance to the path that leads through the park, admiring a beautiful cluster of delicate, amber-colored flowers. Her fingers trace the edges of the nearest petal. When she sees us approaching, she sighs almost sadly and steps back.

She lets Ravod pass her by but throws me a small smile as he does. I like to assume I've seen all of Fiona's smiles, much the way Mads says he knows all my faces. But I can't decipher this one, and it causes something cold to settle uncomfortably inside me.

With effort, I try to ignore it. I have more important things to focus on. I pick up my pace to catch up with Ravod, determined to get every answer I can if it kills me.

11

Of all the fantastical things in Gondal, my favorite so far is the park. Perhaps because it's the closest thing I've seen to what Ma described in her stories.

The wilderness in Montane was already dead, or in its final throes, when I was a small child. The closest I've ever seen to this level of greenery is the gardens at High House. Those were perfectly manicured, though, and to an extent, this park is as well. But there's just enough natural chaos to pretend like it's an actual forest if you ignore the buildings and airships looming overhead.

Everything is green. People blithely wander the cement pathways lined with colorful flowers, unburdened by the pace they keep on the city streets. Birds sing in the branches of the trees and squirrels creep out of the bushes almost close enough to touch. The path we travel curves around a pond, where children throw pieces of bread to brightly colored ducks swimming in the water.

"I don't understand why anyone would want to live in those big buildings when there's someplace like this." I don't realize I've spoken aloud until Ravod turns his head to look at me.

"I used to come here a lot when I was small. I

always thought the same thing." He points across the pond to a large equestrian statue; the robed figure holds a hand overhead where some unseen mechanism, for lack of a Telling, creates a flame that burns in his palm. "I planned to build a fort under that statue."

"Not a bad location," I remark. "I might even consider visiting."

"Oh?" He turns his smile on me, dimples appearing on his cheeks. "In that case, be sure to bring snacks."

I bite my lip to still the fluttering in my chest. "Even with all the amenities of High House, Montane must have been a big change after living here."

Ravod takes a deep breath at my shift in topic. "It was," he says. "People here grow up reading. Learning the history and literature of the land. Believing that it helped shape us as a people. Even the poorest and least privileged of us must be literate to survive. Those who can't are considered uncultured. Simpleminded. Even as a child I knew this."

"And did you think the people of Montane were uncultured and simpleminded?" I frown, on the verge of taking offense.

"Far from it. To me, as a child in a new world, I thought Montane must be *better* somehow, to have evolved beyond such trivialities in order to wield the power of Telling," Ravod says. "A belief Cathal was all too happy to reinforce."

The mention of Cathal makes me shiver despite the warmth in the air. Ravod notices as I curl my arms around myself.

"Having seen both," he continues, his voice growing softer, "I realize now that neither countries are without their problems."

"That's why, hopefully, we can find a way to create meaningful change." I try to draw some measure of confidence from my words, but they feel shaky as they leave my mouth.

"Why do you think I took the *Book of Days*?" he asks.

A renewed shiver creeps up my spine at his words, but for entirely different reasons. The *Book of Days* contains the entirety of Montane's existence, possibly more. If I've learned anything from my misadventures, it's that this level of power is not simply immense, it's *terrifying*. I narrow my eyes at Ravod, concerned, but also trying to temper my curiosity as to what might have been revealed to him in those pages.

His dark eyes reach mine, and I feel a sudden, lurching worry deep within my chest. All this time I thought our greatest fear was putting the power of the *Book of Days* in Cathal's hands. At one point I even worried what its power might do in *Kennan's* hands. I forgot to be concerned about what it might do in Ravod's.

"Ravod," I say, holding his gaze with some difficulty, "where is the *Book of Days*?"

He breaks eye contact to look over his shoulder toward the other side of the park. "We're almost there."

"That's not—" My sentence is cut off as Ravod abruptly pulls ahead of me. Apparently, the conversation is over.

For now.

Ravod leads us several blocks past the park in relative silence. It doesn't take long to see what he is leading us toward.

At a larger intersection up ahead stands an enormous complex, walled off from the rest of the city and only visible through a massive iron gate. The biggest structure I can see from the street looks like a dull gray stone cube. None of the structure is ornamental, standing in stark contrast to the myriad unique buildings covering the rest of the city. Instead, the flag of Gondal—a green rectangle with the sigil of a golden ox—flies at regular intervals from the parapets atop the wall.

Above, more airships than usual patrol the skies, while armored vehicles and soldiers patrol the ground.

"I really hope this isn't a prison," Mads mutters.

"It isn't," Ravod assures him without breaking stride. "This is Axis Keep. It's a military base."

"So, you're handing us over to the military?" I narrow my eyes at him.

He slows to a halt in front of the gate and turns a

serious look on me, one that bores deep into my eyes and is difficult to look away from.

"Why would I do that?" he asks. His voice is as sincere as his expression.

"Then explain it to us," I say sharply. I fold my arms over my chest and plant my feet, making it clear I will not follow him another step. "Why *exactly* are we here?"

The candor in Ravod's eyes is undiminished as he steadily holds my gaze.

"The general wants to speak with you."

I'm still not entirely sure this isn't some kind of trap. But Ravod has had ample opportunity to subdue us once we were in the city. He has the power of the Telling here, after all, and I don't.

If High House taught me one thing, it was to always be on my guard. It's a habit that I'm finding dies hard once acquired.

"Stay close," I whisper to Mads and Fiona as Ravod approaches the sentinels at the gate. "I don't think Ravod is trying to harm us, but we still don't know enough about what we're walking into."

"Should we even be walking in at all?" Mads asks, a frown creasing his features as he glances at Ravod's turned back and the soldiers nearby.

"You are free to leave anytime you wish," Ravod says, making us jump in surprise—which might have been comedic if we weren't so on edge. "But these are the people with the power to actually help us achieve what we want to do. To bring down Cathal. To help Montane. Hear them out, at the very least."

On the surface, his words make sense. If their base is anything to go by, the Gondalese military is certainly formidable. They could be useful.

The thought sends a crackling fear skittering through me. Useful for *what*, exactly? I may only be a simple shepherd girl from the northern edge of nowhere, but I can still deduce that armies are generally only meant to accomplish one thing.

War.

Is that what this has all been the prelude to? Is that what Ravod is planning? What he wants?

My flurry of trepidatious thoughts is interrupted by a loud series of clicks and clangs issuing from the gate behind Ravod. The sounds do not seem to worry him as he begins walking toward the entrance.

The ground beneath us trembles as the enormous gates hiss and grind open, as though an invisible giant were pulling them apart. They disappear completely inside apertures built into the equally enormous wall.

"Staying here accomplishes nothing, Shae," Fiona says, just loud enough for me to hear over the sound of the gate as it finishes opening completely. "I trust your instincts, but it's worth seeing where this path leads."

"We won't have as easy a time getting out if things go south," Mads warns. "Let's play this smart, okay?"

I nod in agreement, and we hurry to catch up to Ravod.

It's easier to see how large Axis Keep is from inside the gate. It creates its own microcosm within the sprawl of Tybera.

The courtyard alone takes a while to traverse, partly because of its size but also because of the unbelievable things to gape at. The closest I've ever seen to something like this were the training grounds at High House. But instead of Bards, soldiers in uniforms identical to Ravod's drill in the courtyard to the sound of barked commands and hissing steam issuing from the machinery. Each group moves in tightly regimented squares. Enormous instruments of war stand at the ready nearby—vehicles like the ones outside, and some even bigger. Still others look like armored suits shaped like a person, but I can't tell if there's someone inside or if they are simply controlled by Gondal's technological ingenuity.

At the other side, a long, wide flight of stone stairs leads toward the cube-shaped building at the center of the compound. Near the entrance stands a statue much like the one in the park but angular and geometric like those in Consonance Station. This one depicts a tall woman in regal armor, standing alone with her hands resting on the pommel of a sword balanced in front of her. Protruding from her back are the wings of an eagle. The metal has aged dark green over time, as though to match the uniforms of the soldiers.

"Ekko, the Winged Conqueror," Ravod explains, noticing my lingering interest in the statue. "Ancient mythology claimed she was the goddess who led the people of Gondal to the river where they founded Tybera, and taught them how to defend themselves. The military, in particular, is very fond of her likeness."

I'm not sure what to say to that. It stirs something dark and heavy in my chest. Something sorrowful.

In Montane we have legends of the First Rider, a similar figure in our collective memory, but he is little more than a distant, nameless, and nebulous tale that parents pass on to their children out of obligation. There is no art, not only for lack of resources, but because no one really knows anything more about the legend, with so many details lost from generation to generation. We have no statues. No stories. No shared history.

"This way." Ravod's melodic voice resonates as we reach the portico leading to the interior of the base.

The interior is almost grand in its starkness. The entrance hall is all dark lines and sparse furnishings, with a tall, flat ceiling overhead. The minimalist decoration lends itself to the sweeping structure, leaving me feeling lost in its enormity. The only color comes from the giant Gondalese flag hanging from the back wall.

The place is busy, at least. It's hard to stick together in the shuffle of the crowd—soldiers, mostly—going about their day.

Ravod marches purposefully through the crowd, which parts for him without seeming to realize it. A few soldiers cast him looks I can't fully decipher and whisper to one another when he passes by.

Beneath the flag are a series of closed doors. Ravod picks one, seemingly at random, and pushes a small round button beside it. He taps his foot absently, watching as a few numbers light up above the doorframe.

The next door over opens, revealing a small, well-lit, closet-like room. A pair of officers step out and a woman steps in. A moment later, the door opens again. The woman from before is gone and an older man steps out.

Before I can ask Ravod what is happening to these poor people, and if the same fate awaits us if we use these doors, a small chime sounds from somewhere I can't see. The door in front of Ravod slides open and several people file out.

I step cautiously after Ravod until we are standing side by side with Fiona and Mads in a tiny room. The door slides shut.

"I don't see a general . . ." Mads casts a confused look around.

"This is the elevator. It uses a motor, a pulley, and a counterweight to take us up or down in the building," Ravod explains patiently as he pushes a button marked with the number twelve. He pauses, looking between us all wearing some version of the same astounded expression. "Did you think everyone in this city uses stairs to get to the top of those giant buildings?"

The room vibrates a little and there's a strange sensation of movement I can't see. Fiona has the most trouble staying on her feet, and eventually resorts to gripping Mads's sleeve to remain upright. The odd sensation continues for several moments until the chime sounds and the door opens into a completely different space.

"Reminds me of High House," I mutter, recalling the twisting passages that send unsuspecting wanderers to different parts of the castle.

"At least here you wind up wherever you set out for," Ravod says wryly.

We are deposited into a large corridor of the same dark, utilitarian style as the entrance but on a smaller scale. It's just as busy, however, and we find ourselves navigating the hall around scurrying officers and their aides.

Eventually Ravod stops at a door, knocks twice, and waits to be admitted by a prim "Enter" sounding from inside.

We file into a small office outfitted with only the barest essentials. Stark white light overhead illuminates the desk at the center. Behind the desk sits a rigid figure in an immaculately starched uniform. The person squints at Ravod through a pair of wiry spectacles balanced upon an angular nose.

"Ah." There is a degree of contempt or suspicion in the tone. "You've returned."

Ravod nods. "It's important that we proceed immediately."

"Is that the general?" I whisper to Ravod, leaning a little closer to avoid being heard.

Ravod suppresses a snort, barely disguising his reaction by bringing his hand to his mouth and clearing his throat.

"Sorry, I should have introduced you," he says, sobering. "This is Ensign Charolais. They are the general's secretary."

I bob my head respectfully and attempt to introduce myself.

"Nice to meet you, my name is Sh—"

"I know everything I need to about you, Montanian," Ensign Charolais interrupts with a curt edge in their voice that reminds me of Kennan. "Please wait in the office. The general will be with you momentarily."

A door is indicated, slightly behind the desk. Fiona gently takes my arm as I proceed toward it, followed by Mads. Ravod lingers by the desk, sharing a few whispered words with Charolais. Both are frowning deeply.

The door swings open into a nicely appointed office. It's unlike the rest of the building in that large, rectangular windows allow in an abundance of natural light. At the center is a stately mahogany desk, cluttered with papers and other things considered foul and heretical back home—books, fountain pens, maps, and inkwells. Our footsteps barely sound on the elegant carpet as we take in the various paintings and trophies of war. A large display case against the far wall boasts a number of elegant swords.

Our attention is drawn back to the door as Charolais silently appears, seeming irritated by the mere sight of us. Presently, they clear their throat, stepping to one side of the door.

"General Ravod is prepared to meet with you."

I try, and fail, to maintain some semblance of composure while confusion spirals through my head at a dangerous velocity. I must have misheard. But my eyes don't deceive me as Ravod walks nonchalantly through the office door. It's not a trick of the light, or a Telling.

Still, it should be impossible. Ravod, by his own admission, spent the majority of his life in Montane. He could have arrived in Gondal only a few days before us at most.

How could he possibly be a general?

Unless . . . The shiver that crawls up my spine nearly makes me convulse. *Unless he wrote it in the* Book of Days?

My gaze meets Ravod's, and I can see that strain of guilt from earlier tightening around his dark eyes. The weight of my renewed questions finally causes my jaw to slacken.

"Ravod . . ." My voice shakes so violently that I can't even continue my sentence.

Fortunately, I don't have to, as a sharp voice pierces the relative stillness.

"That's *General* Ravod to you, young lady."

A woman steps into view from behind Ravod. I'm

unsurprised I didn't see her initially; she's quite a bit shorter than me. She stands with perfect posture despite her age. It reflects in her shock of white hair, styled in a simple chignon at the nape of her neck, and the creases around her mouth and eyes. More accurately, her right eye. The left is obscured behind a metallic eye patch. A deep, jagged scar bisects her face in a diagonal line from the right side of her forehead, behind the eye patch, down her left jaw, and disappears into the tall neckline of her military uniform.

A sharp black eye catches my gaze darting to Ravod.

"My grandson has apprised me of you," the general states, not bothering to mask her inspection of me, and carefully noting my surprised reaction to the word "grandson." I find myself glancing between them again. There's a pronounced difference in their height, but Ravod has inherited his grandmother's sharp features and intense presence.

A realization steals my voice before I can reply, jolting my already dizzy mind. I hear Mads's voice in my head, as clearly as if he were repeating his words right next to me.

. . . *I remember there was someone there. And then there wasn't. But it's weird. Clouded. Like I fell asleep and dreamed the end of the fight.*

I wrote Niall out of existence the same way Ravod did his own parents. Shortly thereafter, all traces of the man began to vanish, most notably from Mads's memory. If Ravod's Telling works in Gondal the way it does in Montane, how does his grandmother remember him?

As though sensing the question in my gaze, Ravod steps forward. "I know this raises even more questions. It's my hope to answer them and continue to find a way to work together," he says.

"Whatever questions you may or may not have are no concern to me," the general says, folding her hands behind her back and striding behind her desk. "My only goal is ending a serious threat to Gondal and its people. If you can aid me in this, as Erik says you can, then I am willing to hear your proposal."

"Erik?" The name falls inelegantly out of my mouth.

The general turns to Ravod, momentarily ignoring any other presence in the room, and says, "I'm not impressed."

"Then you haven't spoken to her enough," Ravod returns, not missing a beat.

The general turns back to me.

"Ravod is our family name," she explains, and something about her weary tone makes me realize it's not the first time she's had to do so for foreigners such as ourselves. "Your culture is more familiar with your use of given names, as I recall. We only tend to use them here amongst family and our closest friends."

Those words sting. It's another reminder of how little I know Ravod . . . Erik . . . Whoever he is.

I take a deep breath and step forward so I'm standing directly in front of the general, with her desk between us.

"You mentioned a serious threat to Gondal?" I ask.

"Indeed," the general says. "A threat originating in Montane."

"How is that possible?" I ask. "Montane doesn't even believe you exist."

"Unlike where you come from, just because a threat isn't believed doesn't mean it doesn't exist."

I narrow my eyes at her, beginning to understand.

"High House," I say.

"I'm told you're the first Bard in a long while to break free of their indoctrination. That is a feat I'm willing to recognize. However, I don't normally find myself in a position to enlist help in military matters from a group of . . ." She trails off, finally finishing her thought with a liberal dose of disdain. ". . . *teenagers*. I'm not entirely convinced you'll be much use to me. My grandson disagrees."

"Shae is more capable than you realize," Ravod interjects. "Not only has she broken free of High House, but she has broken others free as well. Including me."

"He's right," Fiona adds, stepping beside me and placing a hand on my shoulder. "The Bards aren't the only ones who are under High House's control. It's everyone. Shae's bravery and defiance inspired me and Mads to follow her here. *That's* what she's capable of."

"If it's idealism you're after, you might have better luck with the Protesters. I'm interested in results. So, before I leave, I'll offer you one chance to be useful. Otherwise, I must respectfully ask you to stop wasting my valuable time," the general says.

Mads frowns, speaking for the first time. "Be 'useful' how?"

The general casts Mads a withering glare that even Kennan might be envious of. He clears his throat and shifts his weight between his feet until her gaze is directed back at me.

"I want to stop the wasteland that's spreading across the border of Gondal."

With effort, I hold very still and repress my natural reaction to the general's statement. Every impulse I possess demands I exclaim the first thing that comes into my head, and loudly. Instead, I manage to maintain her gaze with what I hope is a neutral expression. I have the very distinct impression that if she senses any surprise or ignorance on my part, she'll simply throw us out of her office. I would lose the chance to make the impact I came here to make. Ravod's faith in me will have proven to be misplaced.

"I believe we can find a way to accomplish that," I say.

The general holds my gaze with her single, dark eye for a moment longer. Finally, she nods.

"I will allow you the opportunity to prove it," she replies. "We shall reconvene here in twenty-four hours. Bring me the *Book of Days*."

"I suppose that could have been worse."

We all make various sounds of agreement with Ravod's deadpan assessment when he deposits us in the living room of his small apartment just off the military base. It's cozy for four people, but still much nicer than a shack in a bog. Or a sewer tunnel. Or a storage bunker in an underground cavern.

Sunlight wanes through the large windows set in the back of the room, which is modestly furnished for Gondal, but might as well be a palace by Aster's standards. Mads looks vaguely surprised when he seats himself on the sofa and the soft cushions descend beneath him far deeper than anything he's probably ever experienced. Fiona grips the windowsill with white knuckles as she peers out the window of the seventeenth story.

Ravod only deigned to disclose that his acquiring this living space was "an arrangement" with his grandmother.

"Feel free to avail yourselves of anything you need here. There's plenty of food in the kitchen. The ladies are welcome to rest in the master bedroom; it's a bit more comfortable," he says. "I'll be back shortly."

"Where are you going?" I ask as Ravod turns and heads for the door.

"I promised my grandmother I'd take tea with her. It was her price for meeting with you," he explains without breaking his stride.

I grimace. "Having met your grandmother, are you sure you'll be okay?"

"I'm reasonably confident I'll survive the encounter." Ravod pauses, his hand on the doorknob, and chuckles over his shoulder, his smile genuine enough for the dimples on his cheeks to appear. "Your concern is appreciated, but I know her weakness and fully plan to exploit it." His voice goes deadly serious for dramatic effect: "It's crumpets."

He offers one more knee-weakening smile before leaving. The soft click of the door closing behind him manages to jolt me back to my senses.

Turning to the living room, I see that Mads has already fallen asleep on the couch. I smile, shaking my head as I pull a blanket off the back and cover him with it.

"It's been a long day," I say with a sigh.

Fiona, still standing by the window, doesn't seem to hear me. She jumps slightly when I step up behind her.

"Sorry," she mumbles, finally letting go of the windowsill to wrap her arms around herself. It's a bit odd—normally when she wraps her arms around others it's the gentlest, most reassuring feeling in the world, but it seems to have little effect on herself.

"You should get some rest," I say. Fiona nods, but it's mechanical. Her pale eyes are unfocused, staring

156 — DYLAN FARROW

past the windowpane and outside into nothing. I place a hand on her shoulder, but even the contact doesn't seem to rouse her from whatever reverie she's found herself in. "Is something wrong?"

She finally exhales a long breath, but she still doesn't turn to look at me. When she speaks, her voice is so quiet I strain to hear it.

"Maybe it's crazy for me to say this," she says. "But I'm worried. About Kennan."

I hesitate, frowning a bit. It doesn't surprise me that Fiona is more concerned about someone else than herself. At least I've had some time and a bit of background knowledge to come to grips with Kennan's hostility. I understand why it's there, even if I dislike it. But Kennan is as cold to Fiona as she is to everyone else. It troubles me that Fiona's concern is for someone who doesn't spare any regard for those feelings. Someone who sees that gift of kindness as some kind of fundamental flaw . . . It irritates me.

"I'm worried about her, too," I'm forced to admit. "Even if she's there by choice, she's still part of our group."

Fiona nods but won't look at me. My words peter out into awkward silence, made somehow more awkward by how rare such an occurrence is between us.

It's mercifully broken as Mads snorts loudly in his sleep. I laugh at the ridiculous sound despite myself. Even Fiona is distracted enough to turn away from the window, but her smile is strained when she meets my eyes. Sad, even.

"You're right, I should probably try and sleep," she mutters.

As she passes me on her way out of the living room, I can't help noticing she's clutching one of the marigolds she was admiring in the park.

Twenty-four hours is not a lot of time to come up with any semblance of a plan to help the general, Gondal, or Montane. The deadline is whittled down considerably when I give up pacing restlessly and pass out in an armchair in Ravod's living room for eight of those precious hours.

It's night when I awaken, but strangely it's not dark. Outside the window, the city is still alive with light and noise.

I take up Fiona's abandoned spot by the window, taking in the sight. The buildings lit up from within create square patterns across the skyline, accented by flashing signs. The airships are illuminated as well. From this vantage I notice there's a whole different level of traffic in the sky; smaller aircrafts zip by and weave through the buildings. During the day they could be easily missed by the naked eye, but as one zooms by the window, I can see them a little better. Most take after the smaller, foot-pedaled contraptions I've seen on the street, but with a slender motor in the back and enormous insect-like wings. They look almost like metal dragonflies.

The sight stirs something in my distant memory.

I recall Ma's stories, although her voice is muffled, like she's talking from inside a bottle. There was one story about a giant insect, I think, that hummed with strange power and let people ride its back.

How could I have known, as a child believing I was hearing a bedtime story, that she was talking about these strange air-treading vehicles?

Nothing in the world is as I believed, I think to myself.

I pull out the locket Victor gave me, opening it gingerly, and gaze at the face inside. My mother's younger self smiles back almost teasingly, illuminated by the false light of the nighttime city.

Get it? she seems to ask.

"Yeah, Ma," I whisper in response to my own silent question. "I get it now."

Another of the dragonfly vehicles slows, near enough for me to see its rugged, goggled driver gauging the movement of the traffic. I watch, entranced, until I notice a hint of red hair emerging from the man's helmet. Before I can consciously connect the threads of who he reminds me of, I find myself recoiling from the window.

Through the glass, I hear the driver and his vehicle disappear into the city. Still, it takes a few moments to slow my racing heart.

He looked like Niall. But it wasn't him. He doesn't exist anymore . . .

Because of me.

The jolt of fear is replaced by the heavy weight of guilt and I blink back tears. I try to remember what Mads said.

You made your decision. And it was a tough call you had to make under a lot of pressure. That you struggle with it says a lot about who you are. I smile over at Mads, still fast asleep on the couch.

As though responding to my thoughts, Mads snores and shifts his position. The sound issues at the same time my stomach rolls over in hunger. The combination finally breaks me free of the dark thoughts clouding my mind.

Ravod mentioned food in the kitchen. I tiptoe around the coffee table, careful not to wake Mads. I'm more used to the creaky floorboards from back home. The plush carpet beneath my feet would probably muffle my steps even if I stomped across the room.

The kitchen is a short distance past the living room, beyond a dark wooden door carved to fit the slope of the stylish archway. My breath catches when I push the door open to find the light is already on.

Squinting through the sudden brightness I look around.

Even the kitchens here are bizarre. I'm faced with an immaculately tiled room, colored in cream and blue, except for the amber light hanging from the ceiling over a simple circular table. There are numerous gadgets placed on countertops and built into the wall, but I don't know what they are meant to be.

As my eyesight adjusts, I realize Ravod is standing in front of one such appliance, which appears to be Gondal's version of a stove. Fire appears in tiny blue jets beneath a trivet on the surface. It is boiling something in a large, metal pot.

Briefly, I consider broaching the subject of Niall with him. The resurgence of confusion and guilt is still a freshly renewed weight on my chest. If anyone could understand or advise me on how to cope with what happened, it would be Ravod. Shame suddenly smothers all my other emotions. I open my mouth but can't bring myself to make a sound.

Ravod glances over his shoulder, holding a wooden spoon, and it takes me a few breaths to realize what's so different about him. For the first time, he isn't wearing a uniform, either Bard or Gondalese. Instead, he sports a simple undershirt tucked into his trousers. A checkered dishcloth is slung over one athletic shoulder.

"I didn't mean to wake you," he says, turning to face me fully, but looking slightly uncomfortable. I can't help noticing the way his entire frame tenses when he notices my gaze flicker to his lean yet muscular, and obviously bare, arms. I force myself not to chuckle at a memory of when he became flustered by seeing me in my nightgown at High House. It makes me wonder if his odd sense of modesty and propriety originated here in Gondal.

"You didn't," I assure him, bringing my thoughts

back to the moment. "I was following the promise that there was food somewhere in here."

"As was I," Ravod says. He picks up a small paper packet from the counter and tips the sandy contents into the pot in front of him.

"Need any help?" I offer, closing the two steps to the stove. The contents of the pot gently bubble, smelling like vegetable soup.

A quiet laugh escapes Ravod as he stirs. "That's the entire process, I'm afraid. But I can use assistance in eating the result if you're interested?"

"Very, very interested," I reply, and my stomach makes a somewhat embarrassing noise to punctuate the statement.

"Have a seat," he says, the corners of his lips twitching up. "I'm actually glad to get a chance to talk like this, after everything that's happened."

I take a seat at the table, finding the rumblings of hunger joined by a number of butterflies at the prospect of spending time with him. Niall disappears from my mind entirely.

Ravod turns back to the stove and stirs his concoction a few more times before using the dish towel to grip the handle of the pot and tip the contents into a nearby bowl.

It's difficult for me to ignore the musculature of his arms as he produces another bowl from a nearby cabinet. With his back turned, he doesn't notice the flush creeping into my cheeks. I cover them with my hands, leaning forward on the table when he turns around and places some soup in front of me. Our eyes meet for an instant that stops the breath in my throat, and I clear it somewhat awkwardly as I avert my gaze.

He knows he has this effect on me. I told him so, not very long ago. The feelings themselves I can handle, or so I've somehow convinced myself. It's the memory of the look of pity on his face when he rejected me that still stings so deeply. I'm not ready to see that again. I keep my eyes fixed on the wall while Ravod takes a seat.

It's probably the freckles, I think angrily. *I have a weird face. I'm too stocky. If I looked like Fiona, that moment might have ended differently. I don't know what I expected. Stupid, stupid, stupid.*

The smell of soup draws my attention back to the table, and I'm grateful for the distraction.

Ravod sets a spoon next to my bowl and takes a seat. We eat in silence for few minutes. Every so often I look up from my food and across the table at Ravod. He keeps his focus on his soup, but after the third time, I find him looking at me.

"Something on your mind?" he asks.

I sigh. Everything I still want to know rushes into my head at once and only creates more confusion.

"I don't even know where to begin," I admit.

His eyes are thoughtful as he regards me. He sets his spoon down and drums his fingers on the surface of the table.

"Well, to start, you are probably wondering how I managed to reconnect with my grandmother," he offers. When I nod, he continues, "It wasn't easy. Because of my original Telling, she had no memory of me. No memory of my parents. I wrote a Telling into a letter I managed to get to her. The written Telling allows for permanency as long as she keeps it nearby."

"I'm surprised," I reply before I can think better of it. When Ravod cocks his head inquisitively, I take a deep breath and explain, "You have the *Book of Days*. Why not just write her memory back into it?"

"I thought about it," he confesses. "A part of me wanted to convince myself that I had already irrevocably altered reality in a way I could not be forgiven for. Nothing would really change about my situation if I did so again."

"But you didn't," I point out.

"I sat for ages in the tunnels beneath the Juncture just . . ." He takes a deep breath and releases it with a heavy sigh. "Philosophizing, I guess. But in the end, I realized something important."

"What was that?"

"Why only make a small adjustment to one person's memory when I could just as easily rewrite the world in any way I wished?" he says. "If I was willing to do one, then I was willing to do the other. And that is the difference between me and Cathal."

"You weren't willing to wield that power?"

"No one should."

A heavy silence falls over the table. I'm not sure

either of us knows how to continue the conversation. Finally, Ravod clears his throat.

"I . . ." His voice trails off in a sigh. "I know it's insufficient, but I owe you an apology."

I pause, unsure if he is going to continue. When he doesn't, I shift in my seat before meeting his gaze. I'm not sure if it's only there because I want it to be, but I see sincerity in his dark eyes.

"You mean for going behind my back, stealing the *Book of Days,* and leaving me at the mercy of Cathal?" I ask, eventually. "Or the part where he punished me by giving me the Blot and I had to fight my way out of High House? Or having to . . ."

It's my turn to trail off. For whatever reason, I can't bring myself to admit what I did to Niall. Even if Ravod is the only person who could understand the punishing guilt I feel when I allow myself to think of it. Instead, I watch his reaction carefully, narrowing my eyes when none of what I said surprises him.

"All of it," he says without hesitation.

"I just . . ." I take a deep breath, holding back the flood of words threatening to escape me. "I want to know . . . why? Didn't you trust me?"

"I didn't. Not enough." His words plunge a knife of ice into my heart. "I should have. But at the time it was too difficult. It's a pathetic excuse, but it's the truth."

"I trusted you." My voice is weak as I fight back tears. I hold fast to the prickling sensation of anger growing beneath my ribs, letting my indignation overwhelm my hurt so he won't see me cry.

His reply is a quiet "I know."

"Well, have you at least changed your mind?"

Ravod is quiet for a lingering moment, a frown creasing his brow as he fiddles with the handle of his spoon.

"Yes," he replies, finally. He seems to debate with himself as to whether he wants to add to the statement before deciding against it.

I allow myself to sit back and take a deep breath. The air between us feels a little clearer than before.

"That means a lot to me," I admit. "We've certainly come a long way since you accused me of trying to steal your horse."

"In my defense, Angelica is a particularly excellent horse."

I laugh at that. I'm only now starting to get better at determining whether Ravod's dry, straight-faced delivery is meant to be humorous.

"Thanks, Ravod," I say. "I feel a lot better about whatever happens tomorrow."

"It will certainly be eventful. We'll talk more before you meet with the general. There's still the matter of why you came here that we must address." He notices my eyes widen in understanding and nods his head slowly. "It's time you saw the *Book of Days*."

Morning light bathed the streets of Tybera, and everyone's mood was a little better after some sleep. There were a few hours to spare before meeting the general, and little planning done over the course of the night. It was decided that the morning would be spent discussing a plan of action at the park. It was not long, however, before Fiona found her way to a dress shop. Shortly thereafter, Mads made a beeline for the duck pond with some toast from his breakfast in hand. And Ravod had to check in with his grandmother before the meeting.

That left me on my own, sitting aimlessly on a bench watching the squirrels play in the branches of a nearby tree, with nothing but my thoughts. As usual, they are not the best company.

Pushing aside downward spiral after downward spiral quickly exhausts me. My gaze drifts to my boots on the cement. It stays there a few long minutes before a pair of worn workmen's shoes I don't recognize stop in front of me.

"Um . . . excuse me?" someone squeaks, pulling my eyes upward to the owner of the voice. My brow furrows as I recognize the young man from the caverns. "It's me. Stot? I don't know if you remember . . ."

For a second, my breath catches, afraid he's here to apprehend me on behalf of the Protesters. He grimaces awkwardly and waves his hand a little by way of greeting.

"Stot," I say. I stand up, surreptitiously checking for any of his comrades who might be sneaking up on me. "What brings you here?"

"I was asked to come find you," he says. He quickly puts his hands up to show he's not a threat. "Not to bring you back or anything. Your friend, Kennan . . . she asked me to bring a message."

I frown. "How did you find me?"

"The Protesters operate all over town. I just . . . asked around."

His halting pattern of speech and deliberate avoidance of eye contact make me wonder what he is so nervous about. For whatever reason, Stot seems far more worried about me than I am about him.

Victor specifically told me to find him, I remember. *He must believe him to be at least somewhat trustworthy.* The thought calms my nerves a little.

"Is Kennan okay?" I ask.

"Oh, she's perfectly fine." Stot gives me a small smile. "She's not even locked up anymore. She talked her way into the group, actually. She's quite knowledgeable. Everyone's really impressed by her."

It makes sense that Kennan would impress them. She's impressive. I'm more surprised that she charmed her way into their good graces. A winning personality would not be the first term I'd consider when describing my former trainer. But when I remember her letting me in, even just that tiny bit, I wonder if maybe this strange place is somehow good for her. If maybe there's a Kennan that I haven't seen yet.

"You said she had a message for me?" I ask, not sure if I believe Stot's word alone.

"Right." He digs in his pocket and produces a crisp, folded piece of paper, handing it over. I unfold it, glancing at the pointy script. "Do you need me to read it for you?"

"No, thanks," I reply.

The message is short, and very . . . Kennan: *I am fine. If you require proof, I can meet you at the Protester rally that is taking place downtown. I'll update you, regardless. I realize this might be a lot to ask, but please don't do anything stupid. K.*

For Kennan, this is practically fond.

I look back up at Stot, who is watching me intently through the curtain of his brown bangs. When our eyes meet, his drop. I fold the note and tuck it in my pocket alongside the page from the *Book of Days*. I seem to be accumulating a strange little collection.

"She says she can meet me at a rally?" I ask.

Stot nods. "There's one happening today. Other side of the park." He points across the stretch of green behind me. "I'm headed that way now, if you want help finding the place?"

There's something oddly charming about his youthful awkwardness that I can't quite put my finger on. Perhaps it's his eagerness to help a foreign stranger and his obvious worry at overstepping in that enthusiasm. It somehow makes me feel like I've known him much longer than a few passing moments. He's different from the rest of the Protesters we met, more willing to give us the benefit of the doubt.

"Sure," I say, offering a small smile in the hopes of putting him more at ease. I'm not sure he even sees it through his hair. He takes a few steps off the path, beckoning me to follow.

We walk in silence across the dappled sunlit grass to the edge of the park. Stot mostly keeps his gaze downward at the ground in front of his feet. Every so often he flicks his head, tossing his hair out of his face, and I catch sight of his bluish-gray eyes.

"Do you miss Montane?" I ask, hoping to break the silence. Find some common ground, perhaps.

Stot shrugs. "I don't remember much about Montane," he says. I think that's the end of the discussion, but eventually he adds, "It's not the land I miss."

"The people, then?" I probe, at the very least hoping to keep the conversation going and prevent the awkward silence from before returning.

"My family." His voice is quiet.

"They didn't come here with you?"

Stot takes a deep breath, shoving his hands into

his pockets. This time, he doesn't pick up the conversation.

I consider prompting him to continue, but his attention is turned ahead to where the park empties back out into the city. A block over, there's a large, noisy crowd gathered on the street. Some hold large signs, each with a slogan demanding sympathy for the plight of Montanian refugees or some form of ambiguous change on their behalf. Others pass out pamphlets that go largely ignored by anyone passing by. It's mostly just a noisy gathering of people shouting over one another incoherently.

So far, the only thing that really makes sense is why they named their group "protesters."

"*This* is the rally?" I ask, turning to Stot as we come to a stop on the other side of the street.

He nods. "We organize them every month. Every so often we get some donations to maintain our setup in the caverns."

"'Organize' seems like a bit of an exaggeration here." I grimace, turning toward the shouting mass of bodies in front of us. "Does this accomplish anything? Doesn't anyone object to them causing a scene?"

"Most of the core group is students from the university. Their parents can afford to persuade the police to turn a blind eye, as long as things don't get too out of control," Stot replies. "It's been this way since long before I arrived." His mouth twists to the side in what looks almost like disappointment.

I think I understand how he feels. They have good intentions, but that's about it. Their energy has no direction, no goal, so it's wasted.

"Maybe it's time for a few changes," I murmur.

No sooner have the words left my mouth than a shift in the crowd catches my attention. A cluster of shipping crates is piled together in a makeshift platform near the edge of the gathering. A lone figure ascends it with graceful ease, drawing the gaze of everyone nearby.

Kennan.

"What is she doing?" Stot asks, cocking his head, hair falling away from his face as he nods in her direction. When she reaches the top of the pile of crates, she cups her hands around her mouth.

"Everyone, eyes front! Your attention!" Her commanding voice carries easily over the crowd and all the way across the street so even I hear her clearly. The writhing rabble goes quiet, most with the same confusion on their faces that is painted across Stot's.

What are *you doing, Kennan?* I ask her silently.

Her eyes, no longer that yellow amber but an earthy brown a few shades lighter than her skin, roam the crowd from front to back. I may have imagined it, but I swear they locked on mine for a second, and it sends an unexpected shiver racing up my spine. The whole crowd seems to have fallen under a similar spell.

Once she's satisfied that she's commanded everyone's attention, she speaks.

"I am a Montanian refugee," she begins. "I stand in a land that a month ago I wasn't sure even existed. I come from a land under the yoke of a regime that denies its people even the most basic of human dignities. I've been in Gondal barely a few days, but it is enough to know with full certainty the reason why High House thinks your way of life is dangerous. Why they would lie to us and try to convince us that your land is nothing more than a subversive myth. You live in a city full of technological marvels with freedoms you merely consider normal. Freedoms my people can't even imagine. You are educated. You are informed. You can hold gatherings, like this one, without fear of reprisal from your government."

She pauses, and the air around her reaches a strange, charged stillness as the rapt crowd waits for her to continue.

"You protest the treatment of my countrymen and call yourselves Protesters. And at its core, that is noble. Yet Montanians still live apart, beneath your city, and your well-intentioned protests go ignored." She continues, "And they go ignored because they alone are insufficient. Showing up and speaking out are not enough. You need to *act*. If you care about my people, if this *truly* matters, you have a moral mandate to rise and meet the challenge demanded by actual change. And when you do, you will become something greater than mere protesters. Whether you remain protesters or become a revolution is up to you."

The last syllable is drowned out by cacophonous cheers that make the pavement beneath my feet vibrate with energy. Kennan steps down from her podium and is engulfed by the crowd, which is suddenly engaged and humming with purpose that was not present before.

I turn to Stot, whose mouth has fallen agape, and a moment passes before he tears his eyes from the crowd.

"That's never happened before," he says. "Not like that."

"That's the entire problem," Kennan says as she approaches us.

"I had no idea you were such a capable public speaker." My eyebrows are still raised, and I seem to be having some trouble lowering them.

Kennan shrugs. "I spent far too much of my life listening to Cathal and his Bards bluster. Change a few words, and demanding a tithe becomes demanding a few ineffectual students take control of their movement."

"Keep that up, and the people of Gondal might start thinking Montanians are something more than just a drain on their resources," Stot remarks, nodding approvingly toward Kennan. "I have to go check in with Emery, but I really hope you'll stick around and keep their boots to the fire." Kennan nods at him, and Stot turns to me. "It was nice chatting with you, Shae."

"Let's do it again sometime," I say, offering him

a smile before he hurries off into the crowd and disappears.

"You two know each other?" Kennan asks.

"He seems like a good kid, that's all," I reply.

"He's certainly curious about you. You managed to make quite an impression on the boy." Before I can ask her what she means, she turns to face me fully. "Did you discover what Ravod wanted?"

I push my lingering questions about Stot aside and quickly summarize the past day for Kennan: the escape from the caverns, the revelation of Ravod's origins in Gondal, his connection to the general, and the meeting we are scheduled to have later today.

"Interesting," she says simply when I've finished. "And you plan to follow through with the military based on what Ravod has told you?"

I nod. "He's been through just as much as we have, Kennan. I believe he's trying to do the right thing."

"And if it's a trap?"

"I don't think it is."

The doubt still sits in a corner of my mind—Ravod already betrayed me once—but I squash it hastily. I think back to last night, sitting across from him at the kitchen table of his apartment, seeing sincerity in his eyes. I can't bring myself to believe that Ravod would turn on me now.

Kennan is decidedly less convinced and rolls her eyes at me.

"Of course. We wouldn't want anything tiresome

like *practicality* distracting you from your weird fixation with Ravod, now would we?"

I feel my face flush bright red at her words, spreading from my cheeks up to the tips of my ears. Part of it is complete and utter mortification, and the other part is rage, as per the norm for my interactions with Kennan. She smirks at me with her usual air of superiority.

"You know, Kennan . . ." I ball my shaking fists at my side, ready to give her a piece of my mind.

"There you are!"

Kennan and I reflexively step back from each other as Fiona's voice carries over to us. And maybe I imagine it, but out of the corner of my eye, I see Kennan quickly smooth away the one stray wrinkle that dared appear on the front of her shirt.

The thought quickly dissipates when my gaze finds Fiona. I almost miss her, barely recognizing my best friend for several moments.

She's completely changed her clothes, and now presents much like the fashionable ladies of Tybera. Like most of the dresses I've seen the past few days, her new outfit is formfitting around her waist, with stylish belts and buckles strategically drawing the eye. The skirt flows back asymmetrically, parting near her knees to show off a pair of tall boots with laces more intricate than anything I've ever seen. Its rich green fabric makes her eyes look even larger and more vibrant than usual.

Of course, nearly every head in the vicinity turns

when she passes by. They did even when she was wearing her Montanian rags. I wonder again how it must feel to be so effortlessly beautiful.

"What do you think?" She does an excited twirl when she draws closer. I realize with no shortage of confusion that Fiona has not directed her question at me, but at Kennan.

Suddenly I feel like I'm intruding on something. Kennan is staring at Fiona, and Fiona is staring right back as if I'm not even standing there. Nothing seems to penetrate the charge in the air between them. Fiona has never behaved this way, that I recall. Come to think of it, neither has Kennan.

"It's very . . . you," Kennan says quietly. The words cause Fiona to deflate a little for some reason. I quickly clear my throat.

"How did you get that dress?" I ask.

Finally noticing I'm there, Fiona puts her smile back on, although it's not quite as wide as before. "I was admiring some of the dresses in the window of a tailor's shop," she says. "Next thing I knew the proprietor gave me this gorgeous dress and was insisting I wear it around town! He said it was 'free advertising.'"

Of course. I don't know what I expected.

"Well, I think that tailor is about to see a *lot* more business because of you," I say, smiling at Fiona, hoping my encouragement will make up for whatever she was hoping to get out of Kennan's predictably chilly reaction.

Fiona's eyes soften, the gratitude in them genuine. "Thanks, Shae."

Kennan sniffs in her usual irritable fashion. "Unlike some of us, I have actual tasks to accomplish. I'm returning to the caverns."

"What? Why?" I frown. "Once we all met back up, I thought you were going to rejoin us to go meet with the general . . ."

"You *assumed* I would rejoin you," Kennan corrects me. "I'm trusting my instincts like you're trusting yours. I want to continue trying to forge an alliance with the Protesters."

"But *why*?" I demand, completely baffled by her tenacity in giving them the benefit of the doubt. "The Protesters are a *joke*! They only *just* became inspired by their *own agenda* when you spoke to them five minutes ago! You can't possibly think they have the means to help us."

"No, I don't think they can help us. Not yet." Kennan's voice is quiet now, almost inaudible over the din of the city. "But my gut says they are *worth* helping. They have potential. I have to see this through."

Without another word, she strides off the way she came, leaving Fiona and me to watch as she joins the dispersing crowd of the rally, then disappears into it.

Respecting her decision is the right thing to do, but I don't understand it. The Protesters have been nothing but unproductive, and not just since we got to Gondal, but for years. They only reinforce the present situation for Montanians, nothing more. Members like Stot are the exception, while those like Emery are the norm. How Kennan sees any potential in such an organization is beyond me.

The thought has occurred to me before, but it thunders in my head with even greater intensity and frustration: *I don't think I'll ever understand Kennan.* It frustrates me even more that I know deep in my bones . . . despite this, despite *everything,* I'm going to keep trying to.

"I really thought she was going to see things through with us . . ." My voice trails off when I realize I have spoken my disappointment aloud. By my side, Fiona stares at the spot where Kennan disappeared before sighing heavily and trudging off in the opposite direction.

Ravod and I agreed to meet outside his apartment after his appointment with his grandmother. I arrive with time to spare after the rally and am left to my thoughts as I lean against the limestone exterior of the tower, the city moving past.

Kennan is doing what she thinks is best, just like I am. I know that. But for some reason disappointment has followed me back from the park. It sits heavily in my chest like a physical weight. I thought we were in this together. Perhaps I'm indignant that Kennan doesn't think my plans or ideas are good enough. To her, I'm still nothing more than a stupid, insignificant peasant. And yet, here I am, still chasing her approval for reasons I can't fathom.

I frown upward, resting my head back and watching the air traffic. I let my thoughts drift away on that current, far from Kennan. A bell rings as a metal chamber full of passengers carried on a series of wires zips past overhead. It nearly collides with a smaller flying machine, whose driver hurls a series of incredibly detailed insults at the retreating apparatus.

I sigh heavily. It's so easy to feel insignificant in a place like this.

No one knows each other here. Neighbors could go their whole lives without sharing a single common struggle. Everyone is just doing the best they can to ensure their individual survival, in accordance with the machine of their society.

Maybe that's what bothers me about the Protesters. They apply their Gondalese outlook to a Montanian problem. I worry that Kennan will start to feel the same and be lost amid the crowds and clanging machinery of Gondal.

"Shae." Ravod's call brings my thoughts back to the ground level. He comes to a halt when he reaches me, giving a respectful nod of greeting. "I hope I haven't kept you waiting."

"I haven't been here long, no," I say.

Ravod gestures toward the sidewalk just past me. "Shall we?"

I push away from the building, feeling a crackle of excited energy ignite in my chest. My thoughts from before are all but forgotten when I recall Ravod's statement from last night.

"Are we really going to see the *Book of*—"

"Not so loud. You don't know who's listening." Ravod cuts me off with a stern look I remember well from our earliest time together at High House. "But yes. I have hidden it not far from here."

I pick up my pace to match the easy distance covered by Ravod's long legs. "Why hide it? Aren't you worried someone might find it?"

"I was more worried about having it on me in the event something went wrong," Ravod says. "Don't worry, I hid it somewhere I knew no one would find it."

"Something in particular you're worried about?"

Ravod shrugs as he walks, pushing his hands into his pockets. "Just trying to be practical."

We fall silent as we turn a corner and travel a few more blocks away from the apartment building. The city's pattern remains uninterrupted until Ravod jerks his chin to point up ahead.

"There," he says.

I follow the motion until my gaze falls on a crumbling old bell tower squashed between a couple of sleek newer buildings. It must have been a sight to see in its heyday, but now it's eclipsed by the enormity of the city surrounding it. So much so that it practically seems invisible. Not a single pedestrian pays it a second glance. Despite that, there's something quiet and dignified about the tower. It only reaches the fifth story of its neighbors, but it seems proud for standing the test of time.

The structure is chained off and warded with a sign. The large warning informs anyone getting too close that THE TYBERA MUNICIPAL COMMITTEE IN CONJUNCTION WITH THE GONDALESE HIGH COURT HAVE DEEMED THE PREMISES UNSAFE.

There's a sudden burning sensation against the side of my leg. Without looking away from the tower, I let my hand drift into my pocket. The page from the *Book of Days* scorches the tips of my fingers and I grit my teeth against the sensation as it subsides as quickly as it appeared.

The page must somehow know that the rest of the *Book* is nearby.

"What is this place?" I ask, turning to Ravod as we come to a stop in front of the tower.

"One of the last remnants of Old Tybera," Ravod replies. "The city has been trying to get it torn down for years but the Historical Society keeps blocking their attempts to get it demolished. Most of the people here don't really care either way, it's just a landmark. They refer to it as 'Lord Ten Thirty' because of the clock."

He gestures up at a large, flat disc at the top of the tower, circled by numbers. Two severely rusted metal prongs stand frozen in place, the smaller pointing at the number ten, the other at the number six.

Without further preamble, Ravod checks our surroundings, making sure we're not being watched. Then he ducks beneath the chain blocking the door. After taking a few steps inside, he gestures me to follow.

"*Open.*" The quiet Telling causes the door to shift slightly where it's been fused in place. Some dust falls out of the cracks as the heavy metal door creaks on its hinges.

Ravod offers me a hand, helping me slip through the gap. His fingers are warm and gentle through the fabric of his gloves and send a small, excited shiver through me. Once inside, he quickly drops his palm away from mine, as if he's been burned by the brief contact. He says nothing as we step into the main chamber, though.

Behind me, the Telling wears away and when I look back, the door is fused shut once more.

Blinking rapidly, my eyes adjust to the dark interior of the tower. It's dilapidated enough that some small shafts of light spear the gloom, and motes of dust swirl through them. There is a decaying staircase spiraling up to the top of the tower, but it looks far too dangerous to use.

For a moment, it reminds me of the Constable's watchtower back in Aster. The last time I was there feels like an entire eternity ago. After Ma died and I tried to convince Constable Dunne of the possibility of foul play.

How little I'd known then. How different things have become.

Still, I find it interesting that a structure dating back to Gondal's history could remind me of a similar one from Montane. It makes me wonder if there's more shared history between our nations than I realized.

"I really hope you're not planning to climb those stairs. I don't think we'd survive," I mention to Ravod. My voice echoes hollowly in the still, dry air.

A soft chuckle escapes him as he steps forward. "In that case, I have some good news," he says, crossing the space to the back, where some rusted old equipment has been long abandoned. He leans into it with his elbow, pushing it aside, creaking against the stone floor. Directly below is a metal trapdoor, nearly invisible save for the layers of dust disturbed nearby.

"What's a secret passage doing here?" I ask, stepping closer.

Ravod issues another Telling, unlocking the trapdoor before heaving it open. A hiss issues before the metal clanks into an open position. A few diamond-patterned metal steps descend into the dark below the tower.

"This place dates to a time when Gondal was embroiled in a civil war. It was designed by a famous architect of the time, who later turned out to be a dissident and harbored his accomplices in secret bunkers built into his work." He takes a small apparatus resembling a hilt from his belt and flips a switch, activating a bright beam of light so we can see better. "More recently, it was discovered by a wayward boy looking for an escape from his home situation."

He casts a knowing glance at me over his shoulder. I can practically see that boy gazing at me through the eyes of his older self.

"You hid here?" I ask, prompting him to share more.

"It wasn't locked down then, so sneaking in was pretty easy. Being somewhat smaller helped, too, I suppose," Ravod states as he begins his descent down the steps, not waiting for me to follow but trusting that I will. "I'm not sure anyone really knows or cares that this bunker is still here. This place . . ." He breaks off as we reach the bottom step and clears his throat, trying to disguise the emotional edge that has worked itself into his voice. "It was my most precious secret for a long time. No one knows I ever discovered it." The corner of his mouth turns upward very slightly in the faint light. "Except you."

"Not even your grandmother?" I ask.

Ravod shakes his head. "She was always very kind to me. But I was never sure she would take my side before her son's. He hid his . . . darker aspects from her rather expertly."

Cathal's face flashes through my mind before I can stop it. His warm smile twists into a sickening, evil grin that wracks my insides and makes my steps falter.

"Sounds familiar," I whisper.

"I know." Ravod pauses, turning to meet my gaze. He hesitantly places a gentle but grounding hand on my shoulder. "People like them tend to take up space in your head. But they aren't here now. We're safe."

I take a deep breath, regaining a measure of calm from his words, clearly spoken from experience. It's nice being able to talk about the scars of the past with someone who understands how I got them. When my feet feel steadier, I offer a grateful nod.

Ravod squeezes my shoulder in understanding. Then he withdraws his hand, a little less hastily than before, and steps away from the stairs.

I press my hand to my leg. The page in my pocket feels like it's afire. But the feeling is weaker, somehow, as if it expended most of its energy on its initial fiery burst, but it's no less insistent.

Almost there, I think, although I'm not sure whether my thoughts are for myself or the page in my pocket.

Ravod's handheld light swerves over a remarkably well-preserved bunker. Anything that used to be down here and was able to be removed seems to have been taken long ago, leaving only a dusty metal cube. A few slats along the walls could be bunks or shelves. Otherwise, all that's left is the carpet of dust that's slipped in over time.

As Ravod strides purposefully to the far corner of the room, I'm reminded sharply of the reason we're here. I'm not sure if the swelling knots in my chest are anticipation, something I ate, or the sudden realization of my proximity to an ancient and extraordinary power.

After all this time, all these hardships, I'm about to see the *Book of Days* at last.

I creep closer, unable to see anything over Ravod's shoulder, but it sounds like he's sliding some of the slats in the floor away. When the noise stops, he ducks down to pick up what he hid there and turns back to me. There's been a shift in his demeanor. He's deathly quiet. Reverent, almost.

In the relative darkness, I can't see what he's holding very clearly. He clutches it with fearful tenderness, unlike anything he's ever displayed. If I hadn't already known it was a book, I might have assumed it was a small, wounded animal or an infant. His breath even seems shaky as he takes a seat on the floor, gesturing to me to do the same.

We sit cross-legged in front of each other, and Ravod uses his free hand to pull out an extension in his light, which transforms it to a small lantern. He sets it down to one side.

"It's much more than a mere book. As I traveled with it, it started to feel more like a companion." Ravod frowns and bites his lip. "I suppose the only way to truly explain is for you to see for yourself."

The slowness of his movements only causes the lump in my throat to enlarge and my heart to pound even louder. Ravod gently places the parcel, carefully wrapped in the black and gold cloth that used to be his Bard's cloak, on the floor between us. With deliberate, delicate movements he uncovers it, one wrapping at a time.

And just like that, the *Book of Days* is laid bare before me.

It isn't until I have the legendary artifact in front of me that I realize I had no idea what I expected it to look like. The object I see is not even close to what I might have pictured.

The leather cover is not only worn but decayed. Any embellishments it once possessed have been damaged beyond the point of recognition, leaving a surface so timeworn that it barely even looks like leather anymore. The corners are charred and crumbling along with the spine and edges of the paper.

I reach forward to gently rest the tips of my fingers on the cover. It's oddly warm to the touch, like it's a living thing. I try to keep my fingers from trembling against its surface. I'm afraid that even the slightest movement will cause it to completely disintegrate.

If I didn't know better, I'd say the *Book of Days* was sick. Dying, even.

I look up at Ravod, questioningly, and he nods solemnly.

"When I took it, it didn't look like this," he says, not even bothering to hide the guilt and fear that edge their way into his words. "I thought the best course of action was to get it as far from Cathal as possible. I never imagined that taking it out of Montane would do this. But it started deteriorating more the farther I traveled."

"You couldn't have known," I say, holding his gaze until he drops it back to the withered book.

"Look inside." His voice is barely more than a whisper.

My hand trembles violently as I open the fragile front cover with as much care as possible. It feels ready to fall off as I lay it open.

At first glance, the yellowed page is blank. When I look closer, squinting in the shadowy light, I see that the words on the page are faded and blurred, like they were doused with water until they almost completely vanished from the paper. There are some small flickers of clarity, but it's difficult to discern whether they are just tricks of the light or my imagination.

At the center of the book are fragments where a page was torn out. I can't decide why, but for some reason it looks more like a painful open wound than a torn scrap of paper. The words closest to the tear are fainter than the ones at the edge, as if part of the book bled out ink when the fragment was removed.

With my free hand, I pull the loose page from my pocket. It's been a while since I looked at it, but it's far more worn than I remember. I unfold it and lay it back in the spot where it had been torn out.

Nothing happens. Ravod does not meet my eyes. I follow his gaze back to the *Book*, where the page has reintegrated with the rest. The stitching is loose, but present, where mere seconds before there was only a torn seam.

The words are a little clearer. One seemingly random piece of text looks darker and more legible than the rest. For the briefest instant I'm almost sure I read the word "grateful," but it flashes so quickly that it could have been nothing.

When I look at Ravod, his face is no longer inscrutable. Pain and regret read clearer than any writing across his features.

"I thought I imagined it," he says, struggling to keep his voice even, "but I heard it cry out when I tore the page. I told you last night I took a moral stance against using it to change reality, but that wasn't the whole truth. When I thought about writing in it, I couldn't shake the thought that it would be . . . violent. Violating. That I'd be abusing it, somehow."

I remain quiet, unable to move or think or breathe. I can see in Ravod's eyes, flashing gold with the lamplight, he has long known the conclusion I'm drawing.

The *Book of Days* is a living entity.

Even being open seems to be a drain on it. The faded blotches shift, erratic and weak, but too often to be imaginary anymore.

I begin to close it, so it might rest, when one final flicker catches my eye. It's a slightly darker, clear word that stands out from the rest of its faded companions. My heart jerks up into my throat.

Kieran.

It's gone in a flash, but the faded stain on the page briefly takes the shape of a small ox.

My hand is shaking too violently, and the book falls shut without a sound. The tremors don't subside, instead spreading from my hands and crawling deep into my core.

Is my brother alive? That isn't possible. I witnessed his slow crawl toward death at the hands of the Blot. I heard his screams. I heard his screams stop.

"Shae?"

Ravod's voice pulls me back from somewhere far away. I take a deep breath and shake my head, trying to clear and reassemble my thoughts in the present.

"The *Book* is weak. Suffering," I say. "I don't know that we could use it, even if we wanted to."

"Agreed." Ravod nods.

I pause as my brow knits. "Why does the general want it?"

"To her it represents nothing more than leverage. Part of the reason Gondal has never come near Montane was Cathal threatening to use the *Book of Days* to wipe them out if they tried," Ravod explains.

"But if she has the *Book of Days*, that threat is eliminated." I finish the thought aloud.

"Exactly. It's an opportunity to act where she could not before."

"So, you're absolutely sure she has no interest in using it? Destroying it?" I direct my question at Ravod but find I can't look away from the *Book of*

Days as I speak. Although it merely sits on the floor between us, I get the strangest feeling that it's listening to our conversation. At the very least, it's aware of it. Perhaps our words are already inscribed somewhere on its pages.

Ravod sighs and sits back a little as he considers my question. Finally, he shakes his head.

"I don't think so. I've gotten the chance to spend some time with her since returning to Gondal. She has a tough outer shell, but underneath there is kindness."

"Sounds familiar." I can't help it when the corner of my mouth turns upward at him.

For a second, Ravod's expression mirrors mine before he continues. "At her core, she's a pragmatist and a patriot. Not a megalomaniac."

"Good to know."

"She's aware I have the *Book*. That's been *my* leverage. And she made a compelling case to entrust it to her. I . . ." His lips thin to a short line as he trails off.

"You want to trust her," I offer, looking back at him.

"Yes," he admits. "But my desire to trust her might not be for the right reasons."

"What do you mean?"

"It's not based on any form of logic. She's my grandmother, my only existing family." He pauses, a deep frown creasing his handsome features. "But it's more than that. I want to trust her because I want to believe that if she's trustworthy it *redeems* my family."

"Maybe the real issue is that you don't trust yourself," I blurt thoughtlessly. My jaw clenches immediately after I speak, unable to snatch the potentially offensive words back.

Ravod stares at me, wide-eyed. Then, to my surprise, he laughs.

"You're right."

I blink several times, processing his reaction. "I am?"

Instead of replying, Ravod looks down at the *Book of Days* and starts wrapping it up. His movements are still reverent, but somehow more purposeful than before. When he finishes, he picks it up and gives it a long, focused look.

"When I navigated the labyrinth ahead of you and stole this book, it was my intention to subvert you. I convinced myself that your trust in me was a necessary casualty of this conflict, and I was doing the right thing. It was arrogant. I was wrong." He pauses with a deep, heavy breath. "All this to say, I meant what I said last night." He extends the *Book of Days* toward me. "I trust you."

The wait in the antechamber of the general's office is shorter this time. Ensign Charolais waves us through from their desk as soon as Ravod, Fiona, Mads, and I step in.

I bite down hard on my lower lip as I cross the room, my hand falling protectively over where the

Book of Days is stowed in a satchel slung over my shoulder. Ravod passes me a knowing glance as he ushers me ahead of him into the office.

"You can do this," Mads leans down to whisper to me from one side. Fiona's delicate hand gives my forearm a gentle squeeze from the other.

General Ravod is seated behind her enormous mahogany desk, waiting for us. It is still cluttered, but this time a large map has been spread over most of the surface.

"You've returned," she says by way of greeting. "Welcome back."

Mads and Fiona are markedly more nervous under the general's sharp, one-eyed gaze. Ravod has reverted to his usual inscrutable countenance.

I find myself at the mercy of a flurry of mixed emotions. Each time I grab for one, it slips away only to be replaced by another. I seem to catch hold of trepidation most often. Even so, I manage a deep breath and step forward to stand across from the general on the other side of the desk.

"I hope we can help, General," I say.

General Ravod's eye flicks to her grandson before fixing me with the full weight of her attention.

"Let's start with the facts," she states, rising from her seat and indicating the map in front of her. It would seem the formalities are over. "This map indicates each point of incursion by your wasteland and its advancement over the past few weeks."

The way she speaks, I would have thought she was

talking about an enemy army making its way over the border. It takes a moment for me to look from the general to her map to realize that that's *exactly* how she views this situation. To her, the wasteland is a hostile foreign force invading her country.

Knowing the nature of the wasteland, I can't say I blame her for being concerned. I trekked across it not too long ago, and the memory of that journey still puts me on high alert against my will.

Hunger, fear, and fire flash in my mind. With effort, I force my shoulders down from where they are clenched below my ears and place two fingers on the desk. The feel of something solid grounds me enough that I can examine the map.

At the top is Montane. It looks so small compared to the vast, brown emptiness I traveled across. According to this map it's only a little peninsula fenced in by mountains. It's no accident that the country is colored by an indigo haze on the map. Despite the actual devastation being a dull brownish hue, the color of the plague on the map was deliberately chosen to indicate the spread of the wasteland.

Gondal lies at the southern border of Montane. The legal separation is denoted by a sharp black line. But the indigo discoloration spreads farther, across five points marked with inky crosses at the base of the mountains. That's where the general is pointing.

Past her gloved index finger, hovering at the border, the indigo spreads to a stop over two landmarks labeled JUNCTION TWELVE and JUNCTION THIRTEEN. She briskly taps the paper over each.

"We have received reports from these junctions that not only has the wasteland spread, a handful of civilians have fallen ill. You can probably guess their affliction." She raises her eyebrows meaningfully as she studies the reactions of everyone in the room.

Only Ravod remains impassive. She's probably already told him about this. But Mads's and Fiona's eyes have gone wide. Even I can't prevent the hitch in my breath.

"The Blot," I whisper.

The general nods. "Just so. It's weaker than the reports I've seen over the years from Montane. But no less insidious. Those without the means to move farther into Gondal have suffered terribly from the disease. Three have died already, and it's only the beginning."

"Shouldn't there be wider panic at news like this?" I ask.

"The Department of Public Health and several squads of my people have suppressed the news for that very reason," the general answers. "That's far from a permanent solution. Unless the spread of the wasteland is halted, and *soon*, there may not be much left of Gondal to protect."

"You'll wind up like us." My voice is shaky. The grim implications of the general's words cause an uncomfortable lump to form in my throat.

"Indelicately put, but yes." The general steps around her desk and past Ravod so she's standing at my side. Her face is set with a solemn gravity that conveys a great deal more than words. "I won't lie, there are those among the upper echelons of the Gondalese government who believe this is a deliberate attack and constitutes an act of war. You were on the inside at High House. I want to know the truth."

It's difficult not to shift nervously under her stare. Even if she isn't accusing me of anything, I feel as though she sees right through me.

"As far as I know, it's not deliberate," I finally manage to reply.

"Yes, Erik maintains this as well." The general's single dark eye twinkles inquisitively, somehow adding a layer of intensity to her stare that was not there before.

"It's the truth," Ravod interjects, his voice level and clear. "Even with the combined power of every Bard at High House, Cathal could not do this. He would need the *Book of Days,* which he does not have."

"Then there is but one clear course of action," the general states, locking her hands behind her back. "If Cathal is responsible for the wasteland's existence and won't—or can't—prevent this from endangering Gondal, he and his regime must be removed from power. The *Book of Days* must be placed somewhere it can no longer be tampered with."

I find myself nodding at her statement. It sounds

much simpler than I know it will be, but this is a goal I can support.

"Can you do that? I know you probably have the means to oust Cathal. But can you *truly* ensure that the *Book of Days* will be safe?" I ask.

"I can," General Ravod says without hesitation. "And I will do you one better. Once Cathal and his Bards are out of the picture, I can ensure that the *Book of Days* is restored to a place of safety in Montane, where it belongs."

"You *really* have no desire to keep it?" Fiona pipes up incredulously.

The general turns to Fiona, one eyebrow raised. "Why would I? Gondal has always achieved prosperity on its own merit. We have no need of the *Book of Days*. I doubt you'll meet any Gondalese who feels differently. It's a point of pride for us that we don't require any special power, only our natural ingenuity."

I don't sense insincerity in her words, bizarre as they seem. This doesn't appear to come as any surprise to Ravod, either. He merely crosses his arms over his chest and leans one hip against a nearby side table, watching.

His grandmother once again takes careful stock of our reactions before her eye falls purposefully upon the satchel slung over my shoulder.

"I know you have the *Book*. You're not as subtle as you believe. I won't force you to hand it over to me," she says. I gulp past the lump choking my windpipe, clutching the strap of my satchel as tight as I can.

"But perhaps I can convince you that it is the right thing to do."

"I just . . ." I trail off.

The general steps closer to me and places a hand on my shoulder with uncharacteristic gentleness. I stare at her hand for a moment before following her arm up to her face. Her countenance is resolute, much like her grandson's, but there's a surprising amount of concern in her expression.

"You don't have to carry this burden, child."

She isn't wrong, I think. There's a small measure of relief to be found in the idea that I can pass the *Book* into the general's capable hands. She made a convincing case to do so, after all.

So did Cathal. A faint whisper of doubt causes me to hesitate. A reminder from not so long ago. I don't have the best track record when it comes to trusting authority figures. The last time I did, it nearly killed me.

I look at each of my friends, hoping they can provide insight. Better yet, they could make this decision for me. Mads and Fiona meet my gaze un-flinchingly, trusting me. Ravod glances between me and his grandmother and back. He wants to trust the general, but won't ask me to do the same for his sake.

I envy them all for not bearing the burden of this decision. But maybe I don't have to, either. Perhaps it's time I allowed someone with years of experience defending her homeland to take responsibility for this monumental task.

Someone Ravod said was always kind to him, who allowed him back into her life and family. If I can trust anyone in power here, it must be the general.

I chew my lip slowly, reaching into the satchel, and produce the *Book of Days*, still wrapped in fragments of cloth. I feel a weight rise from my shoulders as the general relieves me of it.

"Very good," she says. With the *Book* in her hands, she steps back around her desk to where she stood before. "Let us proceed, then."

"What's your plan?" Ravod asks from his perch.

The general does not answer immediately and pushes a button on a small panel off to the side of her desk.

"I'm not leaving anything to chance. In order to assure that Cathal's seat of power is completely eradicated, our bomber squadrons will be targeting the entirety of Montane."

It takes a minute for the gravity of her words to sink in. It's a little like freezing to death. The cold creeps slowly over my skin, then beneath each layer of tissue until I'm coiled completely in its grip.

Several uniformed officers and soldiers suddenly file into the general's office, snapping my attention to the door. Within seconds, the room is full of people. They ignore me and my companions as they silently form a line and stand rigidly at attention in the presence of their commander.

"Thanks to the help of my grandson and these refugees," General Ravod says, pausing to nod toward me and my friends, "you are cleared to proceed with Operation Havoc. Prepare your squadrons for the strike on Montane."

"You . . . You lied? This whole time you were planning to . . . wipe us off the map entirely?" I interrupt.

The general's gaze becomes taciturn once more. "Hardly. My goal has always been the defense of Gondal. You never asked how I planned to achieve it, and as a mere civilian refugee, it's none of your concern. Your part in this is over."

"None of her concern?" Mads exclaims, his outrage overwhelming his trepidation about the general. "You just casually announced your plan to eradicate an entire country! I'd say this is a big concern for all of us!"

"Our families are in Montane!" Fiona adds, tears filling her eyes. "They have nothing to do with High House!"

Their anger thaws the shock that's settled over me, harkening back to the last time this happened—when I trusted someone in power and that trust proved misplaced. Once again, I have been used to further an agenda that is not my own.

"You can't do this!" My shout pulls the attention

of everyone in the room. "Innocent people will be killed needlessly! I didn't give you the *Book of Days* so you could exterminate my people!"

"Your reasons are irrelevant," the general says through her teeth. "Erik, please escort your little friends from the premises."

"No!" I don't wait for Ravod to react to his grand-mother's command. I turn to face her across the desk, slamming my hands down on its surface so hard that the sting of the impact travels all the way up to my shoulders.

Something shackled deep inside me breaks loose. Like an unanticipated storm erupting on a clear day, I am seized by gale force winds and deafening thunder that are the feelings and memories I have tried to keep tethered to my self-control.

I scream, "I've *had* it with people like you! No amount of authority gives you the right to destroy someone else's life! It *definitely* doesn't give you the right to pretend that you're protecting people to jus-tify massacring an entire country! Montane may be a blighted wasteland, but it's my *home*! I won't stand by and let you annihilate what's left of it!"

There's a small part of me that whispers some-thing about using caution, but I can barely hear it in the maelstrom. The only thought that I can hear properly is that I *must* set this right.

I almost try to use a Telling before I remember it's useless. My rage might have shaken the entire build-ing if we were in Montane. All I have here is myself, but even that limitation doesn't cause my will to falter. I will have to be enough.

I launch myself across the desk at the general, swiping for the *Book of Days* still clutched in her grasp.

My fingers brush the edge of the wrapping. Another inch and I can snatch it back.

It starts to recede. That's when I realize I've been grabbed and am being pulled away. The brusqueness of it doesn't even register until I'm forced onto my stomach on the carpeted floor. My hands are pinned behind my back.

"Let her go!" I hear Mads cry, and there's a scuffle I can't see. It ends with both Mads and Fiona being restrained like I have been.

"No need to be so rough, they're only children," I hear General Ravod say as she strolls around the desk. Her polished black boots stop in front of me.

Just like when I first met Cathal. Perhaps it's the pressure of being held down, but suddenly I feel ready to vomit.

"I'm going to stop you," I grind out through my teeth.

"You're quite bold for a Montanian," the general remarks. "I admire that. But boldness can be misdirected. I'll allow you to ponder that from a cell."

I'm hauled up to my feet, where I can now see that I've been captured by two enormous soldiers. Another has similarly apprehended Fiona. It's taken three to pin down Mads.

Anger reverts to sheer terror at the prospect of them coming to harm because of me. I was the one who stupidly handed over the *Book of Days*. I was the one who was so easily tricked again. Only now my stupidity has roped in and potentially damned the people I care about most in the world.

Maybe Kennan is right about me, after all.

For the first time since arriving in Gondal, being unable to use a Telling stings me. I feel weak. Impotent. Useless. A failure.

"Take these three to the prison level," the general instructs her men.

Heart hammering, I cast my eyes about the room for any advantage. There *must* be a way we can still escape.

My eyes lock onto Ravod's.

He still has the power of Telling. He can do something while I cannot.

Help. I try to convey my desperation through my eyes. More than ever, I need him to have my back.

"Erik." The general's voice breaks his gaze, drawing his dark eyes to hers. The room seems to have stilled. The thudding in my chest goes dull, twisting into anguish for Ravod—at my own greed and hopelessness for asking him to choose between me and his only existing family.

If such a decision pained Ravod, he does not show it as he regards the general coolly. It unsettles something deep within me.

"Yes, Grandmother?"

I try to bring Ravod's attention back to me, hoping that if I can only hold it, he will understand what I need him to do.

Are you on my side, Ravod?

The general narrows her eye at her grandson, silently asking him the same question I did. "I trust you don't share your friend's disapproval of the situation?"

"Ravod, you *know* this is wrong. You spent your life in Montane, you've *seen* the plight of its people—we are innocent!" I interject, pulling against the soldiers' grip on my upper arms.

He looks at me for a brief instant and my breath catches. I'm hopeful that this is it. The part where he stands up for me and makes the general see reason. Or maybe he'll use a Telling to create an opening for us to escape.

He looks away.

"I have no objections," he says to his grandmother with a small shrug.

His words are like a knife in my back and send a renewed burst of white-hot fury through me.

I'm not sure if I'm angrier that he lied about trusting me, or that I believed him. Or that I trusted him enough to give him a second chance after he stole the *Book of Days* in the first place.

"Ravod!" I thrash against my restraints. "You liar! You *traitor*!"

The general waves a dismissive hand. "Enough of this. Take them away."

I snarl furiously as the soldiers drag me out of the room. I fight them every step of the way, hurling obscenities behind me. Ravod doesn't even give me the courtesy of looking my way. His face disappears as the office door closes.

A metal door slides shut with an empty clanging sound that reverberates through our flat, empty prison cell. There are no bars on the door, only a small slat, presumably for depositing whatever future meals we'll be given. The single yellow light affixed to the ceiling does little to brighten the dark metallic space. There are several small platforms affixed to the wall for us to sleep on, a sink, and a toilet.

"At least they didn't separate us." Mads's voice is quiet and thoughtful. His brow is furrowed and a grimace tugs at his mouth as he looks around our cell. "They obviously don't consider us to be much of a threat."

"Their mistake," Fiona replies. The barely concealed anger in her voice is jarring and uncharacteristic, as is the tension in her slender frame. I can't blame her for feeling it, though.

"You sound like Kennan," Mads says.

Fiona falls silent at that. She bites her lip and turns toward the wall.

Too little too late. Kennan wouldn't have gotten into this situation to begin with. I can't bring myself to say it aloud. She was right about everything. Especially the part where she called me an idiot. If only I'd listened to her, maybe any hope I had would not be extinguished.

I have nothing left in me. I slide down the wall to slump onto the floor, drawing my knees to my chest.

The shock is wearing off, giving way to a torrent of emotions. The anger I felt from before has abruptly changed course. Instead of charging forward at the general, it veers inward at myself.

I let this happen. When Montane falls to dust, it will be because of me. One stupid girl who made bad choices and trusted the wrong people. And everyone who remains will only remember the general. She'll be hailed as a hero and a savior, fighting to protect her homeland. No one will speak of the innocent lives she snuffed out to ensure her total victory.

It already happened in Montane once before with Cathal. Why would this time be any different?

Not even the *Book of Days* writes our history. Not really. That privilege belongs to those who win wars. Their truest victory is the right to impart their story to future generations. My story—and Mads's and Fiona's—will languish in this dismal little cell.

Staring into the middle distance, I find myself examining and reexamining every choice that brought me to this moment. I alter small details and watch a different future unfold—sometimes better, most times *much* better.

"Shae?"

It takes me a second to realize that Fiona has taken a seat beside me and wrapped her arm around my shoulders.

I can't bring myself to look at her. If I do, I'll only see the faces of her family. Her stern but fair father, and her mother who likes to hum little songs while she cooks. Her elder brothers who dote on their only sister. They're all still alive—for now. The whole town was right about me all along. I *have* brought about their doom.

"How could I have been so wrong?" I hear my voice but can't quite feel myself ask the question. My whole body is numb.

"Shae . . ." Fiona squeezes my shoulder. But her voice trails off. She knows it's the truth and can't decide what to say in response.

"If anyone's to blame for this, it's the general." Mads takes a seat on the bed platform facing me and leans forward on his knees.

"But *I* gave her the *Book of Days*. I made it possible for her to attack Montane with no fear of repercussion," I counter.

"You didn't know—"

"I should have *asked*," I cut him off. I don't mean to sound so curt. Snapping at Mads only makes tears well in my eyes. I take a breath and start over. "I was only worried about whether she would try to *use* it. It should have occurred to me that she didn't need it. All the signs were there, I just refused to see them. Or I was too dumb to understand them. Either way . . ."

My words finally give out. My forehead folds onto my knees, and I'm powerless to do anything more than sob.

"I'm so sorry," I manage to choke out lamely. "Sorry" won't save their families.

Fiona sighs and gently squeezes my shoulder again, shifting closer so she can push my hair from my face with her free hand. Some of the wisps near my hairline require a second gentle swipe where they have gotten stuck to my skin by my tears.

"For what it's worth," she says, "if I were in your position, I would have done the same thing. Like Mads said, you couldn't have known."

"General Ravod played into your desire to do the right thing," Mads interjects.

"I'm an idiot for letting myself be manipulated." I lift my head and meet Mads's gaze. "And it's not even the first time this has happened. I trusted Cathal. I thought of him like a father. And in the end, I led him to the *Book of Days* and put us in this mess. Can't you see how stupid that is?"

"Sorry, Freckles. You're never going to convince me that you're stupid," Mads replies.

"That you trust and want to see the best in people isn't a flaw," Fiona adds.

My retort dies under their combined efforts to comfort me. A little of the hopelessness lifts when I study their earnest faces in turn. They smile at me. Even in a prison cell, when everything seems so hopelessly lost.

I'm lucky to have these friends.

With nothing but time, we spend the following hours either talking or drifting into silence. When my feelings start to overwhelm me, Fiona is always at my side with a shoulder to cry on if I need. Mads is always ready with an offer to talk through the problem. Both have their unique way of helping, and eventually my guilt and self-loathing shift into gratitude and stay there.

Fiona often reminds me that at least we're alive. Mads will respond by stating that as long as that's the case, we're still able to do something about the situation.

The more time passes, the more I wonder if "something" might include breaking out of a Gondalese prison.

There are no windows in the cell. The light never changes. We chart the passage of time roughly, utilizing the constant dripping of a nearby pipe coupled with the intervals when the slat in the door opens and a sparse tray of often-rancid, always horrible-looking food appears. By Mads's calculations, every five hours or so.

By that measure we discern that about three days have passed since we were locked up. No real opportunities for escape present themselves.

But I refuse to let go of what hope I've held onto. Even as the silences between the three of us begin to stretch longer and longer as we grow hungrier and hungrier.

As another silence descends, my thoughts wander yet again to the world outside our prison. Does anyone even know where we are? Does anyone care?

I wonder how Kennan is faring with the Protesters in their cavern. If she's heard anything about what happened to us, at least it might have afforded her a good laugh. I consider whether Ravod regrets his actions. I'm not strong enough to think of him for long. His betrayal, on top of the others, is too raw. I doubt he's even spared me a thought.

All these suppositions inevitably circle back to one question: Has Montane already been destroyed?

A sharp metallic clanging jolts me out of my reverie. I've gotten used to the sound of the slat in the door being opened, and this is not that.

It's the door itself.

Mads and Fiona turn toward the sound like forest creatures wary of an approaching hunter. I realize I must look similar, the way we all unblinkingly watch the heavy door as it hisses and slides open.

"You have some nerve." I can't repress the growl in my throat as Ravod brazenly steps into the cell.

His countenance betrays no hint of disturbance at my words. His hands are folded behind his back in a cool, businesslike manner. He assesses us briefly before speaking.

"I've been tasked with transferring you three to a different part of the facility."

"As though we'd agree to go anywhere with you," Mads says, moving between me and Ravod, glaring icy daggers at him. I find myself grateful—the obstacle prevents me from attacking Ravod outright, and every part of me wishes dearly to do just that.

"You can object, if you wish," Ravod replies. "But your options at present are to come willingly or unwillingly. The choice is yours."

"I'm sure there's no need for violence," Fiona says, placing one hand on my shoulder and the other on Mads's but directing her statement at Ravod. Her eyes flick meaningfully to the weapon holstered at his hip. To say nothing of how he has the Telling at his disposal.

I take a deep breath to steady my anger before I step forward. I keep my eyes on Ravod's, daring him to hurt me more than he already has. But part of me hopes that if I force him to look me in the eyes he will feel some measure of regret. Either way, I hope he squirms.

"Fine." I leave it at that.

He nods, taking a backward step toward the door. His hand has drifted to the handle of his weapon.

"One false move and I won't hesitate to shoot," he says, ushering us out.

Outside the cell, a guard cuffs each of our wrists in turn. When he finishes, he hands the key over to Ravod with a stiff nod and hangs back as we start walking. I glance down at my shackled hands in front of me with a grimace.

The cellblock is long and dark. The seemingly endless hall is all cold reinforced steel and yellow lights. It's eerily quiet. Our footsteps on the metal floor echo around us as we march toward wherever Ravod is taking us.

I shiver, momentarily recalling the sanitarium at High House. By that standard, no place is quite as terrifying. The sounds and smells here are downright pleasant by comparison.

"Where are you taking us?" Mads's question is a welcome distraction from the dark spiral in my mind.

"I'm handing you over to be transferred," Ravod says, somewhat cryptically.

"Transferred where?" I demand, craning my neck to look at him.

Ravod shrugs. "Not my problem."

My head swivels to face forward, mostly so he can't see the tears needling the corners of my eyes. I won't give him the satisfaction of knowing how deeply he's wounded me.

"That's awfully blasé for someone who went through so much trouble to manipulate us into this situation," Fiona states. I feel a certain relief at her words giving voice to thoughts I can't articulate.

"I don't know what you're talking about," Ravod answers.

"I think you do," Fiona says in a singsong tone she reserves exclusively for times when she wants to *really* infuriate someone. "Otherwise, why jump through all those hoops to rescue us from the Protesters? Why go to such lengths to earn our trust? Why enlist Shae to hand over the *Book of Days* when you easily could have done so yourself?"

I bite my lip as I walk, finding myself wondering what Ravod's answers to those questions are.

"Whatever you're playing at, it won't work," he says, sounding almost bored.

A very Ravod answer. I don't know why I thought he wouldn't deflect. I probably just wanted to understand why it was necessary to cause me such anguish. To use my unreciprocated feelings for him—exploiting my affection—to gain my trust. I never thought Ravod to be that needlessly cruel.

As the end of the cellblock looms closer, I realize that it might be time to give up any lingering faith that Ravod was ever on my side. Fiona was giving him an opportunity to explain himself just now. To find his way back. And he refused.

It will be easier in the long run to accept what happened for what it is. More treachery. Another betrayal in a long line of deceits.

Two uniformed guards up ahead notice Ravod escorting us and stand a little straighter as we approach. Behind them looms an enormous circular door locked by imposing metal rods around its circumference. I remember it from our way in, how it hisses, vents steaming as the locks disengage and reengage one by one.

Anticipating their questions, Ravod gracefully salutes the guards. "These three conspirators are being shipped out to the labor camp, general's orders."

I do *not* like the sound of that. Judging from the worried glances cast my way by Fiona and Mads, they aren't thrilled, either.

The guards nod to Ravod and one opens a nearly hidden panel on the side of the wall. With his back turned, I can't see what he's doing, but I hear a series of beeping sounds. A moment later, the mechanisms in the door shift and unlock. With the way ahead clear, Ravod motions for us to proceed.

We're closer to the Axis Keep proper. I was too busy screaming and fighting on the way in to really notice the shift in my surroundings. The soldiers and officers in this area bustle around without paying our group much mind. From what I can tell of the chatter, and the lines of desks and offices, they seem to be involved in myriad investigations. I suppose it would make sense that in a city this big they would need more resources and manpower to accomplish what back home would be the job of a single constable.

With the bright lights, it takes me a second to notice that night has fallen outside the plain rectangular windows. The darkness makes me shudder when I realize I'm about to disappear into it and probably spend the rest of my life in forced labor.

"It's going to be okay," Mads whispers, brushing

his arm against mine, the most either of us can manage with our wrists shackled together.

"I wish I had your confidence," I say, sighing.

Ravod directs us down a series of interconnected hallways. The trip reminds me distantly of our arrival in Tybera—escorted under guard. We are leaving the same way we came. All I can do is not let anyone see how terrified I am. I focus all my attention on that, the one thing still in my control.

Another checkpoint of guards allows us passage outside the Keep. The night air is cool on my skin, and a slight breeze drifts across my face, through my hair. It feels a little strange after being locked up.

This isn't the main door of the base. Instead, we're deposited in a small channel between the main building and the outer wall. Both rise high above to disappear into a faraway night sky where airships float lazily beneath the canopy of clouds, illuminated by city lights I can't see. Back on the ground, our path is lit by a series of austere white lamps.

Only a few token guards patrol this area, and none are terribly interested in us as we pass. They recognize Ravod, however, and greet him with small nods and salutes.

I bite my lip as we walk. A shred of opportunity has presented itself in this mostly deserted area. It would be a long shot. I'd have to move faster than a bolt of lightning if I want to incapacitate Ravod before he can speak a Telling or draw his weapon.

I need a distraction. I look around, trying to be surreptitious. The area is mostly empty save for some litter piled near the sides of the wall. Finally, my gaze comes to rest on Mads and Fiona walking by my side. A very risky plan starts taking shape.

"Fiona," I say quietly, catching her attention. "Remember that time Mads sabotaged your favorite shoes?"

Fiona quirks a pale eyebrow at me. Mads has turned bright red and seems determined to ignore us, keeping his gaze forward as we walk. I shift my gaze from her to him and back, making an angry face and hoping desperately that she will pick up on the cue. She blinks in confusion before a slow smile turns the corner of her mouth.

"That's right," she says, her voice taking on a low growl. "That rash was so bad that old Doc Murphy nearly amputated my feet."

"He did?" Rather than take the bait, Mads is horrified.

Not to be deterred, Fiona shrieks and hurls herself into Mads. I dodge the pair as they stumble into the wall. It's all Mads can do to fend her off, but his protests are drowned out. Fiona scratches at him like a feral cat, the cuffs around her wrists doing little to contain her fury. Between that and the colorful insults I had no idea she even knew, she's caused quite a scene.

The fight affords me enough time to move closer

to Ravod. He's approached the quarrel swiftly with his customary detachment. I wait for him to reach for Fiona before I dart forward and snatch his weapon.

The contraption is strangely heavy as it starts to slide from its holster. I grit my teeth as I clutch it tightly.

A hand closes around my wrist.

"Not so fast."

Suddenly, as he pulls me around to face him, I'm back in Aster, meeting him for the first time. Rain has just fallen after a long drought, and the town has handed over its meager tithe to the Bards already. I might have imagined it, but for a fraction of a second, I think I catch him smiling as though he thought the same thing.

If it was ever there, it is quickly replaced by a grim frown. A lot has happened since that day. Too much.

I open my mouth to say something but am interrupted by the sound of footsteps clattering closer from farther down the alley. It must be other soldiers, coming to back Ravod up. The tiny wisp of hope I harbored withers inside me. The footsteps stop.

A clear, commanding voice rings out through the dark stillness.

"Let them go, Ravod."

I must be imagining things. I crane my head in the direction of the voice and find myself blinking in disbelief.

The passage is still dark, and looks like it's deserted until Kennan strolls into the lamplight. She's finally forgone her Bard's uniform in favor of more casual Gondalese fare: flight goggles perched on her forehead, with a pair of slacks and a button-down shirt that accentuate her tall frame. Somehow, she makes it seem rather effortlessly elegant.

Behind her are half a dozen Protesters who are probably the reason why those guards I was worried about haven't shown up. I almost don't notice them with Kennan's presence commanding everyone's attention.

"Kennan?" Mads and Fiona speak almost in unison, although one seems decidedly more surprised and the other relieved.

Kennan ignores everyone but Ravod.

"You're outnumbered, Ravod. Your men aren't coming to back you up. Time to cut your losses and get out of here," she states, perhaps a little louder than necessary as she steadily points a Gondalese weapon at him.

"Be careful, Kennan," I call. "He can use the Telling here."

"He won't." I can't figure out if Kennan's statement is an assessment or a threat.

I swallow back my questions. Ravod maintains a focused look at Kennan that would have incinerated anyone else. He does not let go of me, his grip on my wrist just below the metal cuff firm but not painful.

I can practically see the thoughts rapidly turning in his head as he considers the situation.

Kennan and Ravod are both poised to attack. This confrontation is at the edge of a knife, the air thick with tension ready to cascade into violence at the slightest provocation. My breath trembles where it catches in my throat. Once again, I find myself hoping against hope that Ravod will read my thoughts and do the right thing. This time, however, I'm not as certain he will.

Eventually, Ravod sighs. He doesn't even look at me as he drops my wrist in the same cold, dispassionate manner with which he abandoned our friendship. He merely spares Kennan one last look of silent warning. Then he backs away, disappearing into the dark the way we came.

My knees give out under me, but the stability of the ground is a welcome relief from the uncertainty moments before. Mads is at my side in the next instant, his large, callused hand on my shoulder grounding me further.

"Thanks." My voice is hoarse. Mads smiles at me a little tightly, still concerned.

I turn to my other side, expecting to see Fiona. Instead, she's rushing toward Kennan and flinging her arms around her neck. Kennan's eyes widen in surprise, and she rests a hand on Fiona's back awkwardly. The embrace lasts a few seconds too long before Fiona finally pulls back.

"You came for us," Fiona breathes out, seeming half incredulous and half relieved, as though this was the outcome she wanted but was too afraid to ask for aloud.

Kennan clears her throat. "Let's get out of here."

She gets no argument from us. The past few minutes finally hit me, and I'm more exhausted than I ever remember feeling. Nevertheless, I allow Mads to help me to my feet, and we follow Kennan and her group back through the alley.

Another group is waiting at the end. They face Kennan as she approaches, giving her their undivided attention.

"We have the prisoners," Kennan says without breaking her stride. "Form up into your secondary groups, stay focused, and make sure the guards are good and confused before you make your getaways. We don't want them tracing our steps."

I half expect the Protesters to question her or start bickering amongst themselves, like before. Instead, they obey Kennan's orders without hesitation. They pair off into groups of twos and threes, disappearing into the shadows surrounding us.

Only a pair of Protesters have stayed behind, flanking Kennan. She addresses them over her shoulder.

"We got what we came for. Let's go."

Nearby, a rope ladder hangs from the top of the wall, surrounded by a pile of uniformed bodies.

"They'll wake up eventually," Kennan says, nodding to the inert guards. She stops and ushers us ahead of her. Remaining poised vigilantly at the bottom, weapon drawn, she waits until everyone has climbed to a safer distance toward the top of the wall.

I can hear distant shouting and warning bells going off down in the Keep as I swing my leg over the side of the wall. I lean down and offer Kennan a hand, which, to my surprise, she accepts.

Hovering in the air nearby are several flying vehicles, the kind that look like enormous dragonflies.

"Climb over and hang on," one of the Protesters instructs, mounting the vehicle ahead of me. Distantly, I recognize Emery's voice. I do as he says, holding on for dear life when I see how high we are. The fear of falling to my death is a small price to pay for escaping this place.

The engine roars to life, humming beneath me. I screw my eyes shut as the vehicle lurches into the sky and we disappear into the city.

Against all the odds, we make it out of Axis Keep.

I sleep restlessly that night. After collapsing onto a cot somewhere in the caverns deep below the city, I find myself staring at a blank wall for a long time. A square of light from the window behind me casts the bare wood in a soft glow, tinged amber from the lanterns outside. I wrap a threadbare quilt around me as though it can provide a barrier against the rest of the world. Eventually, the ball I've curled into feels tight enough, my imaginary defenses secure enough, that I fall into a deep sleep.

That sleep is fraught with dreams both disturbing and outright terrifying, however. People are screaming, fires are raging, and a cage of twisted metal and human bones closes around me. Through it all, a figure stands shrouded by my side, visible only from the corner of my eye. I don't have to see them to know exactly who it is.

Niall. His presence gnaws at me, weighs on me, demanding something from me I can't give.

Then another figure emerges from the dust and ashes swirling in the desolation before me—the silhouette of a man, walking with purpose and confidence. My first instinct is to hope it's Ravod. But when his features come into focus, I recoil.

Cathal steps up to the bars of my prison. The wind, smoke, and ash don't affect him. His clothes and hair are as immaculate as I remember. His white boots alone are stained with the blood that soaks the ground.

I step back, only to feel Niall's gnarled hand grip the back of my neck, holding me in place. Thick, rough nails dig into my skin, stopping just short of breaking through.

Cathal doesn't speak, instead staring into my eyes with a sinister smirk. The message of his silence is clear.

He's watching me. And he will continue to watch as I lose everything that I hold dear. Only then, when I'm finally and completely broken, will he grant me the mercy of death.

I awaken with a start, my skin damp with cold sweat. I don't know how long I slept. Even as I wonder, the images slip from my memory. All they leave behind is a bitter residue of fear, shame, and hopelessness.

The color of the square of light on the wall has changed to a pale blue. I guess the only way to discern the passage of time down in the caverns is by alternating the color of the lamps. I focus on that light, willing the sleep from my body. I don't want to doze off again and risk another nightmare.

Lurching into a sitting position, I consider taking a walk to clear my head. I hesitate as I remember I must look like a mess. I sniff my clothes and immediately wish I hadn't. It's a minor miracle that the whole cavern can't smell the time I served in prison and the subsequent escape.

Thankfully, I spot a basin, a bar of soap, and a ragged but serviceable towel nearby. Beside it is a neatly folded pile of clean clothes, atop which I spot a note. I instantly recognize Kennan's overly pointy cursive.

Clean up and head downstairs when you're ready.

—K.

"Unusually thoughtful of her," I mumble to the empty room as I set about availing myself of the basin. A hand pump sends mostly fresh, searingly cold water splashing into the aged porcelain bowl.

It's not the luxurious bath at High House, but somehow feels just as good as the caked-on sweat and grime of the last few days gets scrubbed off. The cold water instantly expels the last of my fatigue and drives away any lingering thoughts of the terrors that await me in my sleep.

Somewhat more time-consuming is figuring out the clothes Kennan left for me. I've gotten mostly used to seeing garments such as these, but never would have guessed I'd be faced with trying to navigate wearing them. The fashion here favors a plethora of chains, buttons, and buckles, some for utility and most for decoration. After a bit of puzzling, I figure out which is which on the worn leather jacket. The belt of the same material takes me longest, as it not only wraps around my waist, but connects to smaller belts that buckle around my thighs over my trousers. The various pouches it affords me would seem more useful if it weren't such a production to put on.

All I keep from my previous outfit is Victor's locket around my neck, with the tiny picture of Ma inside. I ball my fist around it and squeeze, like I used to squeeze her hand as a child when we walked together.

I pause, my gaze lingering on the pool of discarded clothes at my feet. My Bard trainee's uniform that I escaped High House in. Shedding it feels significant. Like I'm leaving a part of me behind.

I'm not a Bard here. For the first time, I'm just like everyone else. The thought finally sinks in, feeling equal parts satisfying and unnerving.

I shiver it away, remembering that Kennan is waiting for me.

Outside the room is a small antechamber no bigger than a closet, with an open hatch in the floor and a wooden ladder leading down. It creaks uncomfortably as I descend.

The floor below holds an eclectic mix of furniture arranged to provide a sort of communal living space. Along the back wall is a row of ladders leading up into trapdoors like the one I came from.

Most impressive is the window that opens across the length of the room, displaying a broad, panoramic view of the cavern beyond. The colored lights along the walkways twinkle and dance, illuminating the shanties and catwalks and the people who move between them. From afar, it almost looks like moonlight reflected on the dark surface of a lake.

I step to the window, enchanted.

At first glance, the Refugee Cavern looks the same as I remember. When I look a little harder, I begin to see subtle changes.

The mood of the people is the first thing I notice. There's a distinct sound of laughter in the air from various parts of the cavern. The other prominent noise is a little harder to discern, but I know I've heard it before.

My eyes chart a path toward the sound, and I almost fall out the window as I crane to the side. When I discover the source of the noise, I almost fall out the window anyway. I certainly did not see anything like this last time.

A new platform juts into the center of the cavern. A few of the refugees are still completing one side. Groups engage in various training exercises in different areas atop it. Minus the setting, the sight is almost identical to the training grounds back at High House.

"Again!" An all-too-familiar command issued by an all-too-familiar voice cuts through the air. I feel every muscle in my body tighten.

Kennan stands at the center of the platform, somehow running combat drills with three groups at once. She strolls along the gaps between the groups with her hands folded behind her back. Even at a distance I recognize the tight frown on her face, the way her eyes narrow critically as she examines their performance.

There was a period while she was my trainer when I was certain she was trying to kill me. I repress a shiver, remembering her coldness and cruelty. Watching the scene before me makes me realize how close she came to breaking my spirit. I remind myself that she did so to shield me from Cathal. Everything was different then. But, whether she knows it or not, it has shaped who I am now.

One of her students stumbles as she draws level with him, and my breath catches. I know what comes next for the poor young man. If he's lucky, he'll get away with a soul-shriveling reprimand. Otherwise, he faces starting over blindfolded, or with added weights, or both. My jaw tightens as I watch the youth on all fours in front of Kennan, panting, just as I found myself so many times.

Instead, Kennan sighs and shakes her head. She offers the young man her hand and helps him to his feet. From my vantage, I can't hear what she says to him; her demeanor appears stiff and stern, but distinctly lacking in her signature acerbity. Her student appears to listen carefully.

Maybe something is wrong with my eyes. Could I have mistaken another indomitable woman for Kennan?

As though sensing my confusion, she turns and spots me at the window. Her eyes may no longer be the eerie yellow I remember, but there's no mistaking her. She's Kennan, she's just . . . different.

She dismisses her students and strides purposefully across the catwalk that connects the training area to the shanty I'm standing in. The wobbly rope bridge doesn't give her pause; she's grown accustomed to traversing them in the short time she's been here, it seems. Her confidence radiates toward everyone she passes.

"You're awake. Good," she says when she's close enough for me to hear. "There's a lot to do."

I pull a deep breath into my lungs, finding myself standing a little straighter as Kennan approaches.

"Where do we start?" I ask.

Kennan doesn't miss a beat, nor does she slow her step. "I'm calling a strategy meeting. I want you there."

"Wouldn't miss it," I say, hurrying to catch up.

I find myself observing the Refugee Cavern, and Kennan, with new eyes as I fall in step at her side. She must have found something she was missing back at High House. Whatever it is, it seems to be the same thing the denizens of this cavern were so desperately in need of.

Somehow, she's single-handedly reorganized the place in a way I could never have imagined. I realize, like a sudden gust of air rushing around me, that the change in the atmosphere, the mood of the people, the efficiency of the jailbreak she staged back at Axis Keep is all Kennan. She's become a leader, an icon, and—from the looks of it—quite a good one, for the people here.

I wonder if *she* realizes it.

"Montane and its people are in peril. We need a plan." The room falls quiet as Kennan finishes speaking, her brief statement calling the strategy meeting to order.

One of the shacks across a catwalk from where I woke up has been hastily converted into a makeshift conference chamber. Mads, Fiona, and I, along with some of the Protesters, including Emery and Stot, are seated around a large rectangular table. The surface is covered with maps of the city and its various buildings.

No one seems to know where to begin. I'm not entirely sure I do, either. My gaze travels along the lines of the maps. They're drawn to a large square labeled AXIS KEEP. Even just the name makes it impossible to prevent the flood of memories I now associate with that place.

But maybe it's our starting point, I think.

I clear my throat and begin talking before I can

think too much about how everyone in the room is suddenly looking at me.

"Sabotage." The single word leaves my lips sounding far simpler and more certain than I thought it would. Kennan tips her head questioningly at me and I point to the map. "The general's base of operations is Axis Keep. We can disrupt anything she has planned from there."

"You want to go *back*?" Mads manages to ask the question on everyone's mind; there are more than a few eyebrows raised at me.

"Is there any other option?" I counter. The group falls quiet, considering, and the silence lingers when no one can find a better solution.

"What about tipping off Montane? They could marshal their forces, prepare to defend themselves . . ." Emery offers finally.

"And how are we supposed to get word there ahead of the general's bombers?" Stot asks. He shakes his head. "Even if we left right now, there's no way we could warn all of Montane."

"And if we did, they have no way to defend themselves. The only ones who could possibly benefit from that information are in High House, and I wouldn't count on the Bards to defend the villages before Cathal," Fiona points out.

Kennan's gaze lingers thoughtfully on Fiona, then she nods.

"That's a good point," Kennan says. "Shae's idea, risky as it is, may be our best bet. We have an added advantage from the reconnaissance we did for the jailbreak. But only if we act fast."

"The general was paralyzed by the fear that Montane would use the *Book of Days* to destroy Gondal if she tried anything sooner," I add, recalling what Ravod told me at Lord Ten Thirty, the old clock tower. "If we can get the *Book* back, maybe we can trick her into believing we'll leverage it against her."

"That's assuming the *Book* remains in the Keep," Kennan replies, shifting the maps so a detailed read-out of Axis Keep lies on top. "But even that might not be enough to stall an assault if preparations are already underway."

Mads taps his chin with a broad finger, and asks, "Is there someone we can trust in the caverns who knows how to disable those bombers the kid mentioned?"

"A few pulse bombs ought to damage the machinery beyond repair," Stot offers. "We'd have to attach them to each plane individually, though."

"Destroying them would send a clearer message," Emery says.

"And a lot of innocent people could get hurt, which is exactly what we're trying to prevent!" Fiona's outburst launches her to her feet, glaring at Emery.

"That's enough!" Kennan interjects, like a mother scolding her children. "Destruction is counter to what we're trying to achieve but may be necessary as a last resort. What we need to figure out is how we plan to infiltrate Axis Keep, obtain the *Book of Days*, sabotage the bomber planes, *and* not get captured. We've already gotten in over the wall, and they'll be prepared if we try that again."

My fingers drum steadily on the surface of the table, but I barely notice. My mind drifts along a swift current of thoughts as I consider Kennan's words. I follow the lines of the map, letting them lead me from an idea to a plan. When I speak, this time it's with confidence.

"I know what to do."

17

Hours later, I find myself back where I started, standing by the large open window looking out over the Refugee Cavern. This time, however, there's a knot between my shoulder blades that I can't release, no matter how much I shift. It creeps along my entire back, all the way over to my collarbone. My shoulders are bunched up around my ears.

We have a plan, and despite the long shot, it stands a chance of working. I find myself hesitant to count on it, though. So much has gone wrong already—a great deal of it my fault.

Kennan has sent her people off to procure final necessities. The plan can't be enacted until they return. For now, there's nothing we can do but wait for our moment to strike. In my case, that means a lot of quiet worrying.

Adding to my unease is the persistent, annoying thought that going back to Axis Keep might mean seeing Ravod. Whenever that pops into my mind, it sends my other thoughts into disarray. No one has ever managed to crush my feelings quite the way he has.

Preoccupied by Ravod, I don't even notice Stot until he's standing at my side.

"Shae?" he asks, just loud enough to draw me back to the present.

"Stot." I do my best to smile, but it takes too much effort and winds up tight and thin. "Everything all right?"

Stot nods, but the shroud of bangs across his forehead bob with a little more enthusiasm. Our emotions seem to mirror each other.

"Actually, I wanted to ask you a question," he admits. "Are you sure about going back to Axis Keep?"

"It's the only way to stop General Ravod," I reply.

"That's not . . ." Stot sighs, then shakes his head and starts over. "I mean, are you sure *you're* okay going back after what happened?"

I'm uncertain why he cares, but I'm grateful for his concern all the same. It's nice to know that not everyone in Gondal is cold and apathetic.

"I can handle it," I say, but silently I want to add, *I hope.*

Stot squints at me through his hair, but I'm not sure if he can't see me clearly or if he's just skeptical. Either way, he doesn't remark on my statement, instead joining me in leaning on the windowsill.

I can see his face a little better in profile. His features are slender and soft, still torn between those of a child and an adult. I find my focus drawn to his eyes, pale and somehow deeply sad. Maybe that's why he tries so hard to hide them with his hair.

"It's kind of nice down here, right?" he asks, then

grimaces sheepishly. "When you're not a captive, I guess."

"I'm starting to see it that way," I admit, turning back to the view. The lights are changing color again, this time to an ethereal green. Small coordinated groups of what seem to be caretakers are replacing the paper shades around each lantern.

"There's a lot more, too," Stot says. "If you want, I can show you around. I know all the interesting spots here."

His offer is as kind as it is intriguing. Coupled with the sincere, hopeful smile on his face, I find it difficult to refuse.

"I'd like that."

"Great!" Stot's voice cracks a little in his excitement. He beckons me to follow him out of the shack, onto the network of catwalks and bridges.

He leads me along a route that takes us across the center of the cavern, where a dark abyss looms directly below us. I hold the wobbly railing for dear life as his steps cause the bridge to tremble and sway. He glances over his shoulder as I fall behind.

"You weren't always this cautious"—he quickly clears his throat—"were you?"

I'm too preoccupied with the prospect of potentially falling to my death to acknowledge his words, let alone reply. I take a deep breath, shift my grip on the rope, and divert my gaze to Stot.

"I fell out of a tree a long time ago," I finally manage

to say through clenched teeth. Stot doesn't seem like the type to make fun of me and confiding in him will keep my attention away from thinking about the drop. "Can't say I enjoyed it too much."

Stot doesn't immediately reply. He reaches the end of the bridge and helps me onto the platform.

"I used to love climbing trees," he says. "There aren't very many in Tybera, and we're not allowed to climb the ones in the park. Found that out the hard way."

"Maybe if we can change the situation in Montane you can make up for lost time when you go back?" I offer with a small smile of encouragement.

"A lot would have to change for me to go back. Right now, it doesn't look like that's going to happen." Stot slows his steps along the catwalk and turns to me. "Actually, that's part of what I wanted to show you."

We've reached one of the shacks attached to the cavern wall directly opposite where we came from. Stot weaves through the refugees going about their day with easy familiarity. A few call out or wave to him. If his reaction is any indication, he cares deeply about this community, and they him. His usual nerves seem to vanish, a peaceful smile stretching across his face.

It diminishes somewhat when he notices I'm staring at him. "What?"

He's a strange kid. At times he's jumpy and nervous, then he surprises me with his insight. I can see why Victor liked him enough to point me in his direction.

"Nothing. Just . . . taking it all in." I shrug.

To my relief, Stot accepts this answer and opens a door nearby, gesturing for me to follow him inside.

"Here we are," he says with a dramatic flourish.

This space is unlike any of the others I've seen in the Refugee Caverns. It looks like a laboratory. A few small desk lamps illuminate a wide variety of beakers, tubes, and other scientific apparatuses. There's a hum of machinery in the air and a sterile smell, something purely artificial. There are only a few people here, wearing white coats and busily experimenting.

"What is this place?" I ask.

"The lab. I signed on as an apprentice after I arrived. It's not as fancy as the big companies that make medicine here in Gondal, but we get by," Stot says.

"Medicine?" I wander a little closer to the nearest table, carefully keeping my hands to myself. Several test tubes are lined in a row before me, all containing various quantities and shades of a blue liquid.

I realize the answer to my own question. They're looking for a cure to the plague.

Stot nods, leading me through the rows of tables stacked with lab equipment and tests. The harsh light of a nearby desk lamp makes his face seem paler and gaunter. I stop him with a hand on his elbow.

"Did you contract the Blot?" I bite my lip as I peer

past his bangs. In an instant, he looks panicked. He pulls away, and I feel a pang in my chest as I worry that I've pushed too far. His mouth forms a tight line as he runs his fingers over the spot on his elbow where my hand rested. "I had it, too. It was . . ." Even my attempt to salvage the situation falls flat.

". . . Excruciating," Stot whispers.

I look away and nod. I don't think I'll ever be able to forget the searing pain in my veins as the Blot ate at them from the inside out and traveled into my chest. Each cough was a cry for mercy that never came. The torment was so consuming that it clouded my thoughts as ably as the fever.

When I glance back at Stot, I can see his eyes a little more clearly through a gap in his hair. There's an understanding there. He felt that pain, too.

"When I escaped High House, I discovered it's just a Telling," I say.

Stot's eyes flash angrily at that. His jaw tightens.

"It's not '*just a Telling*,'" he snaps. "To minimize it detracts from *everything* our people have suffered. Everything *I* suffered."

I reach for him again. "I didn't mean . . ."

"Don't." He turns away, running his hand through his hair. After a moment, he takes a long breath and releases it. "I'm sorry."

"You don't have to apologize," I say, fighting the urge to wrap him in a hug. Given his wariness at being touched, I doubt he'd appreciate it. "What you went through was horrifying. No one should suffer like that."

Stot's mouth twitches. "You sound like . . ." He trails off and shakes his head. "It doesn't matter."

"Stot, it's okay, you can talk to me," I offer. The way he's speaking makes me wonder if he's ever really tried to talk to anyone about what he went through. "I want to help."

"Why?" His question is barely more than a whisper.

The reason feels as painful as the fear that I'm pushing too far and will wind up doing more harm than good. My voice suddenly feels dry and gravelly in my throat.

"I survived the Blot. My little brother wasn't so lucky," I say. "I miss him terribly."

Stot looks away, staring at the wall. "No parents?"

"They're gone, too. My pa's heart gave out when I was barely old enough to remember him. Ma . . ." I struggle as my voice threatens to give out. Talking about it still feels like I was the one stabbed in the chest instead of her. "Ma was never really the same after the Blot took my brother. The grief was too much, I guess. She just . . . stopped talking. Long story short, she was murdered by a Bard. It's why I finally left my village. To find answers."

Stot doesn't respond immediately. But this time he doesn't tense up or lash out. Eventually, he turns to face me. A tear tracks down his pale cheek and he shakily wipes it away with the heel of his palm.

"Thing is, I can't go back to Montane. Ever. If I do, I'll just get reinfected. The same thing will happen to you. Staying in Gondal only staves off the infection, nothing more," he says. "Unless an actual cure is found, we'll never be free of the Blot. Not truly."

"And Gondal doesn't care about healing a plague that doesn't infect people here," I say quietly. "Even now when cases are starting to appear, the most people seem to be doing is moving deeper into Gondal, if what the general says is true."

"I always had a feeling they'd go for Montane first and ask questions later." Stot shrugs. "They might start work on a cure in earnest after Montane is gone if they think it's truly a threat. Or if they can profit from it. But any results likely will not take place in our lifetime."

He's more of a pessimist than I expected. I suppose living here all these years, apart from the family he misses so much, working to find a cure that means so much to him and never succeeding, would do that. His words twist painfully inside me. He's far too young to speak with such bitterness.

"Is that what the research here uncovered?" I ask.

"We discovered a few things," Stot says. "First, as you said, the Blot is a Telling. It's difficult to craft a scientific solution to a nonscientific problem. Secondly, it's far more difficult to do so with limited resources."

"Especially if you're working on an illness that can't exist here," I point out.

"Exactly. But we have to try. Even if we're just spinning our wheels in the mud. I *have* to believe we'll find a way."

Stot's anger from before has given way to resolve. He gazes somewhere past the beakers in front of us, and it's suddenly much clearer how deeply he's struggled with this.

"Going back to Montane is important to you, isn't it?" I try to ask the brash question as gently as possible.

"It's been all I can think about since Victor brought me here. All I've ever wanted is to see my family again." Stot's words are more of a recitation than a thought.

"You'll see them," I say. "They're going to be so proud of you."

Stot smiles at that. "I hope so, Shae."

It isn't long before someone in the lab needs Stot's help with something. I quietly excuse myself and wander out to the catwalks, turning our conversation over in my mind as I make my way back.

It's my first time navigating the cavern on my own, and I take time to peek curiously around at everything. Foot traffic has picked up some. More than a few times, I hear Kennan's name dropped in passing gossip, with a cautiously hopeful statement following.

I'm starting to put together how everything is organized down here. The larger shacks serve different communal functions and each one is run by a group of Protesters and refugee volunteers. I pass by a large kitchen and dining area manned by a small crew that distributes food to the refugees. They sit at smaller tables spread around the platform to eat before going on their way. Across the bridge is a carpentry shop and a tailor. After those, I spot the small but bustling marketplace and meeting area.

It occurs to me as I weave through the hustle and bustle that the Protesters, or their families, must have funded this, at least initially. In a way, I can see how things became so complacent down here. The refugees are provided for, at least. No wonder they weren't actively seeking to change things. On the surface, it seems like something is being done to alleviate their suffering. Kennan is right, though. It doesn't solve their problems. They will always be second-class citizens.

How long could this last? I wonder. Sooner or later the charity is bound to run out. I don't want to think about what will befall these refugees when that happens. If any of them has the Blot, they'll be unable to return to Montane, just like Stot. They're stuck here, possibly forever, whether they want to be or not.

I climb a flight of steps to the next level, where the

largest shack on this platform has its doors open. I immediately catch sight of Mads, who is peering inside with a mixture of disbelief and awe. He doesn't notice as I step closer and squint inside the shack, curious as to what's captured his attention.

Children of various ages, and even a few adults, sit at rows of desks stacked with textbooks, facing a blackboard where a Gondalese woman is writing the alphabet. She sounds the letters out as they take shape, pausing after each one to let her students echo the sounds back to her.

Such a sight would be considered heretical in Montane. It still sends a small shiver of residual fear up my spine, even though I know the truth. Reading and writing aren't inherently evil, we were just told they are by an oppressive regime. My alarm dissipates as I recall each of the trials that I underwent to learn that it's nothing to be feared.

"You seem lost in thought," Mads says, drawing me back to reality.

"A little bit," I admit. "You'd be hard pressed to find a Montanian who doesn't carry some baggage attached to the idea of learning to read and write."

Mads nods. "Until now, I never even would have considered it."

"Really?" I turn from the classroom to regard Mads. He doesn't seem to be joking.

"I mean, it can't be that hard, can it? You learned, after all," he says, nudging my shoulder with a wide grin on his face.

"I'm getting used to it, somewhat," I admit. "The bigger words still take a little time to sound out."

"And it hasn't been dangerous for you? At all?"

I shake my head. "None of the warnings we heard from the village elders came to pass, if that's what you're wondering. My eyeballs haven't caught fire, as you can see."

"And you're not stark raving mad," he points out with a chuckle.

"True, I found that out the hard way."

Mads sobers a little at that. His eyes search my face for an answer he doesn't seem to think I can give him verbally. "After everything you went through, it's pretty incredible you're standing here at all. I'm not sure I could have done what you did."

"I did what I had to," I say with a shrug.

"It's a compliment, Freckles. Just accept it," Mads says in a tone that means he'll brook no further argument on the subject. He turns back to the classroom, brow furrowing slightly, but more in consideration than apprehension. "Can I ask you something?"

"As long as it's not a marriage proposal." I elbow him in the side, and he laughs. "What is it?"

Crossing his arms over his broad chest, he looks at me. "So, say we save Montane and overthrow High House. What do you think Montane will look like after?"

"That's a very optimistic outlook." My skepticism doesn't cause him to waver, however. He keeps his gaze trained on me, waiting. I open my mouth to reply but all I'm prepared to offer is another quip. His question is so hopeful, so genuine, it deserves a carefully considered answer.

I try to imagine the world he's asking for. A Montane without High House, in no danger of attack by Gondal. It takes effort, but beyond what's so seemingly impossible lies infinite possibility. The villages could become connected by more than the Bards passing through. They could hold on to their resources instead of giving them away in tithes. Telling could be used freely to help people instead of imprisoning them in desperation. Communities could have the chance to flourish instead of cowering in submission.

We could have schools, like the one right in front of us. Maybe even bigger. We could learn. Perhaps we could even stand on equal footing with Gondal someday, instead of fearing and rejecting each other.

"You're smiling again," Mads points out.

He's right. There is something worthwhile in hoping. Seeing the goal in my mind has given me a renewed faith that it's an attainable one instead of an irresponsible wish.

"I guess I am," I say. "And in answer to your question, Montane could use an education."

Mads nods. "I was thinking the same thing. It'll be scary for a lot of people at first."

"If they can swallow the idea that books can kill them, they can swallow the idea that they won't," I say firmly.

"Whatever happens, I'm confident you're going to be leading that change. You're the reason I changed my mind about . . . *everything.* The reason I want to keep helping. Maybe when some of the dust settles you can teach me to read?" he asks. "When we get back to Montane, I want to teach others. Pass on what you gave me."

"What's that?"

He rolls his eyes as if the answer is obvious. "Hope."

"That's . . ." I'm about to say "exaggerated," but the word crumbles under Mads's earnest gaze. It warms up something deep inside me that had gone cold. For some reason, I'm looking forward to what the future will bring, instead of dreading it. "That's the nicest thing anyone has ever said to me."

"Kennan?" I call out. "I was wondering if we could go over the plan one more time—"

I stop short when I hear a painful-sounding crash issue from inside the shack where I was told Kennan is staying. Concerned, I forgo knocking and hurriedly push the door open.

Kennan is seated on the edge of a cot, eyes wide and hair uncharacteristically disheveled. She seems to be trying very hard not to look away from me, as though pure concentration can keep me from seeing anything else in the room . . .

. . . such as Fiona, who is staring up at me from

the floor with the same startled expression on her face. Her blouse is partially open, and she rushes to cover herself while simultaneously trying to hide the bright flush on her cheeks as she stumbles to her feet.

"I was just leaving," she mutters, making haste for the door.

It shuts behind her with a small click, leaving me and Kennan alone in awkward silence. A few seconds pass as my bewilderment dies down enough to allow me to piece together what just happened.

I loosely point between the door and Kennan. "Are you two . . ."

"I'm not discussing this with you."

I let out a laugh. Well, that decides *that*.

"Can we discuss the plan, then?" I ask, pivoting. Kennan is a hornet's nest I prefer not to kick. And I know Fiona. If she wants to confide in me, she will. Otherwise, it's none of my business.

Kennan raises an eyebrow, as though expecting me to probe deeper. When I don't, she gets to her feet and starts fixing the tousled bun on her head.

"Right. The plan," she repeats, the words leaving her lips wearily.

"I can come back later," I say, knowing I overstayed my welcome the moment I opened the door.

But Kennan shakes her head as she secures the last coil of black hair in its proper place with a firm twist of her fingers.

"What is it, specifically, you wished to discuss?" she asks, sounding more like herself.

"I was wondering how we're planning to circumvent the guards on patrol," I reply. "Do we have those mapped out in advance? Or—"

"My person on the inside already took care of that." Kennan waves a hand dismissively, cutting me off.

I blink. "You have spies inside the Keep? You've only been in charge for a couple of weeks!"

"I pride myself on efficiency. You should know that better than anyone," she says. I might have imagined it, but did Kennan just smile at me? If so, it's gone in a flash as she steps over to the desk at the other side of the room. "There's something I've been meaning to ask you."

"What is it?" I bite my tongue to keep the astonishment from appearing too comically on my face. I walk closer to join Kennan at the desk. The books and papers and writing implements resting there barely even bother me anymore.

"Did Cathal ever speak with you about the Telling, more than just the superficial facts?"

I shake my head. "Did he with you?"

"No. But I've been thinking about it ever since we left High House." Kennan sighs. "So much of what that man says is untrustworthy, yet I can't help but look for half-truths and hidden meanings as though they will somehow allow any of this to make sense."

"You believe he lied about the Telling? In addition to everything else?"

"A lie of omission, yes," Kennan says. "I think there's a hidden layer to the power of the Telling that he alone wields."

"You mentioned something like that back at High House," I point out.

"The only conclusion I've managed to draw is that Cathal is different, somehow, from other Bards. As is the power of his Telling."

I pause, digesting her words and carefully looking back on what I know of Cathal. The way he controls not only the power of the Telling, but how it's taught. The careful measure of his words, like he's constantly holding something back. Could that something be the incredible power Kennan is talking about? And if she's right, how do we stand any chance of defeating it?

"His power is closer to that of the *Book of Days*," I murmur. "Somehow, he manages to entrench it deeply in reality. No ordinary Bard could write the Blot into someone the way he can."

Kennan actually chuckles. "Well, listen to you. You almost sound like you know what you're talking about."

I can't decide if she's teasing or taunting me. Perhaps the two go hand in hand when it comes to Kennan.

I shrug. "The real takeaway here is that even if Cathal is defeated, he's made his mark on Montane. That might prove even *more* difficult to get rid of."

"Agreed." Kennan nods, surprising me for the second time in as many moments. "But we'll do what must be done. We have no other choice."

"Look at us, finally agreeing on things." I chance a smile at Kennan. "Better be careful, or we might end up becoming friends after all."

I brace myself, waiting for her defenses to come crashing down around her, as they always do. Her jaw to tighten, her eyes to narrow. But this time, they stop a tiny bit short of the glare I've become so accustomed to.

"You and I are *never* going to be friends," she says. Her words sting, but her tone is softer than normal. It makes me wonder whether she's trying to convince me, or herself.

With that, she strides from the room, and I can do nothing but follow.

The lights are changing to a deep gold as we walk, the catwalks emptying little by little. I can only assume it's because night has fallen outside the cavern. Its denizens are resting in preparation for the new day.

My gut twists uncomfortably. Very soon we'll be infiltrating Axis Keep, and whatever we accomplish—or *don't* accomplish—will change the fate of Montane forever.

"Hey, Freckles!" Mads's voice draws my and Kennan's attention to where he stands nearby along with Stot. Fiona lurks behind them, eyes downcast. "You have *got* to try this. Stot brought a bunch down from the city."

In a flash, a slender glass bottle is in my face. Its contents are clear, with small bubbles rising to the surface.

"What is it?" I ask.

"It's a soft drink," Stot explains. "It's sweet. Non-alcoholic."

I gingerly take the bottle from Mads, sniffing the contents before taking a small sip. As promised, it's very sweet. The bubbles tickle a bit as they wash over my mouth. I find myself reluctant to hand the beverage back to Mads.

"I like it," I say, indulging in one more sip before finally relinquishing the bottle.

Mads forgoes another sip, offering the bottle to Kennan. She scowls. But she takes it, handling it as though it were something rotten. She takes a careful sip, her eyes widening a little in surprise as she turns it over in her mouth like she is sampling a fine wine.

"This is . . . . unexpectedly delightful," she says.

As she hands the soft drink back to Mads, she seems slightly sorrowful. The expression lingers as her eyes meet Fiona's. As if they were too heavy to hold on to, both drop their gazes to the ground at the same time. The silent exchange is loaded, but brief. No one else seems to notice.

"Here," Stot says, reaching into a small crate at his feet and producing two brand-new bottles that glisten happily under the light of the paper lanterns. He opens them deftly with a small pocketknife, causing a small but very satisfying pop each time, and hands one to me and one to Kennan.

Kennan can't seem to help herself and smiles into the bottle before taking a rather large gulp of its contents.

"I can't believe we found something Kennan actually *likes*," Mads says with a chuckle.

"I like things. Certain things. It's called having taste. Something I would not expect you to comprehend," Kennan shoots back. The edge of her mouth is turned upward infinitesimally as she speaks.

Mads laughs, a deep sound from his core that I haven't heard in a long time. Not since well before that fateful morning I worked up the courage to go see the Bards when they visited Aster. It's a deep, exuberant sound that wraps around us all and echoes throughout the cavern.

He slings a muscular arm around Kennan's shoulders, and she rolls her eyes. But she doesn't flinch away or lash out.

For the first time, we all seem to realize that our adventure together has brought us closer than we expected. Despite the odds, we went from a divided, misfit group of wandering youths to . . . something else. Comrades? Quite possibly. Maybe something deeper and even more intricate. Something I have no language for.

Whatever the technical term, it allows for a companionable silence to fall over us. Even the storm clouds over Fiona's head lift as she comes to stand beside me and clinks her glass bottle against mine. She's smiling a little, too, almost despite herself. She sighs and leans her head on mine.

I try to find my own smile, but despite my best efforts, it doesn't quite reach my eyes. It's a beautiful moment yet it feels bittersweet. Incomplete.

Ravod should be here. The thought irritates me, even as the reason for my sudden melancholy crystallizes. His absence is another blistering reminder that he turned against us—against me. That he isn't the person I thought he was or wanted him to be.

It's followed by a cold knot of dread. I hope against all hope that we don't encounter him when we infiltrate Axis Keep. I take a deep breath, trying desperately to strengthen my resolve at the possibility of facing him in combat. Doing what must be done is much harder when it means harming someone I used to care about so deeply. Someone, I'm forced to admit, I still care about despite everything.

I'm not sure I'm ready. I'd rather stay here, in this moment, with the people I care about most.

But much as I may wish to, I can't make it last forever. Soon we will return to Axis Keep. One way or another, change is coming and there's no going back.

_18_

My nerves are already frayed as we emerge from the sewers just inside the wall of the Keep. My heart is pounding loud in five different directions, my ears, my throat, my head—everywhere except my chest, which has gone numb. I tug at the tight collar of the military uniform Kennan's Protesters "procured" for me.

Like the maps of the sewers promised, we're near the northwest corner of the main building. We're deposited in a small alcove reserved, according to Kennan's incredibly precise intel, for maintenance. According to these same sources, the patrols here are fewer, but less predictable. We must hurry.

"Everyone's communication devices on and operational?" Emery's lowered voice might as well be an explosion for how high it makes me jump.

I double-check the wristband he handed me earlier. The small light on the corner of the device is blinking green, which Emery said means it's working. A quick demonstration showed how pressing the small circular button on the front and talking into the three holes above it would transmit my voice to anyone else in our group. I might not have believed it would work if I hadn't heard it myself.

I nod to Emery, along with Kennan, Mads, Stot, and Fiona.

"The others will be starting the distraction at the gate soon," Kennan states, her voice low but no less authoritative. "Once we finish everything up, we meet back here. Anyone not in contact at that point will be left behind."

I try to swallow, but my throat has gone dry. I'm back in Axis Keep. This is really happening.

"I think we all know what to do," Mads says, "so let's do it."

Kennan hangs back as Emery and Mads take point. Their group, along with Fiona, Stot, and Kennan, will break into the hangar where the bombers are being prepared for the assault. Each has multiple devices to plant, the "pulse bombs" Stot mentioned during the meeting. Supposedly, those will damage the machinery to the point of uselessness. They must be impossibly fast, precise, and quiet if they hope to succeed.

Meanwhile, I'm to retrieve the *Book of Days*. I remember the way from our previous visits to the general's office. But just in case, I've been over the route exhaustively since the plan was set in motion. I have no room for error.

"Remember," Kennan says, placing a hand on my shoulder, which snaps me away from my thoughts. "Check in at the northern back entrance."

I almost forgot amid my nerves. I have specific points where Kennan wants to hear from me. The

first is when I get inside. Then when I find the *Book
of Days,* and finally, when I'm at or approaching the
rendezvous. I assume it's to make sure I complete
my objective, either because I have no backup or because Kennan doesn't trust me.

"I will," I reply. She nods once, then disappears
into the dark with the others.

No time to think. If I don't move now, I'll stand
here paralyzed forever. I take one step, followed by
another, in the direction of the northern back entrance.

It's been a while since I was on my own like this.
I grew accustomed to it during my ordeal at High
House, but now it only serves to remind me how
much has changed. I miss the security that comes
with having friends at my back. My fear and anxiety
seem to close in around me without them nearby. I
want Mads to protect me. Fiona to reassure me. Even
Kennan to remind me of what's truly important.

I flatten my back to the cold stone wall when I
hear approaching footsteps, pressing myself urgently
into the darkness as though doing so will force it to
conceal me. The guards are too busy chatting. They
don't see me.

Bolstered a little by the small success, I pick up
my pace. The maps I studied show the entrance I'm
looking for right around the corner.

It's a small, plain metal door. The edges are
rusted. Naturally, it's locked.

Ducking behind a stack of crates nearby, I double

check that I'm unseen. Lifting my wrist to my mouth, I press the button to contact Kennan.

"I'm at the door, but there's a problem. It's locked. I'm not sure how to get in," I whisper into the device.

Kennan's voice is a sharp crackle from the small machine. "Knock twice."

"Are you crazy? Do you want me to get discovered?"

I find myself growing rigid with fear. What I can't bring myself to say is that I don't want to go back to that prison cell. I can't. I can still remember the feeling of my spirit crumbling inside those stark metal walls.

"Trust me," Kennan replies. "Contact me again at the next checkpoint."

I grit my teeth and approach the door. What could go wrong?

Everything. I swallow my fear. I can't falter. Not now.

I place my trust in Kennan and ball my fist, hammering out two sharp knocks on the door. For a few seconds that feel like an eternity, there's only silence. Then I hear a small click from the other side.

Is this some strange Gondalese technology?

I pull the door open wide enough to slip through. The maps say I should be in the service exit to the facility's cafeteria. At this hour, no one will be around. I squint in the dark, feeling my way along a wall that gives way to shelves of canned food.

The lights go on in a sudden blaze.

"Hello, Shae."

The voice, the light, and my panic blend together as I freeze in place. I can't even muster the courage to raise my arm and shield my eyes from the glare. I just squeeze them shut and wince, waiting for whatever fate is about to befall me.

"Remember what I told you about breathing?"

It's okay to be overwhelmed, the same voice says from somewhere within the recesses of my memory, *and it's okay to take some time to breathe when you are.* I know that voice. It makes my ribs twist painfully inward on themselves. My eyes pry themselves open. A familiar figure comes into focus.

I tear my gaze away and cast it wildly around. I grab the first thing I can reach, a cast-iron skillet from the shelf behind me, and brandish it as threateningly as possible.

"Don't come any closer," I warn.

Ravod doesn't seem like he has any intention to. He's standing back on his heels, arms crossed over his chest, watching me flail about like a fool.

"Pull yourself together but do it quickly. There's not much time," he says.

"You mean before your soldier friends arrive to throw me back in prison?" I hiss. "I won't go. I'll die before I let that happen again."

Something dark and sorrowful passes over Ravod's eyes, and he blinks it away. Otherwise, he doesn't move.

"I know you're angry and you hate me. I deserve it after everything you've gone through," he says. "But I want you to know, I never had a change of heart. Not truly."

"You'll forgive me if I don't take your word for it."

"Naturally," Ravod says with a small smile. "But in the interest of time, we're going to have to walk while I explain. And keep our voices down. Getting the *Book of Days* back isn't going to be a simple matter."

I pause, eyes narrowing somewhat. "How do you know I'm here for the *Book*?"

"Because that's what Kennan told me your plan was," Ravod says. "Did you not wonder how she received such thorough intelligence from within the Keep?"

"*You* were her person on the inside?"

"Come," Ravod says, taking a careful step back, indicating the door at the other side of the room. "The disguise I got for you will pass a cursory inspection but won't hold up under scrutiny. Time is of the essence. You'll have to part with your skillet, I'm afraid."

I glance from the skillet clutched in my out-stretched hand to Ravod and back. Reluctantly, I set it down where I found it. I'll just have to keep an eye out for anything that can serve as an improvised weapon, should the need arise. I trusted him twice and was betrayed twice. It's enough to both prompt me to give him one final chance, but also be far more guarded.

Whether I can *forgive* him remains to be seen.

Ravod checks our surroundings as we step into a darkened dining hall. Satisfied we're alone, he gestures to me to follow.

My fear and trepidation at this mission sink to the bottom of my awareness like a rock in a dark pond while something entirely different rises to the surface. A different kind of struggle takes hold in my heart. I'm conflicted, annoyed, wary. It pulls me in several directions at once, and it's only with great difficulty that I dispel these emotions enough to focus on the matter at hand.

We cross the dining hall in silence, but the air is thick and charged between us. It doesn't take long for it to become overwhelming.

"So, I'm losing track—is this the second time I've had to demand explanations from you? Or the third?" The question leaves my mouth soaked in venom.

Even in the darkness, I notice Ravod's eyes drop to the floor before meeting mine. It almost makes me want to take back what I said, but those feelings of compassion only serve to irritate me further, snapping my mouth firmly shut.

"All I can offer you is this: I took a calculated risk in my grandmother's office. If I'd sided with my conscience—with *you*—and got thrown in prison, we'd have stood a much harder time escaping," he says. "There was no time to inform you, and once my cover was in place, Kennan and I decided it was too risky to expose my involvement, no matter how much I wanted to reveal the truth to you. The best I could do was feed them information, help set up their rescue attempt, and maintain the ruse of loyalty to Gondal so I could help you now."

"Seems to me like your 'calculated risks' frequently put my life in peril," I observe.

"Given the choice between putting you in peril, and getting you killed, I will always choose the former rather than the latter. It's not ideal, but . . ."

His voice peters out unexpectedly. Briefly I worry something has gone wrong, but as his steps slow, I find my gaze dragged to his. A faint beam of light from outside the tall windows bisects his features, casting half his face in light and the rest in shadow. It almost mirrors the struggle occurring within him.

"But what?" I prompt. This time, my words bear no bitterness. I just want to know where we stand, once and for all.

"If you're in peril, I can still risk everything to help. If you died . . ." He trails off, but this time he determinedly holds my gaze. He makes no attempt to move closer. As usual, he lets the steadiness in his eyes and the assurance in his voice carry the weight of his meaning. "If you died, I think it would break me. I didn't lie when I told you I trust you. You're the only person who's ever seen me as something more than a burden to be rid of, or a tool to be used and similarly discarded. You've earned my loyalty, simply by believing it was worth earning. And for what it's worth, you've earned far more than that. Any steps I've taken to heal myself from within are directly attributable to your friendship and dedication. That's why I'll never stop doing anything in my power to help you, even if it costs me everything. There is no one I respect and admire more than you, Shae."

Suddenly I'm thankful for the darkness that conceals how red my cheeks must be turning. We're standing a few feet apart but feel much closer. His conviction enfolds my heart without even using a Telling. It takes a moment before I fully absorb what he's saying. It leaves me searching awkwardly for something of my own to respond with, but Ravod waits patiently as I collect my scrambled thoughts. All I seem capable of is saying the first thing I can think of and hope for the best.

"I'm still angry," I admit. "But more than that, I'm . . . relieved. Are you sure you're okay turning your back on Gondal? On the general?"

"Family is more than a place where we're brought into the world, or what's in our veins when that happens," he answers with surprising readiness. "You showed me that, too."

He has a point. I feel the same way about the people I've found at my side when I needed them most. Mads. Fiona. Even Kennan. It's not the same as the family I lost, but they are my family, nonetheless. Including Ravod.

"Don't think you're off the hook just like that, Ravod. But I know what you mean."

"I'll do whatever I must to set things right."

There's determination in his voice. I worry I might believe him. Even so, I hold my ground, watching for anything that might indicate his loyalties lie elsewhere. I won't let him trick me again. That would break *me*.

"It's not that simple," I say. "But for now, just . . . promise me this is the last round of false betrayals and keeping secrets, okay?"

Ravod's smile sends a brand-new burst of electric fire through me. "You have my word."

"Well, then." I take a deep breath. "Let's take back an ancient relic of unimaginable power from your grandmother, shall we?"

The Keep is quieter the farther we breach its dark halls. We pass soldiers and Keep personnel heading to the main gate. The distraction group seems to be doing a good job staging their disturbance. A few guards are gossiping animatedly about it as they hurry in the opposite direction, away from me and Ravod. To them, we look like a young officer and his underling. No one pays us any mind as we step into the elevator at the back of the main hall. I bite down hard on my lower lip, hoping this means our job will be a little easier.

The doors close, leaving us alone in the small compartment. It lurches to life around us as Ravod presses one of the buttons.

"There will be a few small patrols in the hall," Ravod says, breaking the silence first. "Stay close and keep your eyes forward. If they believe we're here on business, they won't question us. If for some reason they do, let me do the talking."

"I'm ready."

The elevator doors open to darkness and silence. It's almost anticlimactic. Even so, Ravod checks the area before stepping out. I follow him.

The path to the general's office is very different in the dead of night. The lights are dimmed so they only illuminate the stark, angular portraits lining the wall. I barely noticed them the first couple of times I traversed this hall. Now that they are some of the only things visible, it's difficult to not shiver a little under the accusation in each stern pair of stylized, painted eyes. I hesitate when a familiar face frowns at me, recognizing a younger version of General Ravod. Her hair is black, like her grandson's, and her face is free of the scar and eyepatch I've come to associate with her. Ravod hurries his pace as we pass it.

He only just found his grandmother after all this time. I feel a pang of sadness, despite myself, at the thought that what he's doing will probably sever them irrevocably.

272 — DYLAN FARROW

"Are you sure you'll be okay?" I whisper to him.

He spares me a glance that is somewhat more loaded than his simple reply of "Yes." I'm about to question him further when the sound of footsteps approaching makes my jaws clench shut.

A couple of soldiers on patrol, quietly discussing the "riot at the gate," pass without noticing us. My heart starts to race anyway, not daring to slow even when the sound of their whispers and footfalls fades down the hall.

"We don't have much time," Ravod remarks as we stop in front of the door to the general's office. He observes the small keypad beside the door, his brow knotted, his lips thinned to a faint line.

"What's wrong? Are we locked out?" I whisper.

Ravod shakes his head but doesn't look away from the keypad. "The door isn't *locked* at all," he explains. "Charolais must be working late."

I try to breathe away my renewed waves of worry as I recall General Ravod's somewhat irritable secretary. I somehow doubt the ensign will allow us to walk into the office, whether we're stealing something or not.

"Maybe you can distract them while I sneak past?" I offer. It's not ideal, but it's better than nothing.

Ravod's dark eyes move in short bursts, and I can practically see the thoughts turning over behind them before they meet mine. He gives a short, stiff nod.

"Wait for my signal," he says. He presses a few keys on the pad.

The door hisses open and he strides confidently through, all trace of his previous consternation gone. I notice it stays open behind him. I step back around the corner into the shadows, peeking out just enough to see what's going on without being spotted.

"What are *you* doing here?" Charolais asks Ravod over a stack of paperwork.

Ravod's casual countenance doesn't falter as he approaches the secretary's desk. "I lost a cuff link this afternoon; I'm retracing my steps."

"A little late at night to worry over a cuff link."

"It was a gift from my grandmother. An heirloom. It's a little embarrassing, to be perfectly honest." Ravod shifts his weight a little. "You haven't happened upon it, by chance?"

I whip myself around the side of the doorframe as Charolais looks up, issuing a long-suffering sigh that I assume is for Ravod's benefit. When I chance another peek, Ravod has carefully inserted himself in Charolais's line of sight, blocking out their view of the door.

"I suppose the sooner I assist you, the sooner you'll be out of my hair," Charolais says with a barely concealed groan. "What does it look like?"

"I can't thank you enough. It's gold with inlaid obsidian . . ." Ravod begins to describe the cuff link in excruciating detail. It takes me a second to notice the faint, lingering resonance in his voice that compels my eyes to flutter closed. The Telling is subtly laced into his description, encouraging fatigue. I

274 — DYLAN FARROW

cover my ears, attempting to drown the sound out. As he drones on, he folds his hands behind his back with one thumb lowered. His monotone reaches a crescendo of boredom, even from the faint bit I can hear, making it difficult to keep from leaning on the wall and closing my eyes.

Presently, he shifts his grip on his wrist, upturning his thumb. It's time.

I move swiftly. I keep to the darkness at the edge of the antechamber, stealing only the quickest of glances at Charolais. The general's secretary is hunched over the desk with their pointed chin propped on the heels of their palms. Ravod notices my distraction and nods vigorously to the office door to hurry me along, impressively maintaining his Telling.

I'm lucky this door is not mechanized and stands ajar, allowing me to slip through to the other side. That same moment, Charolais jolts up with an imperious clearing of their throat, interrupting Ravod just long enough for the Telling to slip into the ether.

"Yes, that's all very *fascinating*." I hear Charolais from the other side of the door. "But I haven't seen anything of the sort . . ."

I must be quick. There's no way to know how long Ravod can keep the conversation going. I take stock of the room in the dim light afforded by the window. The office is much the same, except for the papers on the desk having shifted around a little. I start there, carefully opening each drawer and searching for the *Book of Days.*

The desk is full of files, supplies for the office, and a few knickknacks. Perhaps it was too obvious a hiding place for something so important. I try to remain calm as I search for alternatives.

The bookshelf is another obvious choice, but none of the titles I see even come close to matching the spine of the *Book of Days.* I even try pulling a few out, looking for a false back like I saw in the safe house outside Valmorn.

No such luck. Similarly, my investigation of the floor turns up no loose floorboards. No secret hatch under the carpet. The mechanized keypad on the arm of the chair is alarmingly useful but yields few secrets. Each new failure makes my heart pound faster in my chest. I'm running out of time.

"I just hope my grandmother didn't find it first and stash it in her safe." Ravod's voice is conversational, but a little louder than necessary through the door. "You know, the one behind the painting? She'd lord it over me forever if I lost it."

It takes me a few seconds to realize that while the statement is directed at Charolais, he's not saying this to the secretary at all, but to *me.* There's a safe hidden behind a painting.

I swivel around, coming face-to-face with a large portrait on the wall behind me. I hadn't properly appreciated the beauty of the painting my first two visits. Somehow the colors are starker, the style even more impressive under the beam of false light issuing from the window across the room. The image is in the same sleek, ornamental style as the paintings in the hallway, which I'm learning is a staple of Gondalese art. It depicts a woman in shining armor, a sword in one hand and wings stretching from her back. It's the same figure that's on display outside the Keep. Ravod called her a goddess of conquest.

Carefully, I slide the painting to the side. To my surprise, it clicks into place after a certain point, allowing me to remove my hands from the frame.

As promised, there's a metal compartment embedded in the wall. On it is a numeric keypad, and nothing else. I should have expected another roadblock. My heart suddenly feels like it's suspended by a wire in the empty hollow of my chest.

"You know, those cuff links were a gift to my grandfather, for their anniversary. The fourth sun of the fourth moon. Grandmother's always considered it a special occasion." Ravod's voice is raised meaningfully. Is he trying to hint at the combination? "They were married for fifty years."

"You don't say." I can practically hear Charolais's eyes roll as they reply.

I turn my attention to the keypad, afraid I'm mysteriously about to forget how to read numbers. *The fourth sun of the fourth moon, so the number four fol-*

lowed by another four . . . I press the buttons slowly and deliberately. *And they were married for fifty years, that's the number five followed by a zero* . . .

Nothing happens.

I try the sequence again, and again, nothing.

White-hot panic rises in me. The stress of this entire mission locks me inside myself, unable to move, breathe, or think.

"You seem tense." It takes a moment to realize Ravod's voice is still issuing from the antechamber. "You really ought to try this remarkable tea my grandmother recommended . . ."

He can't keep talking forever. I need to stay calm and think this through. Now is not the time to give in to the churning storm of worry in my gut. With a wish and a hope, I try inputting the password again, this time somewhat desperately inserting zeroes before the fours.

Click.

The safe door swings open, nearly smacking the astonishment off my face.

I can't believe that worked.

I feel around inside, not able to see much in the darkness. Papers. A thicker piece with a glossy finish slides out in my hand. A family portrait, the same medium as the tiny picture in my locket. This one shows an older couple, posed sitting on an elegant couch in shades of gray. A little boy, about four years old, kneels on the floor in front of them, dressed smartly in a tiny Gondalese suit. He has a haunted look in his familiar dark eyes.

I recognize him instantly, and the woman in a crisp military dress uniform a few moments later—Ravod and his grandmother. The kindly older man must have been her husband. The general looks very different in this portrait, both from the woman I met and from the official portrait in the hall outside. A warm smile lights her face and creases her eyes as she rests one hand tenderly atop her husband's.

At first, I wonder if it's a trick of the light, but I could swear I see faded, shadowy smudges where another couple was meant to be seated. There's a messy scrawl on the top corner that reads: *Who is this boy??* It's been crossed out, and below is another, messier note in the same hand, but more recent. It says *REMEMBER ERIK.*

I respectfully replace the picture and renew my search.

Dimly, in the distance, I hear Charolais exclaim something about being unable to work in these conditions and storm out of their office. I try not to let it distract me.

Just when I start to wonder if the *Book of Days* is even in here, my fingers brush something old and leathery at the back of the safe. As though answering my thoughts, the *Book* emerges in my hand. It's faintly warm to the touch, as though it's excited to see me again.

A quick inspection reveals the *Book* is undamaged, although still in its sickly state. I tuck it securely into the empty bag I brought. I let out a shaky exhale. That's one problem taken care of.

Now we just have to get out of here alive.

"Do you have it?" Ravod asks, meeting me at the office door.

I nod, holding it up slightly.

"Great. Check in with Kennan and let's . . ."

". . . forgot my gloves." The antechamber door slides open unexpectedly, interrupting Ravod and revealing Charolais. The three of us freeze with shock. Finally, Charolais starts to splutter, pointing at me, "You!" They turn to Ravod, piecing things together. "And *you*!"

I break out of my shock first, lunging for Charolais. I'm not even sure what I hope to achieve beyond stopping them from raising the alarm. Ravod whispers a Telling that grants me enough speed to barrel into his grandmother's secretary, knocking us both off our feet.

Charolais is surprisingly strong. Their military training seems to kick in at my feeble attempt at subduing them. At the very least, it gives Ravod enough time to intervene just as a boot to my gut sends me flying backward, toppling a nearby chair, and crashing unceremoniously to the ground.

Pain doesn't register immediately, and I manage to stumble to my feet, ready to throw myself back into the fray.

Charolais is headed for the desk, Ravod close

behind. He draws a breath, preparing a Telling, when Charolais collides with the heavy surface, fingernails raking the surface with an audible screech. I rush forward, unsure what they are reaching for, until I see it.

A small red button sits unassumingly on one corner of the desk. Before I can alert Ravod or stop Charolais, their fingertip passes over it, exerting just enough pressure to push it down. Ravod finds purchase in Charolais's coat too late, yanking them backward and knocking them unconscious with a swift right hook.

A red light goes off overhead and a sharp siren starts blaring.

"Get to Kennan and the others!" Ravod orders. I don't like leaving him, not for any reason, but particularly in this situation. He sees my hesitation and gives me a stern look, his eyes somehow darker in the red light. "I can keep the reinforcements pinned here and buy the others time, but you need to get the *Book* out of here."

I try to pull air into my lungs, past my unwilling throat. "Please, be careful."

"I will. Now go."

The next thing I know, I'm racing through the hall, the siren blasting in my ears. A line of red lights seems to point at me, and I know it's just a matter of time before they lead the Keep's protectors in my direction.

I can already hear shouts and multiple footsteps

approaching. I push my sleeve back from my wrist and press the button to contact Kennan as I run.

"Kennan!" I hiss breathlessly into the tiny voice box. "Can you hear me? I'm in trouble!"

"You and me both," Kennan's voice crackles at me. In the background I hear several loud blasts and a similar alarm siren. "An alarm got tripped throughout the whole Keep before we could finish. Get down to the hangar as fast as you can, we're running out of time!"

Finding the hangar is surprisingly straightforward, I just follow the sounds of weapon discharges and screaming. I know I'm close when I start smelling smoke and oil. My disguise holds up, keeping the hurried groups of soldiers from noticing me as I rush beneath a shroud of shadows.

The area breaks off from the main base through a self-contained courtyard, and the entrance to the huge double-doored hangar is in a standoff. Kennan and the Protesters are entrenched behind a hastily constructed defensive line, while soldiers scramble to prepare their next attack.

The Protesters pop up from cover every so often, firing their weapons before ducking. They look terrified. The chaotic sounds of shouts and shots thicken the air. Farther away, I still hear the alarm ringing and machines of war roaring to life.

I slip past the makeshift barricade as a shot ricochets through the air behind me. Another second and I might not have made it. Fiona and Mads spot me and rush to my side.

"Thank goodness you're okay." I can barely hear Mads's voice over the chaos, but it still helps my feet feel more firmly rooted to the ground. Fiona's arms wrap around my shoulders. It's only for an instant, but it's enough to feel reconnected to what's most important.

"Do you have it?" Kennan seems to appear out of nowhere as I catch my breath, and I nod mutely. "The charges are set, but the detonator was destroyed in the firefight. We have to set them off manually."

Stot comes to crouch nearby, adding, "We had to rig them to blow up instead and set off a chain reaction. The explosion is going to be a *lot* bigger and far more dangerous than we planned. People can get seriously hurt."

"How do we prevent that?" I ask.

"We can't. Someone would have to go in and flip the switch on the first set of charges while the rest of us get to safety," Stot says grimly. "It's either that, or we retreat."

"We won't get another shot at this," Kennan replies. Her eyes wander to the huge doors behind us, cracked open just enough for someone to slip through. Fiona's jaw clenches as she notices.

"Don't even think about it." I reach for Kennan,

my hand closing around her wrist before she can jerk away. "We have the *Book,* let's get out of here."

"We'll be saving our own hides while dooming Montane. It's one life versus thousands," Kennan fires back.

Tears prick the corners of my eyes. "But *whose* life, Kennan? These people need you. Montane needs you. And whether you like it or not, you're my friend and *I* need you."

"Get it through your head, Shae, this isn't about you." Kennan snaps her wrist from my hand. "This is bigger than any one of us."

She turns away, preparing to make for the hangar doors.

"Then *I* should be the one to go." I throw myself between Kennan and the hangar, arms flung to either side, daring her to challenge me.

"Get out of my way," Kennan growls. She tries to push me away. I push back.

Somehow, I know the fire in her eyes matches mine as we glare at each other, at an impasse.

This is the right thing to do. *I'm* the one responsible for the alarm being set off in the first place. She wants to think that she can do everything and anything for everyone, but my mistake should not be Kennan's responsibility. *I* messed up. *Again.* But I can still set this right. They don't have to die because of me.

My life is a small price to pay to ensure my friends

get to safety. To ensure that Kennan can lead the Protesters, and that Fiona will be there for her the way they both want so desperately but can't admit aloud yet. And Mads . . .

Wait. Where *is* Mads?

I turn so fast that the battle around me blurs for an instant. The world comes back into focus only to start crumbling around me.

The ongoing firefight and my argument with Kennan gave Mads the perfect cover to sneak away from the group. Right before he slips into the hangar, his eyes meet mine and he smiles at me over one broad shoulder.

"Thanks again, Freckles." I can read his lips better than I can hear him. His voice is a dull echo in my ears as my mind struggles to catch up with what is going on around me.

He's going into the hangar. To flip the switch on the charges. And he's never coming back out.

"No, wait . . ." I shake my head. My feet feel leaden as I try to close the distance between us. "Mads, stop!"

Mads's only reply is to disappear into the darkness beyond the door.

Time slows and stretches. He can't have made it to the charges yet. There's no way he can flip the switch in time. I'll reach him first and shove him out of the way. I'll do whatever it takes. Like a dream, the way ahead seems to elongate when I need it to shorten. Moment after moment, heartbeat after heartbeat passes, and I can't hear anything but my pulse hammering through my body with only one objective—to stop him, to fight with everything I've got to end this waking nightmare.

I'm only a few feet from the door. I can make it.

A blinding light blazes. A burst of heat and force throws me back with a deafening reverberation that shakes the very air around me.

After that . . . darkness.

I remember this feeling. It's a crushing weight that strips everything else away, leaving only an aching numbness. Bit by bit, it takes a piece of me away that I'll never get back. It's a pain so consuming it demands nothing less than complete surrender.

Grief.

The first time I felt it, I was a child being informed that a father I'd known only a few short years was gone forever. He was a kind, comforting presence, one I depended on for things like safety and comfort in the most basic sense.

Next was Kieran a few years later. The baby I'd watched grow inside Ma. The person I'd been promised a lifetime of companionship from. The boy who loved playing with his little stone ox from a faraway land. The Blot ravaged him so slowly and completely that, even in my innocence, I had a notion of what it was I had to prepare myself for. His absence was an ache that took years to dull, enough time to condition myself not to feel it at all unless I thought about it. Children are nothing if not resilient, and I was no exception.

Once half my family was wiped out, I naively convinced myself that I'd finally lost enough. There was no way life could be so cruel as to take what was left from me.

Then Ma was murdered.

That wasn't so very long ago, despite how much has happened to make it feel to the contrary. Recent enough that I can recall in detail how I found her in our home, lying in a pool of blood with a golden dagger stuck in her chest. How it felt to see such violence visited upon someone I loved so dearly and know that there was no way to help her.

Losing Ma was different. I was old enough to contemplate the things we'd left unsaid, and in Ma's case, it was a *lot*. There was an added burden to the sadness of losing her.

Regret.

Losing someone isn't something that gets easier the more it happens—it only gets harder. Each loss is as unique as the person who left. Each time it happens, I'm left a little lonelier than before. Broken into smaller and smaller pieces, patched back together a little less capably. A little less whole.

And now Mads is gone, too.

I'm still in that strange space where I can almost believe that he'll walk through the door any second. I can picture his face with perfect clarity, hear his voice, his laugh, feel his presence. And when he inevitably doesn't appear, I circle back into myself, wounded anew.

The bunker beneath the clock tower, where

we have all hunkered down, has been eerily quiet these past two—or is it three?—days. The space is crowded with people involved in the plan, including the distraction team. Word from outside comes in small bursts from Protesters dropping off supplies when they can. We huddle in the dark, waiting for things to die down.

I've only been able to half listen to the news through the fog of emotions in my head. As far as we know, Mads was the only casualty of what's being called "a brazen act of terrorism," but the violence itself has given Gondal enough cause to panic. Public opinion right now paints a picture of Montanians as violent agitators turning upstanding citizens against the government. Rumors among the civilian populace point fingers at the refugees, and the Caverns are being swept by military personnel hoping to flush out insurgents . . . us.

As dire as that all sounds, it would have been far worse if Mads hadn't made his sacrifice. More would have died, on both sides. What he did was heroic; it just doesn't feel that way when I think about it for too long. I keep returning to the thought that it was stupid or reckless of him, as though rationalizing it that way will make his loss hurt less, somehow.

The others in the bunker have stopped talking about him already. At first, the space was filled with reverent murmurs of how Mads gave his life for the cause. Those words died out as we lingered, and now

290 — DYLAN FARROW

the only acknowledgment of him is the sorrowful glances people direct at me every so often. When I notice, they can't look away fast enough.

I wonder if they blame me for his death, the way I blame myself. If I hadn't messed up and gotten the alarm triggered, Mads would still be here. Guilt might be easier to feel than grief if I can only manage to smother one with the other.

As I suspected, it doesn't help.

Kennan has had her hands full keeping us all under control. More than a few tempers have flared for her to douse. To my surprise, Ravod has been quite helpful to her in this. Most of the Protesters are eager to listen to a fellow native of Gondal. I suppose it's to be expected with tensions and emotions so high in the aftermath of everything that's happened. The Protesters want to go home. This is more than they signed up for. They want things to go back to normal. It's a feeling I'm all too familiar with. Eventually, they will learn, like I did, that there's a point you never come back from—"normal" becomes the illusion it always was, only much less comforting.

Either way, with their hands full, I haven't seen much of Kennan or Ravod. When I catch their gazes lingering in my direction, it's always with a hint of helplessness or, worse, pity.

I've barely moved from this rickety wooden bench. Fiona has remained by my side, with very few exceptions. Sometimes she disappears to bring me food and water I have no energy or desire to procure for myself. With quiet insistence, she has ensured I don't starve or pass out from dehydration. When I start to cry, she wraps her arms around me and waits for it to pass.

I know she has her own grief for losing a friend. I can't say so aloud, but once again I find myself envying that she can set those dark feelings aside for my sake. Meanwhile, here I am being exactly no help to anyone.

Even now, I watch as she sleeps curled up on the floor next to my bench. Some people move around quietly, but most are asleep. Ravod is taking inventory of our dwindling supplies, and Kennan is keeping watch over us all—particularly Fiona—as she sweeps her gaze across the dark bunker. Eventually, she leans against the wall where she sits. Her eyelids grow progressively heavier, and flutter closed.

One by one, the inhabitants of the bunker slow their activity and spread out on the floor, or wherever there's some spare space, and drift off. Stot's in the corner, tinkering with some gadget or other until he quietly sets it aside and succumbs to fatigue. After a while, even Ravod falls asleep, his head resting in the crook of his arm over a pile of supplies.

Right now, Mads would make a quiet quip to distract me. But he doesn't. He isn't here.

I draw a shaky breath, trying to keep my emotions in check as they threaten a resurgence. If it's a distraction I need, then a distraction is what I'll find.

I look around. My attention is pulled to the bag I brought here. It rests on the floor, shoved carelessly halfway underneath the bench. I pull it onto my lap, easing it open and reaching inside.

The *Book of Days* is warm to the touch as it slides onto my lap. For the first time, I'm able to really take it in. It looks the same as I remember, weak and weathered. Somehow, I can feel how exhausted it is. How it's barely holding itself together.

Or is it just mirroring what I feel?

Even though everyone in the bunker is asleep except for me, I don't feel alone now that the *Book* is with me. Ravod was right when he said it felt like a companion. Its presence reminds me of my mother, soothing, patient, and gentle.

As my eyes trace the outline of the *Book,* I sense an invitation. I crook my finger beneath the cover and ease it open as gently as possible.

The first page is mostly blank still. Some words seem to try to break through but are too faint to read. Only dull stains and the ravages of time are immediately apparent. The *Book* is too weak to show me anything.

Even so, I gently turn the page, and suddenly feel a sickening lurch in my stomach.

The paper is covered in thick, bold letters like scars, scratching out words that have disappeared and changing entire passages. These changes are not part of the *Book*—they don't shift, only defile. And as I continue turning pages, I notice they appear on almost every single one.

There are points in the *Book* where smaller, more caring alterations were made in delicate script from long ago. All changes are signed by Bards who bore the title of "First Writer." The smaller, older changes have many different names from across time. Hardly any of these names appear more than twice, except for the writer who swept in with their violent edits. Many of those changes are to cross out or undo the older ones.

My stomach lurches again. I know that handwriting. The signature after each block of changes confirms my fears.

Cathal.

I had no idea the extent to which he'd altered the *Book of Days*. It's sickening to look at. Like he was a butcher carving a knife through its flesh with every stroke of his pen. I take my time, slowly studying page after page in the dim light of the bunker. I start to notice patterns. Disturbing ones.

There's a gentle sensation of calm authority as the *Book* reacts to me. It encourages me to see past my outrage, to remain calm. It weakly guides my line of sight, back to the words "First Writer."

A memory from long ago pushes through the tangle of thoughts rushing into my mind like a small bud coming to life after a long winter.

A glowing hearth in a cozy room. I'm barely older

than eight, and Kieran is bouncing in my lap. We sit alongside Mads and a few other children as one of the village elders regales us with the oldest legend in Montane.

"Long ago, when our land was little more than dark, untamed wilderness, the First Rider came, bringing with him light and learning." This particular elder was silenced for implying that the First Rider taught people things. The fact that I considered that perfectly normal at the time makes me shiver. But her words are reverberating in my mind as I look at the *Book of Days*.

Could the First Rider have been . . . the First *Writer*?

I need to study the passages more closely, and the *Book*'s presence seems to nod knowingly at me. The implications are as boundless as they are terrifying. The land and legends of Montane have been twisted and altered beyond recognition. All by one man.

But the *Book* is here and intact, if barely. Which means it still holds a semblance of its former power. The power of all creation, all reality. I gently turn the remaining pages. Perhaps there's a remote possibility that the *Book of Days* already knows how this story ends.

As I feared, Cathal's changes are there as well, even on the very last page. His final edit reads: *My control is absolute.* And it's signed: *Cathal, First Writer of Montane.*

Faintly, as though it's happening just beneath the

surface of the paper, I see flickers of movement. As words slowly shift into focus, I strain to view them in the dimness of the bunker. They are faint and changing too rapidly to see around Cathal's opaque cursive. I follow line by line to the very bottom, and my breath stops.

The last sentence, the ending of the *Book of Days*, is bolder and completely legible. It alone does not change.

The First Writer destroys the Book of Days.

"Alright, everyone, listen up." Kennan's voice immediately commands the collective attention of the entire bunker. "Our scouts are reporting that the military's search parties are moving away from this part of the city. The time to act is now."

I listen while gingerly replacing the *Book* in its wrappings and place it back in my bag. I was so engrossed, I didn't notice the rest of the bunker wake and stir with activity. Beside me, Fiona sits up and rubs the sleep from her eyes.

"What's going on?" she asks through a yawn.

I open my mouth to reply, but Kennan beats me to it, continuing her statement from a moment ago.

"Time is not our ally. General Ravod will already be mobilizing more forces to continue her attack. Returning to the cavern and endangering the innocent people there is not an option. The time has come for us to return to Montane and take this fight where it truly belongs. To High House."

A chill seeps into the marrow of my bones, growing

colder as I comprehend her meaning. We're going back to Montane, where this struggle will end once and for all. One way or another.

And unfortunately, the *Book of Days* has a destiny of its own. I must bring it to Cathal, of all people, to destroy it.

20

Over the next few hours, Kennan quietly dispatches one small group at a time to the other side of the city, where Ravod says we will find a shipyard. While no one particularly relishes the idea of commandeering an airship large enough to transport our small army to Montane, it's our best option.

"Rationalize it however you must," Kennan says sharply when the plan is laid out. "We have already made our enemies. You can throw yourselves on their mercy, but I wouldn't count on it. Your execution will be a drop in the bucket compared to the lives we stand to save."

Her words still ring in my ears alongside the wind as my group mounts up two by two on the smaller flying vehicles Emery was able to provide. He gives me a small nod of what can almost pass as respect when I see him on my way out of the bunker.

We can't linger outside too long, or we risk being spotted. There's a nondescript alley between Lord Ten Thirty and the neighboring building where several small air vehicles have been stashed for us. I go where Kennan instructs and haul my leg over the side of one. The driver in front of me turns, and my heart skips a beat when Ravod pulls his flight goggles up onto his forehead to meet my gaze.

"I promise Kennan's not still trying to kill you by sending you with me. I'm a very safe driver." He smiles. I'm already seated, but my knees go a little weak anyway. I hastily clear my throat.

"How many times have you flown one of these?" I ask.

"Twice. Well, three times. But the last time didn't count. Damn corner store came out of nowhere." He notices my expression shift as I try to gauge his seriousness. "Better hang on tight."

"I can never determine whether your intention is to make me laugh or send me screaming for the hills." I laugh anyway, imagining him comically swerving to avoid hitting the shop, and his smile broadens.

"The last few days have been hard. It's good to see you smile," he says. Abruptly he sobers, replacing the goggles over his eyes as Kennan approaches us.

"You ready?" she asks.

"As I'll ever be." I sigh, my thoughts focusing on the road before us.

"Obtaining what we need will be the easy part," Kennan says. I notice a slight furrow in her brow that contradicts her confident words.

"Nothing is ever easy," Ravod says, shaking his head. "But I can still use the Telling here, if needed. It will at least be . . . easier."

Frustrated, Kennan and I sigh in unison. It will have to be enough.

Not long after, our group is fully mounted on our respective vehicles. They follow Ravod, and I cling in barely restrained terror to his back. In case of any rogue bodegas, of course.

Holding onto Ravod is no hardship. With my arms wrapped around his waist, I can partially feel the lean musculature of his body through his coat, the steadiness of his breath. Somehow, holding him is even more thrilling than flying high over the streets of the city, zipping effortlessly around air traffic as dawn rises over the towering buildings. I'm glad he's facing away from me, so he doesn't notice how red my cheeks are. I mentally prepare a very solid case blaming the wind just in case he does.

Eventually, we alight on a hilltop near the outskirts of Tybera. Out this far, the towers taper off in favor of factory smokestacks. The air is heavier here, redolent with something I've come to associate with Gondal—with industry.

Spread before us is one of the smaller shipyards in the city, owned and operated by the government. The larger ones are apparently the property of wealthy industrialists like Emery's family and are extremely profitable. This one is still impressively sized, at least to my untrained eyes, and seems abandoned, which must be why it was chosen. The few people I see from our vantage point appear to be engineers and laborers milling unhurriedly about. Rows of airships of various size, shape, and completion stand silently on a flat paved square that's the equivalent of several city blocks.

While the rest of us gather and organize, Kennan confers quietly with Ravod and Emery. From what I hear of their conversation, she wishes to target the speediest aircraft that can accommodate our numbers. Ravod scans our options, finally indicating one with a long, gloved finger. Emery seems to concur with his selection.

I almost don't notice Fiona at my side until she places a hand on my arm and gives it a gentle squeeze.

"How are you holding up?" she asks.

I take a breath, exhaling slowly before answering. "'Holding up' seems like an accurate assessment."

"Mads would probably be hurt if you said you were perfectly fine." Fiona offers a slightly pained smile. "But I know he'd want you to be, in your own time."

"I really miss him." My voice comes out hoarse. The words sting but need to be said.

"I know. I do too."

I blink out at the horizon without really seeing it. Instead, I picture Mads and my mother. I realize suddenly, unprovoked by anything but my own bereavement, that my memories of them are all I have left. It's not enough. I don't know what possibly could be.

"We've *got* to win this, Fiona. For Mads. For my ma." I turn to face her, tears welling in my eyes that I know better than to try to stop. "And when it's over, we have to keep their memories alive."

Fiona nods solemnly. "I want that too, and I'll help however I can."

She's barely finished speaking when I pull her into a hug. There's so much uncertainty in the world. I'm glad that there's one thing I can always count on, and I'm gladder it's Fiona.

"Help! Someone! Mutiny!" The manager of the zeppelin's maintenance team wails as Kennan binds him.

"This isn't a mutiny, you buffoon," Kennan growls, spinning the stout, balding man away from her to secure his wrists behind his back. "It's a robbery."

"Isn't it technically a hijacking?" Ravod points out. The withering look Kennan shoots him only seems to amuse him, but he slips to the back of the bridge anyway, out of range of the conversation.

"Whatever this is, we should probably hurry it up," I add.

I get no argument from the others—the bridge, along with the rest of the ship, is clear of shipyard workers shortly after. The Protesters corral them in a shed, somewhere they will be easily found, but not until long after we've made our getaway.

It was almost too easy. The thought makes me more tense than if something had gone disastrously wrong. I shift nervously before approaching Kennan at the helm. A few of her men have taken the controls and the airship hums to life around us. A gentle current of vibration carries beneath my feet, in tune with the distant sound of an engine awakening.

"This was too easy," Kennan murmurs, just loud enough for me to hear. At least we're on the same page.

"Maybe we're overdue some good luck?" My best attempt at optimism still sounds forced, and Kennan clearly notices, shifting her attention from the front window to me.

"Maybe. Let's hope it doesn't run out before we reach High House," she says, low and thoughtful. With a brisk shake of her head, she slips back into commander-mode. "We already dispatched a great many of the general's bombers, so any pursuit we pick up should be small and brief. The rest of the Protesters are waiting at the Juncture near the border. We'll pick them up and be well and truly on our way."

She doesn't wait for my reply before she strides off to speak with the men piloting the airship. I hang back, my hand resting protectively on the bag slung from my shoulder. A brief sensation of warmth reassures me that the *Book of Days* is safely inside.

As though seeking the source of that warmth, my hand slips inside. I expect to feel the cover of the *Book,* but instead my fingers curl around something cold and small. When my hand emerges from the bag, a small, stone ox sits in my palm. An old friend.

"We're doing all we can," I whisper, half to myself. "The rest . . ."

"It'll happen as it's meant to." Another quiet voice responds somewhat behind me. I quickly shove the ox statue into my pocket.

"Stot." I offer a small smile at the kid standing in the doorway and step closer to him. The wind from outside tousles his hair, sending it flying back from his face for the first time since I met him. "Wow, you really do have a forehead under there."

He grimaces a little, pivoting his body away from me. I can't decide if he's embarrassed or worried about something. Eventually, he turns slowly back.

"Hey, want to see something amazing?"

Before I respond he takes my hand, leading me excitedly away from the helm. I brace myself as the wind outside hits me. The landing is broad enough that I don't have to look down, but the metal railing is worryingly slim. Stot's hand feels like the only thing preventing the wind from sweeping me into the air and over the side of the ship.

At the front of the ship, he releases me. A broad smile lights his face as he steps up to the guard rail. He grips it tightly in both hands, letting the wind whip through his hair as he tilts his face up to the sky.

My heart beats a little faster as I join him, hesitantly at first. The fall is a lot steeper than a mere tree. Somehow, it feels like something even stronger than a Telling is compelling me to step forward.

The railing is cold to the touch as I hold on with blanched knuckles. The wind is equally chilly, and powerful enough that I'll be surprised if I have all my hair after this. The air's thinner here, like it is high up in the mountains back home.

"Shae!" Stot shouts over the roar of sound around us. "Open your eyes, you're going to miss it!"

I realize my eyes have screwed shut against the wind and my own trepidation. I take a deep breath and do as he says.

A cold burst of air rushes into my throat when I gasp. The mechanical metropolis below is even more beautiful from the air. All of Tybera, all of Gondal, is spread below us. Even the tops of the tallest towers look like little more than eager fingers reaching vainly into the sky. From this vantage, it's like I'm watching an anthill. The buzz and chaos of the city is still there, but smaller. The myriad other airships, even the fanciest glittering ones, seem diminutive as we race past them through the sky. A couple on a smaller vehicle wave at us as they zip past.

"I can see why Montane couldn't believe a place like this is real," I shout over my shoulder to Stot. "I still can't believe I got to see it for myself."

"I'm glad you did," Stot replies.

I turn from the view to face the boy. I can see his whole face, and surprisingly, he's not flinching away. His blue-gray eyes meet mine without dropping to the floor or diverting elsewhere. It's not a confident gaze, but it's hopeful. Affectionate. There's something painfully familiar about his face. I can only see it now that he's not hiding from me.

I take advantage of this sudden willingness on his part to look at him truly, fully. As I do, everything he's said to me since we met comes flooding to the forefront of my memory. The sun feels a little warmer as it shines on us, lighting him from behind with a glow of gold in his brown hair.

I swallow thickly. I know why Victor instructed me to find him.

Holding his gaze, a little worried that if I don't the moment will slip away entirely, my hand reaches into my pocket. I take a tentative step closer as I clutch the stone ox. My hand is trembling as I extend it and my fingers uncurl. The little statue glimmers in the light, too solid for the wind to disturb, catching his eye as I hand it to him.

He stares at it, his eyes growing wide. His fingers graze my palm as he picks it up, entranced with a childlike wonder I'd all but forgotten. At my side, the *Book of Days* feels a little warmer, as though confirming what I only now realize.

"It's good to have this back," says Kieran.

"You knew this whole time, didn't you?"

Kieran grimaces at the question. It's so strange how, now that I know it's him, I remember so much more. He made that same face whenever Ma scolded him. For a moment, his gaze diverts, a force of habit I realize, and he turns the stone ox over in his hands a few times before answering.

"I mean, there are only so many seventeen-year-old girls from Montane with brown hair and freckles named Shae, right?"

I sigh and shake my head, a soft laugh escaping me. He has a point.

The wind is quieter on this bench welded to the floor of the deck. We only made it this far after I finally released him from the bear hug that I wrapped him in on the bow, not too far away. The sun is shaded by the upper landing here, making it easier to see him without squinting. I'm pretty certain the bright light isn't the reason we both have tears lingering in our eyes.

"Why didn't you say anything?" I ask.

"I don't know." He chews his lower lip. "At first I was worried you wouldn't believe me. Then I kept trying to find the right time and it just never came. I wanted to, but . . ." He trails off.

"I get it," I say. "There's no easy way to inform someone that you're their long-lost, supposedly dead brother."

He smiles. "True. When you put it like that, I'm not sure I'd have believed me, either."

"So, what really happened, then?" I mimic his posture, leaning forward on my knees and craning my head to the side, almost afraid that if I take my eyes off him he'll disappear, and I'll be left with only this happy dream that he was ever here. "I was told you died from the Blot. The Bards came and burned the house down. We had a funeral—"

"Not Bards." Kieran cuts me off. "It was Victor and his allies. They made a big show of it to keep word from reaching High House. They smuggled me out, I'm not sure how. I was blacked out for most of it. All I remember is that Ma said they would take me somewhere safe. Victor assured me later on that they scared the townspeople enough that they wouldn't mention it again in case the *real* Bards ever came through. You and Ma would be safe."

A silence falls between us as I reconcile what he said with what I remember. It isn't difficult; I was so young I don't recall much, only how it made me feel. I can only imagine my mother that day, agonizing over sending her son, her baby, off to a foreign land in a last-ditch effort to keep him alive. And Victor taking him from his home, never to return.

"No one ever told me," I say, finally. It's all I can manage.

"I figured. You probably would have charged off to try and find me." That makes me smile. After all this time, he still knows me too well.

"I'm sorry it took so long," I say. "So what happened next?"

"Victor brought me through the tunnels into Gondal, probably the same path you used. When I arrived here, the Protesters took me in and kept me taken care of," Kieran replies, turning over the statue in his hands with a faint smile playing at the corners of his mouth. "I was pretty scared, even though they were kind to me. But it took a long time before I could sleep through the night without this little guy. You can buy them on just about any street corner here, but I was very insistent that it wasn't the same. I carried on so much they started calling me 'baby ox,' which gradually became 'Stot.'"

"A baby ox. I feel like an idiot I didn't see it sooner," I admit. "The *Book of Days* even hinted that you were alive. I just didn't put the pieces together."

"You've had a lot on your mind, it's understandable."

"I guess the silver lining is that you've been safe. The Protesters took good care of you, and you found a community, a family with them." Once I've said it, I can't suppress the twisting sadness that forms in my chest. This whole time my brother was alive, but he was part of a family that didn't include me.

"I was lucky," Kieran says softly. He reaches for my hand where it rests between us on the bench and squeezes. "But there wasn't a day that passed where I didn't think about going home and seeing you again. Making that possible."

"Ma would have been overjoyed . . ." It slips out before I can prevent it and hangs awkwardly in the air. Kieran probably didn't even know she was gone until I mentioned it in the Refugee Cavern.

Kieran looks a little sad for a moment and I realize he probably barely remembers her. He was only a small child the last time he saw her.

"I thought a lot about what you said. How she stopped speaking."

"I'm sorry, that must have been difficult to hear. I didn't mean . . ." I bite my lip, stopping myself short. Now that I think about it, hearing about Ma the way he did must have been more painful than I can imagine. After all the time he spent hoping to see her again.

"Shae, you didn't know," Kieran insists. "And like I said, I thought about it. I think she was scared. If she spoke, she probably would have told you everything. It would have put you in danger."

It's my turn to fall silent. I had never thought about it like that. To the bitter end, my mother was trying to protect me.

My next words are little more than a thoughtful whisper. "I think you're right."

"When this is over, maybe we can have a proper funeral for her," Kieran says. "And one for Mads, too."

I let out a long exhale. "That's a great idea." I don't voice my concern that things could still end very badly. I must have hope. For him.

I pull the brass locket Victor gave me from my shirt and unclasp it to show the tiny picture inside to Kieran. He squints until recognition sweeps over his face.

"Wow," he whispers. "She really was a Bard."

"Victor told you?"

"For a few years, we used to write messages to each other. He was my lifeline to Montane." Kieran doesn't take his eyes off the picture in the locket. "It's amazing. You look just like her. Except . . ."

"Except for the freckles, I know." I roll my eyes.

"Remember how she used to say they were fairy kisses?" Kieran laughs. "I was so jealous. I would always ask why the fairies never kissed *me*."

"And I said they liked me better." I laugh too, and it's like nothing has changed in the years we've been apart.

Then the airship lurches downward a little, just enough to break the spell. In the distance, the ground is slowly rising to meet us.

"Looks like we're landing," Kieran says, sighing.

"Kennan said we're picking up additional reinforcements." I slip the locket around my neck as we get to our feet. "Then off to Montane."

"You shouldn't go. The Blot . . ." Kieran seems to know saying so is futile—I'm going anyway—but he says it with the concern of a little brother. I've heard this tone in his voice since meeting him again, and a part of me feels touched that he was worrying about me the whole time.

"I have to," I say. "I can use the Telling to ward it off, at least long enough to see this through."

As the airship touches down, Kieran launches himself into my arms and embraces me fiercely.

"Promise me we'll meet again. In Montane." His voice cracks a little when he says it.

I squeeze him tighter, wishing I could respond with more certainty. If I can't use a Telling, I can at least make a wish.

"I promise."

21

Kennan leans over the hastily procured table at the back of the airship's helm. Between her hands is a map of the known world. Gondal only takes up a small portion just northeast of the middle. Montane is even smaller. Other countries surround them. Places I've never heard of, even in the most fantastical legends.

There was a whole world out there all along.

My reverie is broken as Kennan taps the small icon of Montane twice, reminding me of the here and now. The rest of the world will have to wait until home is safe.

"We need a plan for our approach to High House," Kennan states. "Something better than just showing up and seeing what happens."

"We'll be facing obstacles just in reaching High House," Ravod points out from beside me.

Kennan nods. "Its defenses are exhaustive. Approaching from the air gives us an advantage, but we will lose it quickly if we're not smart. My main concern is the Telling that obfuscates High House from enemies. If we can't counter it, we won't even see the castle. It's impenetrable from the outside."

I remember the voices chanting, how the sound

echoes in a quiet monotone throughout the halls. *There's a constant Telling done by the elder Bards for the protection of High House.* Ravod's voice emerges from my memory. That is what we are up against.

Kennan and Ravod have begun an academic discussion on the particulars of crafting a Counter-Telling to the castle's ancient defenses. I can't understand most of it, even with my knowledge of the Telling. It reminds me how much deeper their combined knowledge and experience are. On the one hand, it is incredible and probably the reason why we stand a chance in facing what we're up against. On the other, it reminds me how much weaker and inexperienced I am by comparison.

I can't let that stop us, I scold myself. *I came this far on what I have, I can do the rest the same way.*

A risky, probably impossible idea starts churning in my head. Maybe we have other options. It's possible, even remotely, that we don't need a Telling to get inside at all.

"Kennan, you said the Telling can't be penetrated from the outside?" I ask, interrupting the discussion.

"That's right." Kennan's frown is less an affront than usual as she leans away from the map, waiting for me to continue.

"Well, what about from inside?"

"I'm sure you've noticed, none of us *are* inside." Kennan arches a dark eyebrow at me.

"None of us, no," I say. "But what about Imogen?"

I hadn't thought it possible, but somehow Kennan's eyebrow raises even higher. "Who?"

"She's my friend." I go on to describe the young servant girl with the wild hair and the little gap in her teeth. I explain how she befriended me when I first arrived at High House. How she helped me when no one else would. A dawning recognition passes over Kennan and Ravod's faces as I speak.

"I remember her," Ravod says eventually. "If you say she's an ally, I believe you."

"That doesn't change the fact that we have no way of contacting her, and even if we did, we have no time to explain the intricacies of what we require her to do," Kennan points out.

"Yes, we do." I punctuate my words by taking the *Book of Days* from my bag and setting it on the table in full view of everyone.

The *Book* has changed since I last saw it. The binding is more secure. The age and deterioration have lessened. Gold enamel peeks through in spots where the leather appears richer. The energy I sense around it is more vibrant. Now that we're closer to Montane, the *Book* is returning to life.

An awed quiet falls over the space. Even the Protesters manning the ship fall into a reverent silence, stealing glances from their positions at the helm. Fiona's eyes are practically popping out of her head. She's stepped closer to Kennan and taken her hand beneath the table. For her part, Kennan looks

316 — DYLAN FARROW

like she's crossed a desert and just seen water. Only Ravod does not react with immediate and stunned wonder.

"Shae, what are you suggesting?" His voice is deliberate and wary.

"If Imogen can lower the veil, Kennan and the Protesters can act as a distraction while you and I seek out Cathal." My confidence builds somewhat as I speak. "All we have to do is contact her, right? If the *Book* is willing, it can help us get the message to her, and Cathal and the Bards will never even know."

"If the *Book* . . . is willing?" Fiona repeats.

"The *Book of Days* is . . ." I grimace, unsure how qualified I am to explain this ancient and tremendous object. The *Book* seems to be listening to the conversation eagerly, as though excited to be the topic. "I know this sounds bizarre, but it's a *living thing*. See for yourself!"

I take Fiona's free hand from across the table, giving it a gentle, encouraging squeeze before I place it on the *Book*'s cover. She looks at me, confused. Then a dawning realization spreads across her features. She feels it, too.

"My goodness," Fiona breathes. "Are all books like this?"

"No, they aren't," Kennan answers before she looks back to the *Book,* then to me. "We have an advantage. I say we use it."

"Just because we have the power to do this doesn't mean we should," Ravod interjects. His eyes flash to me beneath a furrowed brow. "I thought you would understand that better than anyone, Shae."

The accusation stings. I remember what he told me in his apartment in Tybera. *Why only make a small adjustment to one person's memory when I could just as easily rewrite the world in any way I wished? If I was willing to do one, then I was willing to do the other. And that is the difference between me and Cathal.* I recall the clock tower bunker the first time he showed me the *Book. It's much more than a mere book. As I traveled with it, it started to feel more like a companion.* And only moments later he had said, *I thought I imagined it, but I heard it cry out when I tore the page. I told you last night I took a moral stance against using it to change reality, but that wasn't the whole truth. When I thought about writing in it, I couldn't shake the thought that it would be . . . violent. Violating. That I'd be abusing it, somehow.*

I open my mouth to retort but think better of it. Ravod has spent the most time with the *Book.* His attachment and concern are understandable. Try as I might, I can't fault him for his objections. And furthermore, an argument will serve no one. Instead, I take a deep breath, meeting his gaze without flinching.

"Like I said, we must obtain the *Book*'s permission. And only make the smallest, least invasive change possible. I know what the *Book* means to you. I would not be saying this if I thought we had another choice," I say.

"*Do* we have another choice?" Kennan asks Ravod pointedly. What she's really asking is whether he understands we *don't* have another choice. And he knows it.

"We all know this should be the last resort, not a first," I say. "But we have no alternative, and we're out of time. I accept full responsibility for what I'm suggesting."

Ravod is not pleased. He crosses his arms over his chest as I fold the *Book*'s thick leather cover back. His jaw tightens.

"Perhaps the mistake was mine, for placing my faith in you."

The statement sears my heart, and the sensation squirms and festers as silence lingers between us. It pains me in a way no Telling ever could.

The tension is only lifted somewhat when Kennan clears her throat. Her hand is outstretched over the table, a blue fountain pen wrapped loosely in her fingers as she offers it to me. As I accept it, she nods almost imperceptibly.

"You know what must be done," she says.

The pen sits heavily on my palm, as though weighty enough to drag the entire airship to the ground. I take a deep breath, cold air rushing into my lungs past the invisible wound left by Ravod. I try to free myself from all distractions.

I turn my attention to the *Book of Days*. Its attention is directed right back at me as I lightly brush the topmost page with my hand. A strange chill rushes

through the air in response. I'm suddenly, unexpectedly connected to the *Book* in a deeper way than
I was before. Time and movement seem to slow
around me, the light reflecting in a way that reveals
the threads binding the world together.

Do not be afraid. The words appear on the page,
shimmering brightly before they fade. I can feel the
Book's intentions and can similarly sense it understanding mine. It knows what I want, what I need.
Maybe even better than I do.

"I need your help," I say aloud anyway. My voice
is a whisper absorbed by the strange shift in my surroundings.

The *Book* doesn't answer with words. Instead,
shining inkblots spread across the page, and lifelike windows into space and time appear on the
paper. I can see the First Writers and the changes
they wrought through the *Book of Days*. One forged
the mountain barrier around Montane because of
a threat at sea. Another placed High House on the
mountain as a bastion of order during a lawless time.
Yet another made the land arable during a crop fam-
ine. The only commonality was that they all asked
for help, and the *Book* was happy to provide it.

I pause, waiting for the *Book* to add a provision,
such as *that was before Cathal ruined everything,* or
some such. It doesn't happen.

"Does that mean . . ." I swallow, clutching the pen
a little tighter. "Do I have your permission to write?"

Yes.

"Will it hurt? I don't want to hurt you." The question bursts out before I can rein it in. The *Book* is silent as images disappear. Then written words take their place.

Only humans measure their lives in pain. I detect a hint of amusement accompanying those words. I also sense their truth. The *Book of Days* is not bound by the same limitations I or any of my people are. We are just mindless creatures that scurry, when compared to something like the *Book*.

"I need to know," I insist. "Please. I don't want to do to you what Cathal did."

Then do not do what he did.

The words are simple but loaded with meaning. I take a deep, steadying breath.

"I understand."

I sense the *Book*'s gentle approval, like a hand on my shoulder in the way Ma used to comfort me. The words shimmer, fade, and are replaced once more.

If you falter, he will prevail.

With that, the strange communion slips into the ether. I'm still exactly where I was before, but existence has reverted to its natural state, as though it never changed.

"Are you all right, Shae?" Fiona's voice jerks my head up from the *Book*. She and the others are regarding me inquisitively. "Your eyes, they . . . had a strange glow for moment."

"We don't have time to fuss over her," Kennan

interjects, but I see her discreetly give Fiona's hand a small squeeze. "We're running out of time. Can you do this or not?"

"I can do this," I reply.

I twist the cap from the pen. Indigo ink beads at the nib. Once it was the source of fear for an entire people. Now it might be their salvation.

Carefully, I set pen to paper. For several moments, only the distant roar of the airship's engine and the ticking of a clock on the wall accompany the scratching sound of writing.

I craft this, my first written Telling, with the utmost care. I choose my words carefully. Deliberately. I take my time forming each letter as part of the whole. No other Telling I've wrought has been this important.

When I finish, I watch the ink set and dry. I only made a small note, but my handwriting is large and clumsy, very different from the elegant script of those who wrote before me. After a second, a small pulse ripples through the ink and into the world. Reality alters. The *Book of Days* has been changed.

Imogen knows we are coming and will lower the veil.

The room is cast in silence, broken only when Ravod shakes his head, exhaling sharply through his nose. Then he storms out.

Something in my gut tries to pull me after him,

but I stop short of taking that step. Instead, I sigh, trying to exhale my complicated feelings with the air. I'm only somewhat successful.

I busy myself with closing the *Book of Days*. It's more like a real book now instead of a threadbare stack of loosely bound pages. The luster on the cover glints in the light of the overhead lamp when I lift it into my bag.

When I look up, Fiona and Kennan are sharing a meaningful look. Fiona places a featherlight kiss on Kennan's cheek and disperses with some of the other Protesters. Briefly, the venom of Ravod's exit is alleviated, replaced by a peaceful warmth that something good has sprung from all this madness. When Fiona disappears around the corner of the doorway, Kennan's eyes snap to mine and her mouth twists like she's stifling a groan.

"I'm sure you're eager to bombard me with questions? Commentary?"

I shake my head. "Not if you don't want to talk about it."

She looks a little surprised at that. Whatever retort she had lined up goes unsaid. Instead, she steps around the table toward me.

"Actually, there was something else I wished to speak with you about."

I resist looking over my shoulder for whoever she must really be talking to, but Kennan merely waits for my response.

"What do you need?"

"When you wrote in the *Book,* you connected with it," Kennan states. "You could almost pass for one of the First Writers."

The title, spoken aloud, sets off a spark in my chest. "You know about the First Writers?"

Kennan shrugs. "A little. I spent a great deal of time researching the *Book of Days.* The information about it was slim at best and mention of the First Writers was even scarcer. I think I found the last book containing any small detail in the scriptorium. Niall was quick to swoop in and make that particular volume disappear."

"What did you learn?" I ask.

She looks away, somewhere past the windows, to where the darkening clouds rush by. "In ages past, the First Writer was the foremost of the Bards. They were chosen young by the elder Bards for their aptitude, but also their judgment. They were supposed to be the best of the Order. The chosen Bard would spend their youth training and committing to the role. Their mandate was to form the bridge between the *Book of Days* and the rest of the world and there are no records . . ."

She falls quiet, turning her own words over as her gaze drifts back to meet mine. Understanding dawns over her features a moment later.

"Cathal is the First Writer," I confirm.

Kennan nods slowly. "He's been in power so long that the title fell to disuse, I suppose."

"Or he purposefully allowed it to become misinformation, like everything else. It became the 'First Rider.' Perhaps he thought that if people knew there were others in the past, that there would be a possibility he could be replaced." I shudder, recalling his treatment of the *Book*. His edits that gave him total control.

The look Kennan gives me feels loaded with meaning I can't decipher, but she says nothing. When she finally speaks, her voice is quieter than usual.

"That explains the changed nature of the Telling he possesses. The scope of his power. Why his language is so controlled," she says. "He was probably already a powerful Bard. But his connection to the *Book* is what made him truly dangerous."

"The *Book* didn't make him anything he wasn't already." I place a protective hand over my bag.

Kennan narrows her eyes thoughtfully. "Your handling of the *Book of Days* was . . ." She pauses, searching for a word, and settles for ". . . not abysmal."

"You could have stepped in at any time," I say.

"Perhaps, but it wasn't necessary," she replies. "And I don't know that I would have been able to keep my changes subtle."

"What do you mean?"

"Back at High House," she says, "I used to think a lot about what I would do, what I would change, when I finally got the *Book of Days* in front of me. Seeing what it really is . . . was not what I expected."

I recall her speaking passionately on the subject during our time together at High House. Her tone is more subdued now. There's a distance in her voice that speaks to how far this journey has really taken her.

Curiosity overwhelms me. "What would you have changed?"

"That's the thing." Kennan's frown deepens. "I made it my mission to seek out the *Book*. To set things right. I thought that meant vast, sweeping, unignorable change. But mostly, I was convinced that I was the only one who could bring it about. I was going to rewrite Montane."

"And now?"

"Well, that's the other thing. Seeing the *Book* in front of me, just as I always wanted, made me realize . . ." She trails off. "If it had been me making that change instead of you, I would have done the same thing. I wouldn't have passed up the chance to see my mission through. That's why I gave you the pen."

"I don't follow." My brow furrows to match Kennan's.

"When power is all you know, it can be difficult to let go of."

I'm still not sure I understand, but her cryptic answer seems to have more meaning than she's letting on. I allow it to hang in the air and settle. Kennan's gaze drifts to the floor and back to me. Her eyes are starting to fade to the color of a flame.

"Your eyes," I blurt. "They're changing back."

Kennan looks confused, then her face clears with understanding. "We must be getting closer," she says. "My Telling is reactivated."

"Why do a Telling to change your eyes?" I ask.

"I thought you weren't going to ask me annoying questions."

I hold up my hands in surrender. "I withdraw the question."

To my surprise, Kennan snorts a laugh. "Fine."

"What?"

She shoots me another incomprehensible look. "Your effort at self-control is pathetic, but I suppose it's somewhat commendable. I'll allow this *one* annoying question."

"Really?" I hold my tongue before I ask who this strangely agreeable person that I'm talking to is and what she's done with Kennan.

She reaches into her breast pocket with two long fingers, slowly producing a small, tattered scrap of paper. It's folded delicately, but the creases indicate many years of careful touches. She hands it to me.

Somewhat confused but unwilling to sever the strange moment of what I can only describe as familiarity, I accept the paper and gently unfold it. I recognize Kennan's handwriting instantly, but this is clearly an earlier incarnation of it. The letters are more jagged and less skillfully crafted. Even so, there's a faint hum of power connected to it. The Telling.

I read aloud, "My eyes scare you."

Those same eyes are watching me carefully when I look up. Taking my measure, as always.

"You recall I said I grew up at High House?"

I nod, waiting.

Kennan slowly takes back her Telling, returning it to its place inside her pocket. "My parents, sister, and I originally inhabited one of the last manors in Montane. My parents were some of the last real nobles in the country. Their jurisdiction was the town of Taranton, in the west. Unrest led to an uprising in the village that destroyed our home. My first memories are the smoke and fires burning in the distance as we fled to High House. Cathal gave us sanctuary, along with the other remaining nobles who arrived under similar conditions."

"On the surface, that doesn't sound unpleasant," I point out.

Kennan nods. "You understand. Nothing is as it appears in that castle. Most of the nobles wound up killing each other off in petty infights. It was not long before my parents succumbed. It fell to my older sister, Nahra, to continue raising me. I was only ten at the time. Nahra had no interest in participating in the deadly intrigues of the other nobles. She tried her best to bring peace to our troubled microcosm. She petitioned Cathal for help. Bringing about true peace has never been in his interests. Within days of asking, my sister 'mysteriously' contracted the Blot."

I know only too well what that is like. I also know the outcome. If anyone knew Kennan's sister's goals, the fact that she got the Blot made them subversive, something to be avoided at all costs. And anyone close to her would be suspect. It was the same for me and Ma.

328 — DYLAN FARROW

I mutely nod to Kennan to continue. For a moment, I'm not sure she will. She takes a deep breath.

"What was left of the only community I ever knew turned against me overnight. Around that time, I discovered I had the gift of Telling. I was shunted from one dangerous pocket of High House into another. I learned to read and write at the earliest opportunity and made this." She pats her pocket, where her Telling sits safely. "If I'd learned one thing, it was that the surest method to keep people away is if they fear you. And if they were going to fear me, I wanted to control how. So I made sure of it."

"Not everyone turns their eyes bright yellow just to make people afraid of them," I say.

The corner of Kennan's mouth tilts upward. "Is that what you see?"

It occurs to me that the vague language of Kennan's Telling probably allowed for different interpretations depending on who saw her. I see eerie golden eyes.

"Very clever, Kennan."

"Obviously, there are some people with no sense of self-preservation who stubbornly insist on ignoring my Telling." Kennan gives me a somewhat pointed look. "Such as yourself. And Fiona."

"What do other people see?" I wonder.

"Depends on the person." Kennan shrugs. "Fiona says she sees her own eyes. Ravod told me he sees dead sockets, but I think he's just particularly disturbed."

"Mads and I saw the same thing," I realize. It comes out as a whisper.

"You and Mads were very aligned in thought. You both saw the world more similarly than you believed."

Somehow, it's nice to hear that. It helps me feel like there's still something that connects me to him. Kennan rolls her eyes when I smile despite myself.

Yet again, a quiet settles between us, but for the first time since I met her, it isn't charged with animosity. Only a quiet, prickly current that I've come to associate with Kennan. She'll never say it, but I think—maybe—we've become friends after all.

A sudden stabbing, shooting pain tears into me a second later. It forces the air from me. My knees buckle. I reach wildly for the first thing I can find to steady myself, which turns out to be Kennan's shoulder. Her frown deepens to a horrified grimace, but it's not because of the sudden contact.

Blue veins darken on my wrists. The Blot has returned.

Once we are past the mountain range at the southern boundary of Montane, the view from the airship changes rapidly. Small, worrying pockets of decay were visible on the Gondalese side where the wasteland spread, but those were nothing compared to the devastation beyond. Worse than I remember. Clouds of smoke curl on the horizon to the east, and another to the north. The rocky brown expanse I always knew has turned a dull, withered gray. What life the land clung to is well and truly gone.

I should rest while I can. I eye the cushioned passenger seats to my right. Kennan deposited me on them when the sickness flared. But I'm too restless to avail myself of them now, much as I know I should. The ache in my body intensifies as I observe Montane through one of the airship's windows. Tearing myself away from the grim sight below, I perform another Telling to ward off the sickness consuming me. As I flex my fingers and watch the veins temporarily recede, I realize that after a certain point it won't be enough. The thought makes me shiver. I can already feel the plague fighting back. Once we get to High House it will only get worse.

Maybe I'll die.

I'm a little taken aback by how calmly I think it. I have never really stopped to consider the concept of my own mortality. I've thought a lot about that of others—Ma, Mads, even the gnawing guilt I still hold onto about Niall and, until very recently, Kieran. Did I consider myself indestructible? And if it truly comes to pass that I don't make it, what then?

When Pa died, Ma only said he was "at peace." Whatever that means. I find myself revisiting those words as I gaze out the window without really seeing anything. Are she and Mads at peace? And what happens to people like Niall, who were removed from reality entirely? What happens to the people who remove other people from reality? Does someone like that even deserve peace?

It feels unlikely—impossible, even—to imagine I can simply drift into eternity without a fuss after everything that's happened. All the mistakes I've made.

Not to mention everything I've left unfinished. Montane is still imperiled, due in no small part to my meddling. And even on a smaller scale, I only just became reunited with my brother. I finally connected with Kennan. But I need to set things right with Ravod, who has been carefully avoiding me in the hours since I wrote in the *Book of Days*.

The *Book of Days* . . . My hand drifts to my bag, where the *Book* rests calmly—almost *too* calmly given the circumstances. I could easily open it and know my fate in detail. Surely facing whatever fate awaits me at High House would be easier if I know it for certain?

"Attention, everyone." Kennan's voice issues from a device above the door of the small cabin. "Is this . . . I can't hear anything. This is really speaking to the whole ship?" There's a muffled voice in the back, reminding her to speak into the machine. Kennan clears her throat and continues, "We are approaching High House. Know that I believe in each and every one of you. Now, get ready for a bumpy landing and a big fight for the soul of Montane."

Imogen came through for us. Freezing wind bites my face and sends my hair into a frenzy about my head as a huge ramp in the cargo hold is lowered midair. The airship jostles, making it difficult to maintain my footing, but I can see High House. And it's getting closer.

Cathal has marshaled every available person to defend the castle, it seems. There are tiny figures on the battlements below, readying war machines. Trebuchets and bows along the defensive line have already started firing at the airship.

"The airship won't hold up very long under an assault like this!" I call to Kennan over the wind. She's shoving large crates down the ramp to fall on our attackers below.

"It doesn't have to," she shouts back. "It just has to get us over the ramparts. If High House has any vulnerability, it's most likely being infiltrated from within."

The airship jostles again, nearly making me lose my footing. I cling to an exposed pipe in the wall to remain upright as the ground beneath me regains equilibrium. At the end of the open ramp, the training grounds outside the Bards' Wing of the castle are visible, almost close enough to reach.

As though she read my mind, Kennan hands me a length of rope and quickly anchors one end to the wall. Ravod and Fiona have joined us in the hold. Ravod meticulously refrains from making eye contact with me, but Fiona marches all the way up to Kennan and me, placing her hands on her hips.

"Let's go," she states.

My eyebrows nearly shoot off my head as my heart seizes in sudden worry. "Fiona? No. You can't."

"I'm coming along. I purposefully waited until now to say it, so you have no time to waste arguing with me." Her voice is resolute. I remember that same tone in her words the day she informed me she was coming with me to Gondal. Reluctantly, I must admit that she deserves to see this through as much as any of us.

I sigh. "Just promise that you'll be careful. I can't lose you."

"Never." She squeezes my forearm. It stings from the residual plague deep within, but I bite my tongue against the pain.

Kennan's concern is only barely concealed as

Fiona turns to her. Most of their conversation is silent as Kennan cups Fiona's face in her hands with a gentleness I've never seen her display. Likewise, I've never seen such naked adoration in Fiona's eyes before as she locks her gaze on Kennan. Kennan whispers something to Fiona. I can't hear what, but it makes her smile.

Normally, I might have found myself jealous of Fiona for managing to find love and romance when I can't, but it's difficult to manifest such pettiness when she's clearly the happiest I've ever seen her. I can't help feeling a small, warm glow at this unlikely thing happening to unlikely people at an unlikely time. It's fragile and beautiful, and well deserved, for both my friends.

I shuffle away as the moment between them grows intimate. I notice with a little amusement that Ravod is still leagues more awkward than I am. He stands off to the side, trying to pretend he's alone in the cargo hold. His face is the brightest red I've ever seen.

"I hope you'll excuse them for assaulting your delicate notions of propriety," I say, nudging him very softly with the tip of my elbow.

The jab was intended as playful, but Ravod keeps his gaze trained on the horizon. "I don't know what you're talking about."

"Then why are your cheeks so red?" I ask.

Ravod sniffs irritably and still refuses to look at me.

"It's the wind," he says.

Before I can reply, the ship shifts to hover as close to the ground as possible without landing.

"It's time." Kennan's voice makes me turn as she tugs the rope. "Be safe. All of you."

"You're not coming?" Ravod asks the question for us. Only Fiona doesn't seem surprised by the news.

"These soldiers need a commander. I've assumed that mantle, and it's my responsibility now. I may not get the glory of chopping the head off the snake, but I'll make sure the body is incapacitated. While you get to Cathal, I'll decimate his forces. We won't get another chance. Our victory today must be absolute," Kennan says with her signature calm self-assurance. "Go with the others. The aircraft will draw their fire and buy you time to get inside."

Kennan's resolute stare holds me in place a second longer. Her eyes are pale gold once more and burn with resolve, conveying something she can't with words alone.

The Protesters aboard the airship pour from the cargo hold ahead of us. I feel Kennan watching as we slide down the rope onto the sturdy ground below. Somehow, I still feel it when the airship pulls back.

Ravod, Fiona, and I watch as the airship's engine charges to a deafening roar. High House's forces have lobbed countless projectiles and flaming arrows at it, puncturing and battering the hull beyond repair. The assault continues as the airship builds speed, heading for the tightest cluster of enemy soldiers at the ramparts.

Right before the ship reaches its destination, a dark figure, the last passenger of the airship, leaps from the still open ramp onto the battlement. She lands nimbly, throwing small blades to clear the path in front of her of enemies. Seconds later, the airship crashes into the side of the castle, and chaos ensues.

"Let's go." I hear Ravod behind me, his voice quiet and distant, but still urgent. I tear my gaze from Kennan. Ravod has already turned his back and started for the entrance to the castle nearby.

The battle for High House has begun.

The castle interior is strangely quiet. Most of the fighting is taking place outside and the sounds of the skirmish are muted through the walls. They've replaced the sound of chanting that used to quietly echo through the halls, so faint it could be missed if you weren't paying attention.

Aside from the odd servant rushing to evacuate, or a patrol of guards heading to back up the forces outside, we hardly pass anyone. Like during the crisis at Axis Keep, they are too preoccupied with their own problems to notice us. My heart beats faster and my skin feels like a cold shell. I slip back into the same innate condition that I had that night—survival.

Or maybe it's the Blot sending that freezing burn through me. As I suspected, it's stronger here.

Resisting it with a Telling is more difficult the deeper we travel into the bowels of High House.

I can't help also remembering the last time I snuck through these halls warding off this plague. Mads was with me. The absence of his steadying presence feels physically painful. It joins the current of chaotic emotions and sensations swirling through me, and my heart feels too tight in my chest. I take a few deep breaths to calm myself.

"Where are we going? And how do you know we're going the right way?" Fiona whispers to us.

For the first time that day, Ravod meets my gaze and shares a knowing look. The castle itself possesses a strange power, exerts a will of its own, that brings people to their destination. With the *Book of Days* at my side, I can feel the intricate connection these powers share. The *Book* and the castle are two parts of a whole, working in tandem. Ravod's eyes soften, as though he's thinking the same thing. Then he abruptly seems to remember he's still angry with me and shuts down, diverting his gaze.

"There's an old rumor that the castle will lead certain people where they need to go," I finally reply to Fiona, but I'm watching Ravod as I speak. He was the one who first said that to me.

Fiona's eyes widen a little, and she shakes her head incredulously, but she doesn't argue.

"I never thought I'd set foot here," she murmurs. "It's nothing like I imagined."

"This isn't exactly a normal day—" I cut myself

off to prevent a cough that threatens to surface from speaking.

"True," Fiona replies. "But the stories we heard in Aster made it seem like it was a bright, sacred, beautiful place . . . it's still majestic, but it's so much colder and darker."

She tilts her head, taking in the high vaulted ceiling lost in darkness above. Next her eyes flick to the rows of austere marble statues, each in its own darkened alcove, that line the floor of the same material. The shadows are deep and lengthy around us, and the faint light causes them to stretch unnaturally. She's not wrong. I thought something similar when I first arrived. Like the whole place was set up to trick me. To make me question myself and everything I know.

In a way, it was.

My reverie is abruptly cut short as we turn a corner and a slim figure barrels headfirst into Ravod, causing both to stumble.

In the dim, flickering light, I catch sight of a mass of wild, dark curls. Imogen's unruly hair has finally broken free of the cord she used to tie it back at the nape of her neck. She looks even younger with her hair flying about her face. She squints at us before recognizing me, and a broad grin splits her face, revealing the familiar gap between her two front teeth.

"Shae!"

I'm nearly knocked off my feet as she launches

herself at me. The sickness within my body painfully protests the contact, but the fullness of my heart simply doesn't care. This girl is responsible for making our return possible, at great personal risk to herself. Not even the Blot could bring me to deny her a hug.

"It's good to see you, too, Imogen." I half smile, half wince.

"I've been worried sick about you!" She finally draws back, looking me over. Then her eyes drift to Ravod and Fiona. "Where's Mads? Is he here? Is he okay?" The silence that falls answers her question. An icy lump threatens to choke me as I slowly shake my head. Imogen's large, brown eyes glisten. She sets her jaw. "And you? Are you hurt?"

"Not hurt. But I'm running out of time. I need to reach Cathal. Do you know where to find him?"

"I overheard some of the Bards say he's gone with a few guards to someplace called a 'sanctum.' But I've lived here my whole life and never seen or heard of such a room before," Imogen says.

"I know where that is," Ravod says. "I can get us there."

"Is there somewhere safe you can go until the fighting stops?" I turn back to Imogen.

"I'm not hiding anywhere." The girl seems insulted I would even suggest such a thing. "There are still servants throughout the castle that need help escaping. I'm getting them out before they can get hurt. Then I'm going back for the agitators."

"Agitators?" I ask in unison with Ravod and Fiona.

"Lord Cathal's been . . ." Imogen grimaces. "He's not been himself. A lot of people have been saying—very, *very* quietly—that's he's become unhinged. Paranoid. The Bards have been going out to make sweeps across the entire country. He's been looking for you, Shae. He's obsessed."

"I don't think it's me he's looking for, not truly." My hand drops to my bag. "It's the *Book of Days* he wants."

"Whatever the reason, he's been apprehending a lot of innocent people and accusing them of harboring or working with you," Imogen explains.

"The agitators." It makes sense now. I highly doubt I've ever even met any of these poor people.

Imogen nods sagely. "He's been spreading lies about you, that you misused the power of the Telling to turn people against High House."

"I don't require anything as complicated as a Telling to turn people against High House," I say, unable to help a rueful laugh. "All it takes is the truth."

"These agitators might be willing to throw their lot in with us if we ask," Ravod states. "Having a few helping hands inside the castle, either fighting or sabotaging the Bards, would be incredibly useful."

"I thought the same thing," Imogen says. "And I'm sure they wouldn't mind some payback."

"Do it," I say. "But make sure anyone who can't or is unwilling to fight makes it to safety."

"You got it!" Imogen grins. "I've never been in

charge of stuff before today. It's no wonder people enjoy it so much."

"Please be careful, Imogen," I remind her.

"I promise I won't go mad with power." She holds up a hand and crosses her heart with charming sincerity. "You should hurry. Finish this. For Mads. For all of us."

I hug Imogen one more time. Without another word, she dashes off into the darkness at the far end of the hall.

"We should keep moving," Fiona says, placing a gentle hand on my arm.

"This way," Ravod says, ushering us on.

We follow him down a series of increasingly intricate dark corridors. Through a secret passage behind the false back of a large fresco. Down past the tunnels behind the waterfall. Back into a secluded, long-abandoned courtyard. Down another hallway.

There are no torches or daylight this deep in the mountain. Ravod whispers a Telling that makes the stones glow faintly as though there were a torch following us overhead. Functional, but it does little to raise anyone's spirits. The task ahead bears down heavily upon us, even more so than the darkness.

Each winding pathway raises the tension in the air. Every step makes the Blot more painful, the warding less useful. I sense a mounting dread from the *Book of Days* at my side that mirrors the blank resolve on the faces of my friends.

At last we reach a flight of tall stone stairs leading

to a double door at the end of what feels like the longest, darkest corridor.

Cathal's sanctum.

My voice trembles as I ward the Blot away one more time. The weakness in my body, like I'm one hundred years old rather than seventeen, informs me that the cause is very close.

Beyond that, nothing is certain.

"How kind of you to offer your unconditional surrender in person, Shae."

Cathal stands at a dais atop a steep flight of stairs at the back of what must be the largest room in High House, and by High House standards that's saying something. Hollowed under the mountain is a vast chamber, almost the size of the Refugee Cavern under Tybera. This one, however, is marble and hewed by unparalleled workmanship.

It's not just any room, either. It's an ancient, massive complex of a library. The books here are too numerous to be read in one lifetime. At a glance, I see categories covering mathematics, science, engineering, philosophy, astronomy, history, and beyond into subjects I've never heard of. Knowledge that could not only uplift Montane, but maybe even push it ahead of Gondal by decades. It figures that all this time Cathal was hoarding a colossal repository of hidden knowledge.

The tall, amber-colored windows carved into the mountainside mimic stained glass, figures in different shades of gold depicting a story lost to our people. I can't help noticing that one bears a striking resemblance to the Gondalese war goddess, Ekko. She

346 — DYLAN FARROW

stands beside one figure in a version of a Bard's robe, and another I don't recognize: The three place their hand upon the open pages of a book. The light that window casts creates a pale halo outlining Cathal's otherwise dark frame as he watches us enter.

I dreaded seeing him for so long. Now I know why. Half of me still can't fully believe that he betrayed and hurt me so profoundly. It still remembers him as someone kind and caring. My mentor. The other half just writhes in pain while the wound he left is torn open, fresh as the day he inflicted it.

I have no idea how to convince this man, or trick him, into destroying the *Book of Days*. But I must. Somehow. And I won't leave until I do.

He gestures casually to the Bards standing alert by the door we had burst through. They stand down reluctantly, allowing me, Fiona, and Ravod to pass into the chamber and to the foot of the steps leading to Cathal's pedestal. Another gesture sends them away completely, probably to help their brethren in the battle outside. Cathal seems confident he can handle three wayward youths, only one of whom is a fully trained Bard.

"We're not here to surrender," I state, planting my feet on the elaborate marble floor as though my willpower alone will make me unmovable. I can't see Cathal's face very well in the light, but he cocks his head slightly in what seems to be amusement. "We're here to hold you accountable. It's time you faced justice for your crimes."

"My crimes? And what might those be?"

There is no hint of irony in his measured voice. Chills creep up my spine alongside the realization that he really, truly believes his innocence. That the resistance to his regime was born of outside malice rather than a reaction to his corruption. From the top of his dais, he sees invaders and terrorists, threatening the order he so carefully constructed. We are the villains in his story, however warped that is.

I square my shoulders and resist reacting to the pain that shoots through the muscles fighting to keep me upright. The warding is wearing off. Another one might not even be effective this close to Cathal, the source of the Telling that is this sickness.

I take a deep, equally painful breath. "Your subjugation of Montane. Your pillaging of our resources. Our sanity. Our dignity. Our reality. And not least of all, our right to an education. To learn, and grow, and thrive. Instead, our land is dying and our people with it. We strive only to see the fruits of our efforts, quite literally, taken away, so you and your Bards can continue to live here in opulence. It needs to stop. It must. If you don't, there won't be anything left of Montane to protect."

The sheer effort of speaking drains my stamina to the point where I collapse to my knees on the last syllable. My hands are deep, inky blue and shake where they rest on my thighs. Dark veins wrap around my arms, as familiar as they are terrifying.

Maybe I wasted my effort saying what I did. But I had to say it.

The Lord of High House sneers. "Are we assigning blame? Because from where I stand, you and your pathetic revolutionaries are guilty of quite the number of atrocities. Your violent jailbreak from this very castle? Your subsequent evasion of justice? Assaulting the Bards who I sent to bring you back? Inciting sedition? Acts of terrorism? Your theft of the *Book of Days* pales by comparison, do you not agree? You claim to want to protect Montane, yet you are the one who is actively seeking to destroy it."

I hear the tap of Cathal's boots on the steps as he descends toward us. My vision has started to blur intermittently, and it takes a few breaths after he stops on the last step for his feet to come into focus.

I force myself to look up at his face, even as I feel my muscles scream in protest, my bones aching with the effort.

In many ways, he looks much as I remember. But his eyes are different. Bloodshot from lack of sleep. The set of his jaw is so tight I think his face might shatter. For a long moment we simply stare at each other.

"Spare me the theatrics. I know why you are here." A thin smile spreads across Cathal's face, too wide to look completely natural. His eyes flick to the bag at my hip. "Why you are really here."

"And why is that?" My voice grates out of my throat as though I were breathing fire.

A low humorless chuckle escapes him. He regards me the way a disturbed child who just pulled the wings off a fly might.

"You wish me to destroy the *Book of Days*." There's a glint in his eyes as he watches me try to stifle my surprise. He continues, "You have it here with you. Surely by now your feeble intellect has cobbled together the truth of the nature of my bond to it. I can sense it in that bag you are carrying. It is mine, after all."

"It's not yours," I reply. "This power was only ever on loan. It belongs to no one."

"That logic is precisely why I'm the one who controls the *Book* and its power and not you." He rolls his eyes. There's a tremble in the ground. In the air. For the briefest of seconds, his legendary discipline has slipped. He recovers it quickly. "If you truly understood it, you would have used it as it was meant to be used. You might have written yourself into my position. Or sent me to the bottom of the ocean with a pen stroke. Or perhaps"—he pauses to sneer—"you might have stayed true to form and simply done to me what you did to Niall."

I grit my teeth. He's baiting me. "Maybe the difference is that I'm not obsessed with power and domination like you."

"Someone must be, or there would be no society," Cathal states. "I tried to explain this to your mother, you know, when she mounted her little insurrection and demanded I destroy the *Book*, just as you are now. I will say to you what I said to her: *It won't happen.*"

There's another tremor in the otherwise still air between us. For the first time, I catch a faint glimpse of Cathal's true power—the power he carefully controls when he speaks, because when he doesn't, it splits the seams of reality. It tugs at the *Book of Days,* and I sense a quaking, primal fearfulness in the *Book*'s response. A sense of what is happening having happened before.

"Give me the *Book,* Shae. Everything can go back to normal. I will see to it that your friends will be treated fairly as prisoners of war. That your own fate will be met swiftly and painlessly. You have my word." Cathal extends a hand, expectantly.

My gaze travels from his hand to his eyes. I am well versed in the worth of his word.

"Never."

The growl in his throat is impatient, betraying his seldom-seen building fury. We might not last long if he brings the full might of it to bear. I need to find a way to end this, and fast.

Before I can think or move, Cathal advances on me. My body is too sluggish to react.

He's cut short as a pale, willowy figure steps confidently in front of him. Fiona swipes at his face, and the light catches on something silver gripped in her fingers. The teeth of a little silver comb. When it comes away, a few drops of blood adorn the sharp tips.

"You should take the hint," she says. "Montane is done with you."

Cathal staggers back, clutching the gash on his face. When he manages to compose himself, his stare is disbelieving, as if he is noticing Fiona's presence for the first time. He says nothing, backhanding her and sending her reeling to the floor alongside me. Even as I feel the sting of the strike in my heart, Fiona just glares at him with steadfast conviction.

"History does love to repeat itself," Cathal muses, almost to himself. "I've seen it countless times in the *Book of Days*. And I live to see part two of the time Iris confronted me alongside Martin and Victor." He nods at me, Fiona, and Ravod in turn as he recites their names. "Are you going to do as they did? Scurry away with the *Book* while you can still hide it from me until the next round of would-be rebels try again?"

"You can end the cycle here, Cathal." My voice is tight as I resist the urge to cough.

"I most certainly will," Cathal hisses. "I took a great deal of satisfaction in ending Victor's miserable existence once you were kind enough to flush him out of hiding for me. I suppose I owe you some small measure of gratitude for allowing me to wipe out the last remnant of your mother's resistance. Today, I will finally purge yours and bring peace back to Montane."

"You are insane," I say. I struggle, trying to stand, and fail so that I only stare at him.

There was a time when I believed he would bring peace to Montane. That he could. But now . . . Seeing him hunched over the stain of his blood on his palm, eyes flashing like those of the feral creatures of the wasteland, I see something entirely different. A soulless husk of a man who exchanged his humanity for power. Such a person is more dangerous than any cornered animal.

"And you . . ." he begins. The warped smile returns to twist Cathal's features. "You've become somewhat less of a blunt instrument during your little adventures, haven't you? Very clever to employ a servant in your scheme to lower my defensive measures around the castle. Placing knowledge just outside my reach. Just as Iris did when she concealed the *Book* from me. I knew only what you told your little friend, but not what she planned. I did not think you capable of such subtlety. But the fact remains. Iris tried to stand against me." Cathal straightens somewhat, and the cold fire in his eyes blazes with greater intensity. "And she *failed*. So will you."

"No, she didn't." The tremor in my voice comes from anger now, not weakness. It gives me enough strength to push myself to my feet. "She didn't fail, because I'm Iris's daughter and I'm going to finish what she started. And Victor wasn't the last remnant, either. A fighting force of fed-up Montanians—sorry, *agitators*—were just freed from your jails. They will continue the fight, too. You can never stop all of us. That's one power you don't have and can't give yourself."

Cathal's eyes lethally focus on me as I speak, while Ravod skirts the distance around us, coming up from behind him. I keep talking long enough so that by the final syllable, he is poised to incapacitate Cathal.

"You always were the clever one, Ravod," Cathal sneers, catching Ravod's arm. He pulls Ravod's body over his shoulder like it was made of paper. A faintly audible Telling forces Ravod to the ground on his back with an agonizing slam.

"Ravod!" The scream tears through my raw throat carelessly and I stumble in their direction but fold into myself as an uncontrollable cough wracks me. Fiona is at swiftly my side, drawing my arm over her shoulder, keeping me mostly upright.

I can't summon the strength to ward off the Blot anymore. Even if I could, I feel in my aching bones that it would be weak and wouldn't last. Fiona's worried gaze flicks between me and Ravod, prone on the floor in front of Cathal, unable to determine which of us is in more immediate danger.

"We've got to wait for an opening," I whisper, my voice so hoarse I'm not sure Fiona can even hear me. "If we don't play this smart, he'll kill us all."

"And sneaking up on him obviously won't work," Fiona replies in the same hushed tone while Cathal remains intent on Ravod. "If only we could turn his advantages against him."

I turn to Cathal, biting hard on my tongue. Waiting for my opportunity. I just hope it arrives before I succumb to the sickness ravaging me.

"I remember teaching you that little maneuver." The coldness in Cathal's voice seems at odds with what he's saying—a disparity that I now realize exists in the opposite direction. He can also appear warm without feeling anything whatsoever. He looms over his victim, a saber that was not in his hand previously touching the side of Ravod's neck. "I never quite understood what caused you to break from the fold. Shae I always had a feeling about, with her history and all. And despite her prowess, Kennan was always a little unstable. But you? I was prepared to offer you a place as my right hand, Ravod."

"He's lying." My words grate out, just loud enough for them to hear. Only Ravod looks in my direction. "You *know* he's lying."

"Am I?" Cathal steps back. Suddenly the saber that was in his hand is nowhere to be seen, as though it was never there to begin with. "And how many times has Shae withheld the truth from you? About her motives, her plans? Did she ever disclose how she escaped justice when she followed you?"

The fever in my body suddenly goes to war with the pit of ice that manifests in my gut at his words. He doesn't know what happened to Niall. I never talked to Ravod about it. I should have, but . . .

"Ravod, I can explain . . ."

"She used a scrap you left of the *Book* to write Niall out of existence," Cathal finishes. There's no hint of triumph in his voice, only cold facts that speak for themselves. He follows it with a meaningful look at Ravod. "Quite a fate, wouldn't you agree?"

"How . . ." I scramble to collect my thoughts. "How do you know that?"

My question catches Cathal's attention, and he looks from Ravod to me with a glint in his eyes that enrages and terrifies me.

"I am the First Writer of Montane. I'm inextricably linked to the *Book of Days*. What it knows, I know," Cathal states. "I knew what you did even as you did it."

"I was fighting for my life." It's a weak justification, but the only one I have.

"And by your logic, who are you to decide who lives or not? Who exactly is allowed to alter reality, according to you?" Cathal asks, tipping his head in mock curiosity. "You say I'm a liar, but we all know you're not above a little hypocrisy."

His voice sounds different when he's speaking without the usual filter of his control. He sounds . . . human. And for once, Cathal isn't lying, not completely, and it's like a razor slicing into me. It takes all my willpower to look Ravod in the eyes. There's conflict in his gaze. He shouldn't have found out like this. I should have told him everything when I had the chance to.

356 — DYLAN FARROW

"I know I have a lot to be sorry for and . . . I *am* sorry, Ravod," I manage. It's pathetic, but mercifully, Ravod doesn't look away.

"It's a bit late for that, Shae." Cathal clicks his tongue. "But you, Ravod, I'm willing to hear you out. We're reasonable men, after all."

Momentarily, I'm back in General Ravod's office, my heart in my throat, as Ravod is made a similar and equally compelling offer to toss me aside. I can only watch, mute and numb, as he gets to his feet, wondering if history is about to repeat itself. The deeper cutting question I try to ignore is if I even *deserve* Ravod's loyalty.

"Shae has the decency to feel guilt and seek forgiveness when she does something objectionable," Ravod says. "She's not perfect. She'd probably be the first to say so. But you set the bar pretty low. Shae might be many things, but at least she's not a pompous megalomaniac."

Without another word, Ravod lunges at Cathal. This time a sword is in *his* hand. Cathal barely has time to register the insult or the attack. Within seconds, the sounds of exchanged blows are reverberating through the otherwise still air of the sanctum.

It feels like crude nails are being driven into my skull with a cruder hammer. I nearly pass out but Fiona catches me, breaking my fall and helping me down to the ground gently. The Blot is claiming me. I don't have much longer to live. It breaks my heart, but the possibility of respite from this pain feels like a blessing.

"Hang on, Shae . . ." Fiona's voice breaks. Tears are streaming down her face as she grips my hand between hers.

Even if I knew what to say, I can't find the strength to respond. My head flops feebly to one side. The figures of Cathal and Ravod, locked in combat, slowly come into focus. Rage at my incompetence grips me. I can't help Ravod—I can't even help myself. I feel like a fool for thinking I could help Montane.

Cathal has a clear advantage. Ravod's skill and power are impressive, but Cathal wields the Telling with complete effortlessness. The kind of ability that only comes from being the most powerful Bard in Montane, chosen to inscribe the *Book of Days* itself and become forever linked to that wellspring of cosmic power. His lips don't even move; he doesn't need to speak his Tellings, he can simply think them.

Step by step, Ravod is driven back. Against the barrage of Cathal's coordinated Tellings and skilled physical tactics, Ravod struggles to maintain the blade in his hand while defending himself. Cathal pushes the fight further in his favor, summoning orbs of flame to strike his opponent. Ravod is only barely able to repel them.

With effort, I look up at Fiona. I immediately wish I hadn't. The look on her face isn't one I'd ever want to see, especially not from one of the most important people in my life. She stares at the fight unblinking. Her green eyes are glossed over with unshed tears that reflect Cathal's fire Telling but none of the light from within her.

She's lost hope. That single thought is more painful than the combined efforts of the plague ravaging me.

"Save your strength," she whispers to me, and I can feel as deeply as the rot in my bones that she's putting on a brave front. She gathers me in her arms, letting my head rest on her lap as she holds me.

If I must die, at least it will be in the arms of my dearest friend. This is the sort of thing one wishes for in forging such friendships—someone to be by your side through thick and thin to the bitter end. In a world that was so needlessly damaged and cruel, I was blessed with a friend like Fiona.

But this isn't how it was supposed to end.

The *Book of Days* is warm beneath the palm of my hand, resting in the bag at my side. Its gentle reminder that I tried my best seems more like a rebuke. But that, I know, is just my anger speaking.

Ravod cries out as he's knocked back. His focus and energy depleted, he grips his bicep, where the fire has disarmed and scorched him. For a split second, his eyes meet mine and I almost expect them to be blazing with the same fury that's kindling within me. Instead, I'm met with a gaze that looks defeated and apologetic. A look that conveys nothing but sorrow that he's reached his limit and can't do more.

Cathal stands over him triumphantly. A renewed orb of fire hovers between Cathal's hands, larger than the previous ones. I can almost feel Cathal's arrogance and malice pouring into it. It's an attack he's not intending his victim to survive. He even casts me a look, making sure I'm watching, that I know how completely I have been conquered.

If only we could turn his advantages against him.

I came to this place with a purpose. I promised I would not leave until it was achieved. That has not—*cannot*—change.

"You're right." In my semi-delirious fever state, I momentarily think Fiona is repeating herself aloud. I realize she hasn't when she looks at me, confused.

"Shae?"

I grit my teeth in advance against the onslaught of agony that breaks over me like a wave when I push myself off her lap. I still can't stand . . . but I don't have to.

Time feels slower in the urgency of the moment. Like when Mads disappeared into the hangar. Perhaps he's with me now. Guiding my hand into the bag at my hip. I close my fingers around the soft leather cover of the *Book of Days*, pulling it forth.

As Cathal launches his final attack at Ravod, I summon the very final fragment of bodily strength I possess. This might be the last thing I ever do, but it *must* be done. I hurl the *Book of Days* away from my body and into the fire.

"No!" Cathal cries, eyes widening in realization as the *Book* connects with his Telling. The final will of the *Book* is exerted, and it ignites immediately, faster than normal, crumbling into ash. The embers float very slowly to the cold floor and extinguish.

And like that, the *Book of Days* is gone.

"What have you done?" Cathal's hiss breaks the silence. He rounds on me, eyes feral. He is about to step closer but stops.

Before I can question his hesitation, I feel it, too. A tug. From somewhere inside me. It happens again, stronger this time. There's a strange, shifting sensation in the fabric of reality. It almost feels like the world is about to crumble. It builds . . .

. . . and then flickers. The phenomenon lasts only a second or two. All it leaves behind is a residue of understanding that reality is irrevocably changed, for the last time.

I can't see properly. My head is swimming, shifting my surroundings in and out of focus, like the feeling that comes right before vomiting. I can feel the sickness moving, but instead of burrowing deeper into my body it's shifted course.

Then, like the detonation from the hangar at Axis Keep, it explodes from me. From the pores of my skin, the corners of my eyes, my nose, and up through my throat. Waves of dark indigo surround me.

The Blot is quite literally pulled from my body . . . and into Cathal's. The dark blue wave pushes itself into him in one painful, instantaneous burst before it subsides.

Cathal and I stare at each other. The veins beneath his skin are a shade too dark; the white parts of his eyes are tinged blue. He hunches over, unable to maintain his usual flawless posture. But he is staring at me with a look I've never seen on his face. Disbelief.

He opens his mouth, possibly to speak. But he never gets the chance.

The windows darken, then shatter. The doors burst open. A swarm of ink, pulled from every corner of Montane, from every victim it was ravaging, has been diverted to its creator, all plunging into Cathal. The mass of shifting, aberrant disease forms an inky barrier around him until it is fully absorbed.

All that is left when the storm subsides is a plague-infested shell of a man. The sickness has eaten through him completely, exposing crumbling indigo bones beneath rotted flesh stained the same color.

His body jerks and twists. Then it falls to the floor.

I get to my feet. I'm dazed, but my body, purged of its affliction, feels stronger than ever.

Fiona rushes to stand and places a hand on my shoulder as she looks me over. I can't find the words to speak my gratitude, so I place my hand over hers. She knows what it means. Ravod stumbles to my side, slightly out of breath. Relief courses through me, a familiar warmth kindling a glow of elation, seeing that he's all right.

"Are you . . ." His voice is soft. "Are you okay?"

I nod. "You?"

Ravod nods and takes a deep breath. He's about to say something when movement at the doorway catches our attention.

A group of shell-shocked, incredulous Bards are gathered there. The commotion caused by the Blot descending on this part of the castle must have summoned them. I don't need to ask, it's obvious from the looks on their faces—they saw everything.

"Don't just stand there," I order. "Go to the courtyard. Stop the fighting."

I feel foolish issuing commands to the Bards, but to my surprise they rush to comply.

"We should go, too," Fiona says. A smile appears on her face. "Kennan will have lots to say about this, I think."

I can't decide whether to finally breathe a sigh of relief or to return her smile. My response is an odd mix of both.

The three of us head to the door, where we're greeted by the sound of running footsteps. Imogen skids into view. There's a smudge of dirt across her cheek, a small gash on her forearm, and her uniform is torn and disheveled, but she looks otherwise unhurt.

"Shae! You have to come quick!" she exclaims.

"Slow down, Imogen." I try to steady her, placing my hands on her shoulders, but it seems to have little effect. "What is it?"

"Ships!" Imogen squeaks. "Huge ships! Like the one you brought! Only there's hundreds! In the sky! *And they're heading straight for us!*"

The training grounds are quieter than when we left them, but nearly unrecognizable. The airship that crashed into the side of the castle left deep, jagged tracks in its wake. Fiery debris from projectiles and rubble alike litters the ground, and although the smoke is lifting, the air is still thick with ash and embers.

There are bodies everywhere. Many—*too many*—are lifeless.

But my message was received. The fighting has come to an end. Some of Cathal's forces are fleeing the castle. Others remain and join the surviving Protesters in searching for and tending to the wounded.

High House is surrounded by more than a dozen hovering airships in the darkening sky overhead. They are nothing like the commercial crafts we saw hovering over the city—these are black, armed, and armored. The Gondalese flag is proudly emblazoned on their sides. They are instruments of war. Some are lighting the ground with bright spotlights, much like in the city. But this time they illuminate the destruction of High House, bringing it—and the contrast between the two nations—into stark focus. Farther back, I see the silhouettes of smaller crafts surveying the area.

They are not making a move—for now.

A tall figure strides toward us through the wreckage. It takes a second for Kennan's identity to fully register. Fiona recognizes her immediately and the two rush toward each other as though pulled along an invisible tether.

"You seem no worse for wear," I point out, concealing my complete and utter relief. I know how Kennan reacts to sentimentality.

"I'm a little insulted you'd believe otherwise," she replies, halfway into Fiona's hair as the pair embrace. "The *Book*. Is it gone?"

"It's gone. Cathal, too."

"So that only leaves our uninvited guests." Kennan's yellow eyes flick upward to the airships. A worried silence falls over us.

When I glance over, Ravod is giving me a strange look. His normally neat hair is disheveled, and silken black strands fly haphazardly across his forehead in the gathering wind. The bout with Cathal did no favors to the state of his clothes, which are torn and burnt in places. There's a small cut on his cheek. Yet somehow, he is still difficult to look away from.

He seems like he's about to say something, but a blast of noise cuts him short. One of the Gondalese airships has descended gracefully to the ground and the roar of the engine is amplified by the surrounding mountains.

A ramp descends from the bottom of the airship in a cloud of silver steam. When it lifts, a group of five soldiers appears and heads to ground level. Behind them walks a shorter but commanding and instantly familiar presence.

General Ravod comes to a halt with her hands folded behind her back. No one seems brave enough to approach her. She silently surveys the carnage through her one sharp, dark eye with little surprise and a hint of familiarity. But it isn't what she's looking for, not really. Her inspection comes to an end as Ravod, Kennan, Fiona, and I approach her.

"One of you led this assault?" she asks without preamble and all her usual pragmatism.

Kennan steps forward without hesitation. "I did."

The general gives Kennan a quick once-over. "I've been briefed on you. A radical insurgent who goes by 'Kennan,' correct?"

"That's correct," Kennan replies. "And as you can see, this is a Montanian matter, and one I have in hand. You and your forces may return to Gondal."

For once, the general seems surprised . . . and also slightly amused. She looks Kennan over again, as though reassessing her.

"Is that so?"

"There is nothing for you here. Montane is a wasteland. The *Book of Days* and Cathal are gone. Does Gondal really want to shoulder the burden, and the expense, of taking on Montane's problems? I've seen how your country treats my people. If you can't be bothered to take care of them on your land, what makes you think you should take care of them on ours?" Kennan says.

The general's face is tight, but it almost looks like she's trying very hard not to smile. "You're quite the arrogant one, aren't you?" she says. "With the *Book of Days* gone, as you say, how do you really intend to stop us from taking the situation over? We are better armed. Better equipped. Better organized. What will you and your little band of teenage rebels accomplish that the Gondalese military can't?"

"Is that a threat?" Kennan's fingers tense at her sides.

I step forward and clear my throat loudly, which brings the full weight of Kennan and the general's attention to bear on me. "I believe we can reach an agreement here," I say.

"Is that so?" The general cocks her head slightly. "I'm curious why I shouldn't place you back under arrest."

"Because this isn't Gondal and you have no authority here," Kennan says. "I want to hear what Shae has to say."

I indicate my gratitude to Kennan with a small nod before speaking. "The *Book of Days* is gone, but in its place, we have access to a secret repository of knowledge that Cathal kept hidden. We're willing to share this with Gondal, amicably, if you agree to leave us in peace."

"This outcome benefits both Gondal and Montane

without the threat of further hostility." Ravod finally speaks up. "You must admit it's the most practical solution."

"An interesting proposition," the general admits, pausing thoughtfully. Her sharp eye holds my gaze before turning to Ravod. "You realize there's nothing stopping me from taking this information by force?"

"You'd be starting a war," Ravod points out. "And war is expensive. Montane may not be as technologically advanced, but you've seen for yourself they are resourceful and, above all, tenacious. They will not submit without a fight. Those resources could be better spent directly for the benefit of Gondal."

General Ravod crosses her arms over her chest, her expression impossible to read. "I will be launching a full investigation into this, and shall discuss it with the powers that be," she says after a long silence. "I make no promises that I won't return if they see the benefit lies strictly in our favor. If not, you may expect to be contacted by our diplomats."

"I suppose that's fair enough," I reply. "I hope you will encourage them to see the benefits of a peaceful solution."

"I will do what's best for Gondal," she replies. "But I will take your position into consideration."

With that she turns to Kennan, extending one hand halfway between them. Kennan grips it firmly in hers and they shake briefly.

"I'm interested in seeing what you do, Kennan," the general says with a curt nod. Then she turns and heads back up the airship ramp, not breaking her stride as she speaks over her shoulder. "And I will be expecting you for tea in the near future, Erik."

"Yes, Grandmother," Ravod says. A small smile plays at the corner of his mouth.

The others disperse as the airship roars to life and lifts back up into the sky to join the others. Within moments, they are retreating into the distance as nightfall shrouds the sky.

A blanket of stars and silence folds around High House. No one is thinking of victory, just tending to the wounded and restoring order. It's a quiet, somber atmosphere that settles over the castle. Less like a celebration and more like a memorial for the cost we paid to get here. A greater number of lives were sacrificed for this change, more than the ones that took place this day. We owe it to them to make sure it was worth it.

Even so, there's a tangible, almost electric current beneath the surface. Something more powerful than a Telling, as though a breath of renewed life has crept in through the cracks of the wreckage. I dare to wonder, to believe, that it's the first fragile, embryonic stage of hope.

My fingers brush the locket hanging from my neck. Suddenly I realize what Ma meant about being at peace. I open the little pendant, and her smile from the picture inside puts something inside me to rest, also.

I'm proud of you, Shae, she seems to say.
"Thanks, Ma," I whisper back.

It feels like I'm standing on the balcony of a different High House. As early morning sunshine washes over the castle grounds, it's hard to believe I once felt such fear and insecurity within these walls. Seeing the remaining Bards join forces with the Protesters to rebuild has breathed new life into the place.

Sleep has been in short supply this past fortnight. This time, it's not because of nightmares or guilt or grief. There's simply so much to do. There are recovering wounded to tend to, rubble to clear, enemies to root out, and word to be taken to the villages. Slowly but surely, it's getting done.

From my vantage point, I can see as far as the wasteland beyond the foot of the mountains. Small, scattered patches of green emerge in parts of the expanse. Very small and trepidatious, like the rest of us. Three days ago, there was a small thunderstorm. The first real rain in Montane to take place in . . . I'm not even sure how long.

If I had to guess, I'd say that the destruction of the *Book of Days* resulted in only reversing Cathal's changes. The castle is a building that doesn't play tricks on its inhabitants. The weather has been unpredictable. New life is emerging from the desolation. The Indigo Death is extinct, never to return.

His control has been well and truly severed. I will probably spend the rest of my life wondering if the *Book* did that intentionally, its final act of service to the land it was bound to for so long. Or even just to spite Cathal.

The Telling is gone. Or, more accurately, changed. Many Bards, myself included, have noticed with a little experimentation that, since the battle, no new Tellings have been possible, though old ones may be undone. Many are unsure how they feel about it. I never wanted it, never grew dependent on it. For me, it's a relief.

The only thing I've truly realized is that some answers will never be known to me. I must accept that, however grudgingly.

It only takes an instant to change everything. The past two weeks have been full of instants. I take a deep, cold breath of fresh mountain air and bring myself back from the view to examine the small silver comb in my hand.

Fiona set out to return to Aster yesterday. I'm not sure when I'll see her again, although we promised each other that it will be soon. Her absence dimmed the light here a little. But she'll keep her word and eventually return; I'm not the only one at High House she's invested in. Kennan was most displeased to see her go but grumbled her understanding. She was forced to admit Aster was uniquely fortunate in that regard, that it had Fiona to help guide it forward.

Even without Fiona, Kennan has had her hands full. Predictably, she took charge of every effort she could get her hands on. Also, predictably, each project she touched has been wildly successful and morale grows exponentially by the day. I'm not sure if she's aware of the rumors, perhaps Kennan started them herself, but there's a growing faction of her supporters who wish to see her install her own government. Everyone here accepts her command readily and without question.

Everyone except the Bards. For some reason I've noticed they insist on deferring to me. They're calling me the First Writer. I hate it. I've said numerous times that it's a terrible idea, which amuses Kennan endlessly. I've had no choice but to follow her example as a leader and try to send them where I think they'll do the most good. Most are dispatched to the villages to provide aid. Others have been sent with the Protesters to Gondal where they will help any refugees who wish to return to Montane.

I'll see Kieran again soon. The thought brings a smile to my face.

My reverie is interrupted by a knock on the door. I turn to see it open, revealing Ravod in the doorway.

"Is this a bad time?" he asks.

I shake my head, unable to prevent my smile from spreading somewhat. It even reaches Ravod. There's no Telling anymore but seeing that expression on his face makes the air warmer, somehow.

Ravod shifts his weight, but true to form he

doesn't move closer. "I couldn't find you in your quarters. Kennan said you fell asleep here after conferring with her last night."

"The sofa in here is dangerously comfortable," I say with a nod to the piece of furniture I succumbed on a few hours ago. I'd awoken with a light blanket draped around me, but I know better than to outright accuse Kennan of such a thing. "You know, Ravod, this isn't technically my bedroom, and these aren't technically my nightclothes. You can come in without feeling like it's improper."

The tips of his ears redden and his smile turns sheepish as he steps into the room.

"As you command, First Writer."

"Please never call me that."

He chuckles, crossing the room. His gaze momentarily strays from mine to the embroidery project I started earlier. I almost rush to cover it—force of habit—as he slows his pace, tilting his head with a small, appreciative smile.

"It's quite lovely," he says, coming to a halt not far in front of me as I step into the room from the balcony.

"I missed sewing. It's nice to have a normal hobby again." I try to shrug as casually as possible, hoping to quell the heat rising in my cheeks, but I only manage to jerk my shoulders awkwardly.

"Normal will be a pleasant change, I think," he says. Then he sobers, his smile becoming a small, tight grimace. It suddenly seems harder for him to look me in the eye. "I, ah . . ." He takes a breath before making eye contact again. "Actually, I wanted to find you because . . . Well. Before I leave. To say goodbye."

It feels like a heavy boulder is sinking inside me as he says that. I only barely conceal it.

"You're returning to Gondal?" It's less a question and more of a realization. One more painful than I imagined it would be, if I'd imagined it was going to happen at all.

Ravod takes a deep breath and nods solemnly. "I've given it a lot of thought. I didn't decide this lightly."

"I know."

"I . . ." He breaks his gaze to examine his boots, hands still clutched tightly behind his back. "If I'm being totally honest, I would have left sooner, but . . ." He trails off for a moment that nearly stops the beating of my heart for some reason. "I have to make amends back home. With my grandmother. It's probably going to take a *lot* of meeting up for tea, a lot of awkward conversations. But they're worth having. And very overdue."

"Make sure you come armed with plenty of crumpets," I advise.

"You remembered." His voice is a disbelieving whisper directed at the floor, and I almost don't hear it.

"I'm going to miss you." I keep my voice quiet to prevent it from cracking, and even then I'm not entirely successful. Ravod looks up at me, saying nothing. His eyes roam my face while the rest of him is motionless.

"You could come with me, you know," he says after a moment. "My grandmother says she'd be willing to overlook your . . . transgression."

"No way she called it that." I muster a little smile.

"I believe her exact words were 'laughable attempts at misconduct,'" Ravod says. "But the offer stands, if you wish."

I blink at him. There's a wistful, almost optimistic tone that's crept into his voice. Like he *wants* me to accept his offer.

"I can't, Ravod," I say. "For the same reasons you can't stay. My place is here now. Helping Kennan. You know that."

He's not disappointed, much to my surprise. He only nods. "I understand."

"That's it?" I raise an eyebrow, feigning offense.

"No." Ravod is smiling again, but it's subtle, with that same quiet wistfulness from before. "That's definitely not it. We'll see each other again. At least, that's my hope."

"Mine, too."

"Perhaps"—he draws his lower lip beneath his teeth and takes a very small step closer—"on that occasion, you might allow me to take you to dinner?"

My heart thumps once, heavily in my chest, before beating so fast it could power an airship on its own. My voice isn't forthcoming for a few excruciating seconds.

"I'd really like that, Ravod," I manage, finally.

There's a slight shift in the intensity in his dark eyes as he gazes into mine. He wouldn't be Ravod without his signature restraint, but the way he looks at me is completely unguarded. Without him saying a word, I can see respect, admiration . . . *affection.*

Without looking away, he takes my hand gently in his. He holds it delicately, as though it is precious and he's afraid to break it as he draws it closer to his face. His warm breath lingers on my knuckles before he turns my hand over at the last second. He only looks away when his eyes close, as though performing an act of reverence. His lips are soft and equally warm as they brush the inside of my wrist, first featherlight and then deeper. I feel their absence keenly, until they are replaced by the breathy whisper of his voice.

"You can call me Erik," he says, finally opening his eyes and looking back at me down the length of my arm.

I'm not sure I'm capable of saying anything in this moment. For some infuriating reason, this seems to please him. He releases my hand and steps back to the door with one final smile over his shoulder. He passes Kennan on his way out, nodding once to her with respect as he turns the corner out of sight.

For now.

My skin tingles pleasantly where he touched me. I trace the spot he kissed on my wrist with the tips of my fingers, still ascertaining that it was real.

"That was *sickening*." Kennan's voice breaks the silence.

I roll my eyes at her. "You say that, but I think you're secretly taking notes for when you next see Fiona."

"Notes on romance from Ravod?" Kennan laughs. "Well, I suppose stranger things have happened. I'm surprised, actually."

"By what?"

Kennan cocks her head, watching me appraisingly. "I would have thought you'd leap at the chance to ride off into the sunset with him. Instead, you prefer to stay here."

"That's right," I say with a smile. "I want to help my friend rebuild our home."

For once, Kennan doesn't correct me and hiss that we're not friends. Because that's exactly what we are.

Instead, she strides past me back onto the balcony. I follow to find her producing a small slip of paper from her breast pocket. Her Telling. She leans on the ledge, examining it. Then she rips it in half and releases the severed scraps of paper into the wind.

"Fear has no place in what we're trying to do," she murmurs as she watches the paper disappear along the current of air. She turns to me. Her eyes are dark brown and deadly serious. "I say 'we' because this is bigger than any one of us. It will take a while to reshape this place to match our vision for it."

"You don't have to give me the pitch, Kennan. You know I'm behind you," I say.

"I'm saying it because I'm not blind and I'm not an idiot. I can see that people have come to rely on my apparent competence. I will lead if I must, but I don't wish to do it alone," Kennan replies.

"What do you mean?"

"I'm implementing a power structure. Stability is important," Kennan says, maintaining her measured gaze. "I want you to be a part of that. I'm setting up a council, people I can trust who share my vision of a unified, peaceful, enlightened Montane and will work together to make it happen. People are already calling you the First Writer of the Bards. I'm asking you to step into that role in an official capacity."

I know my eyes are wide, but I can't seem to stop them widening farther.

"Okay," I say.

"Okay?"

"If that's what you think is best, that's what I'll do."

Kennan scoffs, but a small corner of her mouth is turned upward and only half in relief. "I should have known you'd make this something drippy and sentimental."

"You asked me to join your council. You knew what I'd bring to the table." I chuckle.

Kennan rolls her newly dark eyes again, and they

settle somewhere out in the distance. "This . . . What we're trying to do . . . It's going to take a long, long time."

"Our whole lives, probably. And then some," I say. "But it's worth it. Even if the work is never done."

As silence falls between us, I join her, leaning on the balcony railing and casting her a smile I know she sees out of the corner of her eye. Along with the quiet, a sense of pride and purpose emerges, like the green life reawakening in the wasteland.

We stand together, looking out over High House, and Montane beyond.

EPILOGUE

Twenty years later

"All right, students. Eyes front, if you would be so kind."

The young professor stood at the head of the classroom, tapping the large blackboard with the tip of his chalk. The sound reclaimed a few of his young students' attention from the sunshine spilling through the tall classroom windows and onto the neat rows of wooden desks piled high with books, paper, and writing implements. The spring afternoon outside was, admittedly, a singularly glorious sight. The professor made a mental note for the following semester: Making history the last period of the day was an amateur mistake.

"Now, as I was saying," the professor continued, "there was a certain degree of upheaval after the Battle of High House. Civil unrest took root for several years. Even today, there remain pockets of discord from the massive, sweeping changes that took place. Can anyone name just one of these changes?"

A few students raised their hands. The professor pointed to a girl near the front.

"The Telling's gone," she said, surreptitiously covering the doodle she made of a fire-breathing, flying horse in her notes.

"That's true and not true," the professor replied. "The nature of the Telling was permanently altered, so those who had the gift are only able to undo Tellings that previously existed. And with every Telling that's reversed, some say the land thrives a little more. It's even theorized that in a few more years there will be no more Tellings left to remedy. The Order of the Bards is already shifting toward becoming the guardians of history, spreading knowledge, fighting injustice, and helping Montane however they can. It's been argued that a new 'Telling' has emerged, that the Bards 'tell,' as in share, the story of how the Montane we know came to be. Anyone else?"

A few more hands rose, and this time the professor selected a boy a few rows back.

"The University?"

"Yes, excellent!" The professor beamed. "The Maddox University of Montane was established shortly after the battle. It now stands in the middle of what used to be the wasteland. The library hoarded in the sanctum of High House paved the way for it to become one of the most comprehensive centers of knowledge and enlightenment in the world. Does anyone remember the names of some of its alumni from last week's lesson?"

Every hand went up. The professor pinched the

bridge of his angular nose beneath his glasses with a sigh.

"Besides me."

Half the hands lowered. The professor called on a girl at the back.

"That famous doctor."

"Can you be a little more specific, please?"

The girl grimaced. "Karen . . . ?"

A few of the other students snickered quietly until the professor silenced them with a look.

"I suggest you review the reading a little more thoroughly next time, Sophia," the professor replied. "Kieran Shepard is one of the most renowned physicians in Montane, specializing in infectious diseases. Anyone else?" When a few eager hands rose in response, the professor selected a boy sitting off to the side.

"My ma says she attended the University with Director Imogen."

"Yes, the current director of the University is also a prestigious graduate," the professor said with a nod. "And she was my professor before that. A very gifted teacher." He paused, letting some of the students finish taking notes. "Moving on, last week we talked about the structure of our government. That was all set up in the aftermath of the Battle of High House by . . ." He trailed off, looking for hands. One girl's shot up faster than the others.

"Queen Kennan!" she answered before the professor could prompt her.

"Yes, that's correct." The professor nodded, smiling. "Kennan became the first queen of Montane, and we'll be covering that in more depth next week before your exams, so pay attention. She enacted many of the changes we take for granted and stepped down after a term of ten years. This paved the way for each queen going forward to serve for exactly one decade . . ." He paused to write on the blackboard. "And each queen is selected by the council Kennan set up. They oversee the various aspects of the government and advise the queen directly."

The eager student raised her hand again. "What happened to Queen Kennan afterward? Did she really disappear?"

"No, of course not. She married the former constable of the town of Aster and they live together in retirement," the professor said. "It's considered common knowledge that Kennan adopted a lot of the same policies that made Aster a thriving business hub from her wife. Now, back on topic, not all the unrest that occurred after the Battle of High House came from Montane. Today, Gondal is our ally and trading partner, but there was a time when diplomatic relations stood on shaky ground. A treaty known as the Tybera Pact was negotiated by Gondal's ambassador to Montane, Erik Ravod—"

A grinning, dark-haired student near the front turned to his classmate and whispered loudly, "That's my dad!"

The professor soldiered on. "—aided by the First Writer of Montane, Shae—"

"That's my ma!" Another barely concealed whisper issued from the boy.

"Are you quite finished, Adam?"

Adam quickly snapped to attention with an innocent, if precocious, smile. The professor returned to addressing the class with a sigh.

"As your classmate so discreetly pointed out, his mother is still the First Writer of the Bards, and a member of the Queen's Council," the professor said.

A bell tolled in the distance, interrupting the lesson one last time, indicating that the school day had come to an end. All eyes turned expectantly to the professor; a few children shifted anxiously.

"Class dismissed. Please read chapter eleven in your textbook for tomorrow." The professor smiled as he seated himself at his desk. The students rushed happily to collect their things and dash to the door.

"Bye, Teach!" Adam waved over his shoulder as he pulled on his elaborately embroidered jacket and joined his classmates.

That child is a handful, he thought to himself.

The classroom grew quiet as the professor turned his attention to grading papers and planning for the next day's lesson. Outside, the laughter of his newly liberated students was slightly muffled, but still audible. Just another day, with more to come.

ACKNOWLEDGMENTS

2020 was an . . . interesting year to write a book. A lot of truly amazing people helped make this one possible.

My incredible agent, Emma Parry, was the angel on my shoulder, encouraging and guiding me through the process. A mountain of gratitude to Lexa Hillyer and the wonderful team at Glasstown for their dedication and support, in addition to their awesome creative chops: Olivia Liu, Maha Hussain, and Brandie Coonis, thank you.

Wednesday Books took a chance on a new series by an unknown writer, and I am truly lucky for the opportunity to work with the incredible *Hush* and *Veil* team. Vicki Lame, my editor: a million thanks, from beginning to end; these books exist today because of you. Production editor Melanie Sanders and production manager Lena Shekhter, thank you from the bottom of my heart for all you do. I am so grateful for the skill and artistry of designer Steven Seighman, and the jacket and mechanical design of Ervin Serrano and Olga Grlic. I'm amazed by your work—thank you for making this book stunning. Mary Moates, publicist extraordinaire, it was such a treat to work with you. Marketing stars Alexis

Neuville and Brant Janeway, my thanks for getting *Hush* and *Veil* into the world. Lauren Hougen, whose diligent and insightful copy edits whipped *Veil* into shape, a million thanks. And editorial assistants Angelica Chong and Vanessa Aguirre, for all your hard work, thank you.

Ryan Mazie, the best publicist-turned-friend in the world, my eternal thanks for your empathy, patience, and savvy. Lynn Nesbit, your belief in my writing in the very beginning got me to where I am now: published author of this duology. I hope I can continue to do you proud.

Over the past year, I owe my sanity in large part to the friends who, despite distance both social and otherwise, stayed connected. Misha and Victoria, my international squad. Katherine and Emma Pascal, and my godmother, Casey, for a lifetime of love and shenanigans. Michelle Wong, for checking in with me and chatting into the night. Priscilla, my soul sister, thank you for all the hearts and flowers.

To my family, for their love and support, both over the years and specifically while I endeavored to finish a novel during a pandemic, I love you. Mom and Sue, I dedicated this book to you because this story, at its core, is about continuing a mother's legacy. I am who I am today because of you both, and I'm so fortunate to have such strong, remarkable women in my life. I'm also grateful to each of my siblings who stood by me over the years.

And of course, a shout-out to my husband, the love of my life, for everything (especially keeping our daughter out of my hair while I tried to write). You are a real-life superhero. And to Evangeline, my continual inspiration, your mom loves you so much.